LAURA LUKASAVAGE

Moonlight Changes

First edition

ISBN: 978-1-7366905-1-2

Editing by Josie O'Brien
Cover art by Laura Lukasavage

This book was professionally typeset on Reedsy.
Find out more at reedsy.com

For my daughter Bella, who gave me the push I needed to pursue my dream. Everything I do, I do it for you. You are my heart, my whole world. Thank you for being my little girl. God blessed me and made my life whole when he gave me you.

Contents

Acknowledgement

A special thank you to my editor, Josie O'Brien, for without her this book would have been a lot worse off.

Also, to everyone who never stopped believing I could do the impossible and to all my followers, for without you this dream wouldn't be a reality.

<u>Dark Inheritance</u>

Moonlight Secrets (1)
Moonlight Legacy (3)

<u>Standalone</u>
See You On The Other Side
Enough Is Enough

<u>Darkness Awakening Series</u>
Will's Awakening

I

Part One

Chapter 1

Amberly

"What did you see in this dream?" My mother's voice has never felt so far away.

"I don't know if I would call it a dream. It felt more like I was there, physically. I think, I astral projected myself there," I pause and turn my attention to my mom, "in the same way our ancestor, you told me about when I was a kid, was able to travel."

For the first time, she looks at my father, who hasn't stopped pacing around the room since I woke up. I can see the tension radiating off his body into the atmosphere around us. My mother's gaze returns to me.

"They were only stories, Amberly. Passed down from generation to generation. I don't believe there is any truth in them."

I've seen that look before. There is something she isn't telling me. My mind starts racing and I know the one thing I can say to make her believe that this wasn't just some dream, "So that man, with the scar that ran down the side of his face from his eyebrow to his lip. He wasn't real?"

For the first time, I see fear in my mother's eyes. It is not the normal kind of jump off the cliff into the water fear. The 'my world is forever changed' fear. My father stops pacing and walks over to her side, he places his hands on her shoulders to comfort her.

His eyes come to rest on me.

"This man, is he the one you said is coming for you?"

"It is more complicated than that, Dad," the words just slip out before I can think to stop them. We exchange the briefest of smiles with each other before either of us makes a big deal about it, I continue, "He and the other man mentioned someone else, someone in charge, and they said something about him wanting me. I think they said his name was Vladimir."

I can feel the tension radiating off my mom's body as she begins to shake and the intensity of the situation sinks in. Something I said was worrying her.

"Mom, what is it?"

"That name."

I stand, slowly at first, testing my leg, watching as I add more weight so I know it's sturdy enough, then, I look up and walk across the room to my parents, "What about it?"

The realization is clear on her face when she looks me in the eyes, "I've heard that name before."

I can hear the fear in my mother's voice as it reaches out to me across the little space that's left between us, "Growing up there were stories, many stories, that we passed down to our children but there was one that our parents always made sure we knew like the back of our hands. That story was the one about the seven."

I've never seen my mother so lost in thought. I can see her focusing hard on her words before she speaks. Her hands are knotted up in the bottom of her shirt as she slightly rocks back and forth while my father still tries to calm her. I can tell she's still uneasy.

She looks at me before continuing, "The story of the seven was told throughout the forest. Every village has its version of the tale."

She stops talking and rocking at the same time and without another word she reaches up to her shoulder to take my father's hand in hers. I can see how even the smallest touch calms her, and I'm suddenly reminded of Julian. However, right now there are more important things at hand; my love life can wait a few more hours.

Growing up there weren't many stories my mother told me about our ancestors, other than the ones about different powers our leaders would have but haven't had in many generations. I would ask her why the leaders didn't inherit those powers anymore, and she would always say the same thing, 'the link to the powers vanished', whatever that meant. I honestly think she didn't know the answer so she just came up with anything to shut me up. But no matter how hard I search my memories I can't recall her telling me anything about the 'seven'.

"Mom?"

Her eyes return to mine and she can see the question in them, "The easiest way to tell you about the seven is to say that they were the first," she looks to my father as she says, "The first shapeshifter," then to me, "witch, angel, demon, fairy, natural and healer."

Before she can get out another word, I interrupt with my first set of questions, since I'm sure there will be many more tonight, "What's a natural? And what's a healer?"

"A healer was someone who healed any nature of injury or illness. A cut, broken bone, or even things like a broken heart or an uneasy mind. They could bring the dead back to life but with a cost to them." She pauses for a moment to give me one of her serious looks before she continues, "Like I've taught you magic always comes with a cost. From what my parents taught me if the healer wanted to fix the mind or the heart it would not affect them. However, when they healed a cut or broken bone, they would take the injury themselves but heal quickly. But bringing someone back from the dead, that's what would take the most from them."

I couldn't help but interrupt her again and ask, "Take the most from them? What do you mean?"

She smiled at me before continuing, "Each person they bring back would take a little of them. Meaning, after bringing back so many people from the dead they would get weaker and weaker, then, eventually, they would start to heal slower and slower until," she pauses to look over at my father sadly and I know this is a talk she never wanted to have with me, "until, they took the place of someone they brought back."

"You mean they died?"

"Yes. However, over the years the healer-power became weaker and weaker in each generation until that power, like most of the others, died off." She pauses again and walks across the room to get a drink. She returns to the seat in front of my father as she takes a nice long sip, "and a natural, well they are a little more involved but the least complicated way to explain them is that they control all the earthly elements. Their power never loses energy because they are restored from the earth itself. That alone made them extraordinarily powerful. They weren't altogether unstoppable even when the earth restored their powers. They were not limitless. The person controlled the power, not the other way around. However, the stronger the person, especially the mind, the stronger their power was. Add that to their siphoning power and they were almost unstoppable."

I can feel the skin between my eyebrows crinkle up and I'm sure the question is plain on my face. My mother lets a laugh escape between her lips, and I know she's noticed too, "By siphoning, honey, I mean they could take someone else's powers for their own. Either just enough to use for a short time or even years or they could take one's power entirely."

"So, if they were unstoppable, what happened to them? What happened to all these other villages? I mean I know the witches and shapeshifters and even the fairies are still around, but I've never heard of the others. And what happened to the seven? Who are they? Where are they? And what does this have to do with what happened eighteen years ago and what I just saw?" I pause, taking note of the overwhelmed expressions on my parents' face, "Sorry, I was doing it again."

"It's fine, Amberly. I love how interested you get in something new you're learning about."

A knock on the door interrupts our conversation. As I turn to face it, I hear my father tell whoever is on the other side to come in. Much to my dismay, it's Angela. Not that I'm unhappy to see her, I was just hoping to see Julian.

"I'm sorry to bother you but we kind of need you out here, Aaron."

My father stands for the first time in minutes as he walks towards Angela, "Everything alright?"

The smallest of smiles creeps onto her face, "Well, Julian is kind of in his own world, and I need some help getting the people from Jocelyn's village settled, and then there were a few things I would like to talk to you about."

Before my father can turn her away my mother reaches his side and puts her hand on his arm saying, "Go do what you need to do. I'll be here with our daughter trying to fill in all the blanks while we wait for you to come back."

With a small smile, my father leans down to kiss my mother on the forehead before he leaves the room with Angela. My mother turns back around to face me with happiness radiating off her. Since we've gotten here, she has become someone I've never known before. She is not my mother, at least not the mother I grew up with. She's so different and I don't even know what words to use to try to describe what has changed. Being with my father, and being around him again, has changed her into someone I always wanted her to be. She's so happy and it makes me happy to see her like this.

"So, to answer your earlier questions," she returns to her seat before continuing, "as far as I know the other villages and tribes died off and there aren't any more naturals, healers, demons, or angels alive..."

"What about Vladimir? What is he? Because up until eighteen years ago he was still alive."

"Vladimir is the first original demon. As far as I know, he murdered off the other six, hundreds of years ago."

I can't hold in my surprise, "What! Why?"

"Some said it was because of his thirst for power, others say it was over jealousy. He had fallen in love with one of the seven, but she did not love him in return. She fell in love with the shapeshifter and that sent him into a blind rage."

I can feel a rage forming in my gut for reasons I don't understand, "How could someone do that? I mean didn't they all know each other? How can you do that to someone, let alone someone you know?"

I can see the sadness creeping into her eyes, "Yes, they all knew each other. They grew up together just like you did with Logan and Troy. They were meant to be the protectors of our kind because they were the strongest. They developed the rules on how and where to live, as well as our job protecting the humans from the rogue creatures roaming the world." She pauses to look down at her feet, for what reason I don't know, before continuing "There were always seven. With each generation fourteen more would be born with a distinctive birthmark that distinguished them as one of the new seven protectors." She pauses again and looks back up at me, "or the destroyers. Seven good and seven evil, that is how it always was. Until he killed off the original six and then turned on their descendants. Then everyone went into hiding, made their villages and kept to themselves in the safety of their homes with numbers to protect themselves."

"So, if you had this mark, that's how people would know you were born from the Originals Bloodline?"

She nods.

Does that mean...

"Every generation born of the seven had it. That's how we would be able to identify someone as being born of the new seven."

"They knew just by the mark?"

"Yes and no. They waited until the child was older and started to show their powers. Once they did that's when they would know for sure they were to be one of the seven and they would know which of the seven based on which powers they would have."

"But how would they know if they were good or bad?"

"There was never a way to truly know, at least not until they were much older. Once they came of age and started using their powers and you could see what kind of person they were at heart, that's when it would become obvious."

"Was it always so cut and dry? Like 'hey, she's good,' or 'hey, he's bad.'"

My mother smiles at me as she replies. "No. Sadly it's quite easy to be wrong about these kinds of things. Growing up a person is always changing, learning, and becoming a new version of themselves." She lifts her hand slowly to tuck a piece of loose hair back behind her ear, "As you grow you make mistakes, you rebel. It's just a normal process and sometimes because of it, it can be easy to think the wrong way about someone."

I nod in understanding.

I try to absorb everything she's said so far about the original seven and what Vladimir did but the only thing I keep going back to is the birthmarks. Seven good and seven evil, seven protectors and seven destroyers. Is that what the birthmarks on me, Troy, Logan, Angela, and Julian are? And what about Celine and Cole from Angela's tribe? Are we all part of this, has our ancestors' blood been fighting to come back and in us? If so, are we the protectors or the destroyers?

I look up at my mother, afraid to ask the question that is invading my mind. "When was the last time someone was born with one of these marks?"

I see something like fear in her eyes. Does she know? Of course, she does, she is my mother. She had to have seen the mark on me at some point, right? Maybe it's something else I'm seeing in her eyes. Maybe her fear is about everything else we've spoken about.

She lifts her arm and places her cup against her mouth and takes a long sip. This is when I realize this isn't something she's going to talk about, not right now. Meaning, she knows.

Chapter 2

Aaron

"What's going on with Julian?" I ask Angela as she makes her way outside the cave entrance, with me directly behind her.

"What do you mean?"

I lift my hand to my eyes and rub at them feverishly, "Angela, please don't play coy with me, not right now. I know he's in love with my daughter." I remove my hand from my face and return it to my side as I look her in the eyes, "He asked me to help make Amberly hate him. What's going on?"

I've known Angela so long that I know every facial expression she makes and usually what they mean. However, she's holding something back, but I don't know what. The only thing I know for sure is it has to do with Julian and my daughter.

"I know the pack rules and I know how you must be feeling but please listen to what I have to say," she pauses, waiting for me to say something but when I don't, she continues, "We've both watched Julian grow these last few months and we know his track record with girls in the past isn't the best."

A half laugh, half moan escapes my mouth, she lifts her hand to silence me before she continues, "I know, I know. He has never been good in the girl department, or even love for that matter. He has always blocked himself from letting anyone in because he's been too afraid to love. He can take the physical pain that comes his way, he welcomes it, but he can't take heartache."

I shake my head, "I know this."

Her hands become fists at her side like she's begging me to be heard. "So, she changed that. She found a way to get in and break down those walls. You can't tell me you haven't seen a difference in him?"

"I would be lying if I said I didn't."

A small smile creeps up on her face, "He never told you this but for years he would watch her."

I can feel the uneasiness in my stomach rising. I close my eyes and take in a slow breath of the cold night air. It fills my lungs and when I slowly exhale it takes a lot of the unease with it.

Angela studies my expression before she continues, "What I mean is when he was younger, he started feeling something. A pull, he called it."

I open my eyes wide, "A pull?"

She nearly jumps out of her skin before she speaks again, "He told me that the pull led him to her and that he wasn't sure why, but when he found her, he would just watch her. Watch her play with her friends and he got to know her from afar. He saw the beauty in her strength and her determination.

He fell in love with her when they were only children. Watching her helped him learn to slowly open his heart and feel again, but more than that, for the first time he started to care again."

"Why is this the first time I've heard about this? Why didn't you tell me he used to take off?"

"I don't know. I guess back then I could see he needed the space, the distance."

I rub my eyes. "Something could have happened to him while he was out there by himself."

"We were young. I didn't think much of it at the time."

I nod in understanding.

"I don't know if you remember him disappearing early in the day and returning late at night many nights in a row."

I nod again.

"He would come in and lay in the bed next to me and when I would ask him where he had been at first, he said nothing but after a few months he finally started talking to me about her."

"What would he say?"

She smiles lightly. "He would tell me how this pull had led him deep into the forest and when he laid eyes on her for the first time, it stopped."

"The pull?"

She nods.

"It just stopped?"

She thinks before she speaks again. "Well, he didn't say it stopped, more like it lessened."

"So, he continued to feel this pull?"

She nods. "Yes. But it wouldn't be as strong when he was around her, when he was away from her, he would feel it stronger. Like he needed to be wherever she was. But when they were together, the closer he was to her the less the pull would be."

"So, he still feels it, even now?"

"Yes. But something is different now. He told me when he touches her it's like his hands are on fire and then it spreads through the rest of his body."

"In a painful way?"

"No, he said it was more like the feeling woke him up, made him feel stronger."

I sigh, not ready to hear this. I just got my daughter back. She's still a baby to me, I can't think about her with anyone.

"He came to care for her so strongly in no time at all."

"Why didn't he say anything?"

"He didn't know what to make of it himself."

"He should have said something. What if he was seen? What if someone followed him back to the cave one night."

She looks at me sadly, "But they didn't. We are all fine. Nothing bad happened."

"But it could have. You have both seen firsthand how cruel this world can be, he should have been more careful."

I can see my words awoke a hurt in her she had pushed down for many years and I sigh, mad at myself. Her words pull me back. "He was young, he needed to escape the world he was living in his mind. The past that he continued reliving repeatedly every night."

I look at her in confusion. "So, he cared for her and 'the pull' more than the pack?"

"No, he did care about the pack and us, but this was someone outside the pack, someone he never met face to face. And this person took away that hurt that was boiling inside him. He was engulfed in this feeling. It filled all the anger and slowly took the hurt and replaced it with something else. He cared for her strongly." She looks away as she takes in a deep breath before continuing. "He saw the gentleness in her with the animals in the forest and with her friends. He knew her deepest thoughts, wants, and needs and he sensed how alone she felt."

Sadly, I ask. "She felt alone?"

She nods.

"I should have been there."

"You are now and that's all that matters."

I nod absently.

"As time passed, he realized he could hear her thoughts sometimes and that's when he learned she didn't know the truth about you, her father. He knew her deepest wish and he wanted to grant it for her."

"What was her wish?"

She smiles at me knowingly. "She wanted to feel whole, understand who she was, and she knew something was missing, and more than anything she wanted to know what it was. That's when he decided to approach her and bring her here. So, she could get her answers."

She closes her eyes and this time it's her turn to let out a long sigh but before I say a word she continues, "He fell in love with her long before the day she came to our cave, long before any of us even knew she existed and since then that love has only grown. Finding out she was your daughter was the hardest thing for him to hear in years. He tried to keep his distance from her but then her feelings were made clear to him, first in her thoughts and then in her actions and it became impossible for him to keep his distance from her."

Oh, man.

"When he saw her kissing that guy it destroyed him, but he took that as his way out. He knew you wouldn't approve, and he didn't want to let you down, so he came up with a plan to make her hate him before you learned of his feelings and became angry with him. He looks at you like a father and he never wanted to let you down. He knows what she means to you, and the pack, and he would never jeopardize that."

She takes in a breath slowly. "All I'm asking is if there is a way, any way that you could understand."

"Angela."

"Yes."

"I may not have a choice."

Her confusion is obvious when she asks, "What do you mean?"

"I mean, they are connected. They are as we call it, foreordained, and because of that I can't get in the way, no matter how badly I want to."

"Foreordained?"

"It means that long before even I was born, they were destined for each other."

"I've never heard of that word before."

I closed my eyes, suddenly feeling very tired and drained, "That's because for hundreds of years, no one in the pack ever met someone they were destined for and because of that, like most things, it got left behind. Only the pack leaders would share this information with the new pack leader, and we were told to not speak of it unless there ever came a time when we believed it happened again."

"So, because they are, what did you call it?"

"Foreordained."

"Right, just because they are foreordained, how does that make it ok for them to be together? I mean if she's the pack leaders' daughter."

I felt the frown take place on my face before I could stop it, "Because it is one of our most concrete pack laws. When a wolf meets someone, and their connection is that strong. When they feel the pull and can talk with one another in their minds, then you know they are connected in the highest form."

"But what is the law exactly?"

"It states that if they find one another nothing is to interfere, and their union is to be protected by the pack."

"But what if someone in the pack connected with a human or someone in one of the other tribes?"

"It wouldn't matter. The connection is the most important thing."

I could see her interest in the topic as she thought of her next question. "So, this connection, what's the purpose of it?"

"I'm not entirely sure myself. All I know, from what was passed down to me, is that their uniting is vital for the pack's survival."

"How so?"

"It is said that they would become the strongest among us once connected and that their union could bring a," I paused not wanting to even think about my daughter and this next part being in the same thought or sentence, "child that would strengthen our pack tenfold."

"OK so the child would be stronger, why does that matter?"

"Well, they also said something about that child having more power than us, a different power but also the parents themselves would become much stronger in the union, more than the whole pack combined. Bottom-line is its pack law and anyone who couldn't follow our law was meant to be cast out, and as Alpha, I have to hold up our laws the most. No matter how I feel about it."

I can tell Angela is trying to hold back a smile from spreading across her face, but she isn't having much luck. She loves Julian, as do I and all she's ever wanted was for him to be happy and to find someone to break down the walls he put so high up around him, "That means they can be together? I mean if she wants to be with him too then they have your blessing?"

"Yes."

The word makes my stomach uneasy again. I know Julian will protect her and I can tell he cares for her, but she is my daughter. I feel more protective over her than anything else in my life, and I know his history with women, and I'll be damned if he does that to her.

"I'm sorry, Aaron."

I smile at her. "Sorry? For what?"

"I know this can't be easy for you and I'm over here smiling."

I place my hands on her shoulders as I smile down at her. "Don't ever feel you need to apologize for being happy for someone else's happiness in our pack. I understand and I'm happy he finally learned to let someone in. I just really wish it had been someone else's daughter."

She looks up at me and sees my half-serious expression, and she starts to laugh. In moments I'm laughing along with her. It's going to take some time for me to completely fall in line with Julian being with my daughter, but if he makes her happy that's all that matters. I already know he would do anything to protect her and really, what else could a father ask for?

"Just remember he's changed."

"I'm trying to."

She smiles. "I don't think there is anything he wouldn't do for her, you know."

"I know."

"Good."

I smile.

"So, Julian could become your son-in-law." She smiles up at me.

"Not funny."

"Hey, you might as well get used to the idea now don't you think?"

I shake my head. "Nope, too soon."

She laughs. "Fine."

"So, from here on out I would like to know as little as possible."

She smiles. "Understandable."

"Good. Don't think I can handle that yet."

"Well, she is eighteen."

"So?"

She laughs. "So, time to get on the boy train Daddy dearest."

I frown.

"What?"

"Too soon."

She laughs, "Oh, come on. You're no fun anymore. What happened?"

I chuckle. "I guess I'm getting old."

She waves my words off with her hand and says sarcastically, "You? Old? Never."

"Now who's lying to whom?"

She smiles. "Hey, I'm not lying. You can't get old. You are not allowed. I forbid it."

"Well, I guess it's a good thing we don't age like humans do then."

"You can say that again. I have to keep my figure."

I frown at her. "Since when do you care about your looks? And for that matter when did you get so...girly."

She crosses her arms over her chest defensively, "I beg your pardon."

I raise my hands in a retreating manner and smile. "I didn't mean anything by it. I can see that you're different. Since they got here you've changed. You're not as grown up. You no longer act like a leader. You act like a..."

"Like a teenager."

I rub the hair on my neck sheepishly. "Yeah."

"Well, Aaron, in case you forgot that's what I am."

"I know."

She looks at me almost hurt. "Do you?"

"Yes. Honestly, I was starting to worry that you were growing up too fast. That you weren't able to have normal teenage years."

"Then what's the problem?"

I look at her with concern. "I'm simply curious, why the sudden change? And why now?"

"I don't know. Maybe it's because I'm around people my age who don't expect me to lead them. It's refreshing for once."

"I'm sorry if I ever put too much responsibility on your shoulders."

She places her hand lightly on my arm and smiles. "Aaron, I owe you everything. I owe you my life."

"That doesn't mean I should take it over."

She shakes her head. "You didn't."

"Are you sure about that? Sometimes I wonder if I did more damage than good."

She releases a long sigh. "Aaron. I would have died without you."

"If I didn't come along someone would have."

"We don't know that."

"I guess we never will."

I can see the sadness in her eyes when she says. "I don't want you thinking you failed me in any way because you didn't."

"I'm not so sure about that."

"Aaron. You saved us, you gave us a home, someone to look up to, to learn from. You gave us a pack."

I look away from her before I speak again. "I also gave you too much responsibility for someone so young."

"No, you didn't. You ensured we felt needed. You gave us purpose again."

"But now look at you."

She looks at herself shyly. "What about me?"

"You seem. Confused."

"I'm anything but. I love who I've become, and I owe that to you. I

18

wouldn't change anything. I learned and grew and now I get to be a regular teenager, even if it's only for a little while."

"I wanted more for you. For both of you. And I can't help feeling like I didn't deliver."

She throws her arms around me, taking me by surprise. "You did more than that. We have a family here. I have a pack," she pulls back to look up at me, "a father, a brother and Julian he has all that and now someone to love and love him back."

In my worry for Angela, and her recently bizarre behavior, I had forgotten all about Julian. "You better go find Julian now and let him know he has my blessing before he goes off and does whatever stupid thing he had planned."

I see the joy leave her face so quickly that it takes me a second to process it. "You're right. I completely forgot he was planning something. I hope he wasn't stupid enough to do anything yet that we won't be able to fix."

She goes to turn away and I yell after her. "We?"

She looks over her shoulder and smiles.

Kids.

Chapter 3

Jocelyn

"Vladimir was in love with the Natural, Aadya. He loved her since they were incredibly young and no matter how much he tried to win her affections she never felt the same way for him. Instead, she fell for the shapeshifter, Johnathan."

I want to keep talking because I'm afraid of her asking me about the marks again. I do not know how to tell her... or even... what to tell her, for that matter, because I don't know the truth. Her birthmark was the second thing I noticed about her when she was born. The first was her face, eyes, and smile, which had me the moment I looked at her.. But the second I saw the mark my heart stopped; I've been living in constant fear for her since that day. And now hearing his name after all these years, that fear has only grown in my chest. If he's still alive I know he will be coming for her and by sheltering her and not teaching her more, I may have just made the worst mistake in my life.

"So? OK, she didn't love this Vladimir guy and fell in love with someone else. Why would he kill the woman he supposedly loved and everyone else he grew up with? How can anyone be that cold, that heartless? I would never think to hurt anyone I love or once loved over something, so stupid."

"Honey, there is no way to entirely understand someone else's actions. We can only understand our own, and as I have said, these are just stories and rumors. We don't know what the truth is. You say you could never see yourself hurting someone, but until you are in those shoes you never really know what you're capable of. If you felt that person was everything to you and someone took that away from you, let alone someone you knew, you don't know how you would react. You might hurt them without even realizing you've done it."

"Okay, you may be right. It's true, we don't know what's real and what's a made-up story. We don't even know for sure that he's still alive, and that the rest of the seven are dead?"

"The only way to know for sure would be if we went out looking for the answers," I pause to look at her and know what she's thinking, "which I don't suggest we do." I can see the excitement leaving her eyes and I know she understands what I'm trying to say so I start to relax. "There's something I want you to try on me, Amberly."

"What?"

Thankful for the diversion I continue, "I want you to go into my mind and go back to that day."

The uncertainty is plain on her face, "I don't know how to do that?"

"I'll help you."

21

Stubbornly she folds her arms over her chest, "Mom, that's not even one of my powers."

"After today I know it is. There are so many powers you have now that I did not know about. Going back in time like that, reliving that moment in spirit form while your body was still in the present, and being affected by it, tells me that much."

She unfolds her arms and shifts her weight in her chair to move herself a little closer to me, "What do you mean? What other powers do I have?"

"For now, I know for sure that you can astral project into different times, read minds, and control someone with your mind. I'm sure you will have psychic dreams, like premonitions. You can also go into someone's mind and travel to a memory of theirs and live it with them like I'm asking you to do. There is a lot you can do that I'm sure we don't know about still, but these things I'm sure you can do after today."

Skeptical of what I'm telling her, she asks, "But how is this even possible? No one else in the village has those powers. I mean you, me, Logan, and Troy, have different powers than everyone else but none of you have that many. So, why would I?"

For the first time since she was born, I can feel the necessity of this path for her. We need to learn what she is capable of, and I need to teach her how to use all her powers so she can use them against Vladimir when the time comes, which I'm hoping it never does. And now I am starting to have conversations with her that I've feared having for her whole life, "Because you aren't like us, honey. You are born of two villages. Something that has never happened before, as far as we know. You are half witch and half shifter. You're the first of your kind. And because of that your powers could be endless."

"Doesn't it scare you? What I might be able to do? I mean, I'm scared of myself. You are telling me I can control someone's mind."

I can understand her fear more than she will ever know. Growing up I was the strongest in our village and I could do things no one else could and I never knew what I was capable of. Most of my powers I learned about on my own and my parents were no help since they had no idea where my powers were coming from. It was hard knowing they were afraid of me and what I was capable of and I would be lying if I said I wasn't a little worried about my daughter but not for the reasons she thinks. I am worried because I don't know what powers she has or how to teach her to not only use them but control them.

"You are gifted, and I always knew you were meant for great things and your powers will help you get to where you are meant to go in this life. You were meant to be a leader and now it's time for you to learn how to do that. You need to be strong enough to learn and to fight if the time comes. Your pack needs you; our village, your friends, and your father and I need you."

"But being able to take away someone's free will, being able to control their mind. How could that ever be a good thing to do Mom?"

I closed my eyes and let out a breath I hadn't realized I'd been holding, "It's only a dangerous power if you let it be. You are in control. You know what's right and what's wrong, and I know you'll always keep that in mind when you use it."

We remain silent for what feels like an eternity and then she sighs as she closes her eyes and says, "Fine, I'll do it." She pauses again but only long enough to open her eyes and look at me.

"I'll take you back, but you have to walk me through how and what I'm supposed to look for."

I smile at her with pride. "I will and it's more like you're going to get my mind back there so I can relive it and hopefully get some answers for us."

Her worry for me is written all over her face, "Mom, are you sure about this?"

Hesitantly I reply, "No, but it's something we need to do if we are going to get some answers."

I can hear the urgency in her voice when she says, "Mom, he doesn't want any of you though, he wants me. Wouldn't it be smarter to just train me and then I can leave so I won't put anyone else in danger?"

I'm consumed with anger, worry, and pride in my daughter as I reply, "Don't you ever think that way! Anywhere you go I am going with you, whether it's my life or your life in danger, that's how it works when you have a child. And I'm sure your father would feel the same way."

She looks away from me and I can see sadness in her eyes. "He barely knows me, and he has the pack to worry about."

I place my hands on hers. "It doesn't matter if he knew you eighteen years, five years, or a day, he is your father and he loves you. I know we never talked about your father and that was all my fault, it was too painful for me but that shouldn't have mattered. I should have buried that hurt for you and for him and I should have talked to you about him."

"I understood why you didn't."

"I know but I also know part of the rift between us was because I wouldn't talk to you about him."

She smiles at me. "Mainly it was because I knew you were hiding things from me and you wouldn't fess up."

I smile back. "I know but the main thing was your father. All the secrets had to do with him and because of that our relationship wasn't what I hoped for. I feared the day you would ask me about him. About our family, when instead I should have embraced it and I should have shared with you all the wonderful things about your father."

"Well, there's no time like the present."

I look down at my hands as I go back in time to memories I locked away for so long, "Your father was the one who brought up the subject of children all those years ago. He always wanted a big family."

"Really."

I nod. "Yes."

I look back up at her as she looks away from me as the sadness returns to her expression.

"There's nothing he wanted more than you. The joy he showed and felt in the moments he knew we were pregnant was the happiest I ever saw him, and I knew your father for many years before I became pregnant with you. So, losing you, losing us, I know it was his greatest sorrow, as it was mine. I don't want you to ever think that because your father doesn't know you, as well as I know he wishes he did, that it would make him love or care for you any less. That isn't true. Yes, he has the pack to worry about, but I have no doubt in my mind that if it came to you or them, he would step down as alpha and choose you every time."

I can hear the surprise in her voice when she asks, "Really?"

"Yes."

She looks down at her hands and I can see her getting lost in thoughts I wished to always spare her from. The silence builds in the space between us, I can feel it growing so I smile at her and say, "You are more like your father than you are me."

She looks up at me with surprise. "Really?"

I smile. Guess we are doing one-word answers again. "Yes."

"How so?"

"Well, you get your stubbornness from both of us." I feel my smile grow. "But your heart, your courage, your need to always pick up a book or be in the forest. Your love and compassion to not only humans but the animals in the forest. That's all your father."

"I thought I got a lot of that from you."

I shake my head. "I wish I could take the credit."

I can see the fire returning to her eyes. "OK, Mom." She smiles at me, "I'm ready. Let's do this. I'm ready to fight. Fight for this life, for us, I want to get to know my father and I want him to get to know me. I want to finally be where I belong."

I feel the pride and worry for my daughter boil over and I do everything I can to keep it from showing as I take her hands in mine and we smile together in silence.

Chapter 4

Julian

From where I sit, I can still see them. Logan and Troy. I don't know why I'm even bothering, but I want to keep them in my sight for some reason. The thought of Amberly being with him turns my stomach but I know it's what needs to be done. I can sense how she feels about him and I can tell he would take care of her, but for me, it's not enough.

The thought of her in his arms every night, his lips on hers, his hands wiping away her tears, him being her home, her safe place. It's eating me alive. I want to be all those things for her and more. But she grew up with him, she's known him her whole life and she's known me, what, a few short weeks. How could I expect anything different? How could I want anything different? I know I can't be with her, as much as I want to, so I should be happy that the person she will be with is someone like him. Someone who knows her cares about her, loves her. He's everything I can't be for her and I think that's why I hate him, because I would give anything to be him.

All these years, watching and listening to her. Learning about her. The thought of only losing her in the end, for it to bring us here to this place of emptiness makes me angry.

When I went into the woods all those years ago, I never expected to find her but more than that I never expected to want her or for her to have this power over me. She consumed me, my every thought, every need, every want. Every moment I wasn't with her felt like torture, I felt the emptiness without being around her. I felt the loss of my family more deeply when I wasn't near her but more than that I felt the loss of her too. I could feel this empty place where there had always been one but when I saw her it was gone. Filled. But, when she wasn't around, I felt her absence harder than anything, and that emptiness that had been there before her was a whole lot bigger without her.

I can feel it now.

The hole.

The emptiness.

I need to fill it.

I need to fill the void.

But I already know the only thing that can do it is something I can't have. Her.

I can't be selfish with her. I love her and because of that, I need to let her go. I need to let her be happy even if it means being miserable. But being near her, watching over her is better than not having her in my life at all. We can't be together, as much as we both want it, we can't have it. It's not allowed, and I can't go against my pack, my Alpha. Not after everything he's done for me. I owe him more than that. As much as I want her, I know what needs to be done and it needs to be done now.

I need to let her go.

I need to make sure he is worthy of her love and that he will love her as I would have and protect her when I cannot. I need to make sure he is ready.

Chapter 5

Jocelyn

My eyes feel pasted together as I try to pry them apart. I can smell smoke and the night air, and I know I'm back. Part of me does not want to open my eyes but I know I have to, in order to find a way to hopefully save my daughter. I can hear my parent's voices in front of me. I can feel the cold soil under the palms of my hands.

As I finally get my eyes to open, I see a white light coming in my direction, but it doesn't come for me, it's aiming for my parents. As they fall and hit the earth, I can feel my heart shattering all over again. The men take no notice of me as they turn their backs and start to walk away. I turn my attention to the right where I know Aaron's body lays limp on the ground. The feeling of losing him is overwhelming for me and I must remind myself that I'm in the past and he is safe and alive somewhere in the room next to my sleeping body. Knowing we need answers I let go and let my body go through the motions of that night.

I stand feeling the anger and sadness emanating from me like a time bomb. I lift my hands to my face, finding the moisture covering my cheeks as an earth-shattering scream parts my lips sending everyone around me flying backward, landing with sickening sounds. Just when I feel the scream will never end, I fall to my knees and go silent. I sit there for what feels like an eternity before reality finally sets in and I know for the safety of my unborn daughter I need to make my way back to the village and try to pick up all the broken pieces around me. As I stand and make my way back toward the village, I turn to take one final look at my parent's limp and broken bodies on the ground as another tear makes its way down my cheek. Then my eyes wander over to Aaron one more time as I can feel my heart breaking in my chest. I close my eyes and whisper "Goodbye," before I turn away for the last time and make my way back towards my village knowing what needs to be done once I get there. For the sake of my daughter, the only family I have left, I need to come up with a story and implant it in everyone's minds and I need to place a protection spell around the whole village to make sure none of these people, if they come back, can get in.

* * *

Jocelyn

The world around me starts to blur as my subconscious makes its way back to my body. I try to leave all that hurt and anger behind as I open my eyes to see Amberly and Aaron both sitting next to me.

Amberly's voice shakes and I know that took a lot out of her. "Mom, I'm sorry I couldn't hold it any longer."

"Don't apologize, honey, I got what I could. But sadly, I saw nothing in my memory that could be of help."

I slowly move into a sitting position and dizziness fills my brain. I look over at my daughter searching for signs of the toll her magic took on her but other than her shaky voice she's showing no sign of fatigue.

Confusion and disappointment are clear on her face, "I don't understand. When I went back their Lurch and Onyx made it sound like their whole plan was ruined after that night. And we need to know what they meant by that. I know it has something to do with me, they made it sound as such. We need to know the reason why it was so important to kill me back then. That might be the key to stopping him."

"I'm sorry honey I wish I had more but right now all I saw was what I already knew and already shared with you both. Maybe we can try to go back tomorrow, to before I passed out or maybe to when I returned to the village. Maybe there's something there I'm not that I can't remember."

"There has to be something. This doesn't make any sense."

"I know you're frustrated honey and I promise we will find the answers. Tomorrow."

"But what if we can't."

Aaron looks at us and speaks for the first time. "One way or another we will find the information we need. We won't let anything happen to you."

I smile at him. "Your father's right. Right now, the most important thing is rest. We all need some time to reboot if we plan on trying again tomorrow."

"Do you think we will find anything? Is there anything to find? What if somehow, they covered their tracks, and we found nothing yet again?"

31

"There's something there, something we are missing that I'm sure of. But I don't know where to start. I wish I did. The only thing I know for sure is we need to find it, the missing link and in time I know we will. We will finally put an end to whatever it is that Vladimir has been planning all of these years."

She looks up at me with a grave expression on her face. "What if we can't stop him? What if he won't go away or stop killing until he's killed me?"

"We won't let that happen."

"But if that's the only way to protect everyone I love if we can't stop him."

"Don't you dare finish that sentence young lady, you aren't just a chess piece to us, you are our daughter, and you mean a lot to everyone here. Whatever Vladimir wants is nothing in comparison to what we feel, and we will find a way to protect you."

She looks away and says her next words so low that I strain to hear her. "That's what I'm worried about."

"What does that mean?"

She looks back at me angrily. "It means I won't lose anyone I love, not to protect me. I couldn't live knowing it was my fault that someone I love was killed."

I place my hands on hers and give a squeeze. "We would happily lay down our lives if it meant you would be safe."

"I know and that's what I'm worried about."

"As a parent, it's not a question. You will do anything to protect your child. I pray one day you can understand and see for yourself because I feel it's then and only then that you will understand all of my actions these last eighteen years, and the actions that your father and I are now going to take."

"I can't lose either of you. Not when I just found you both."

I look at her confused. "Both."

She looks at me sheepishly. "As you said earlier, we never really had a relationship, not until we came here, not until you knew my father wasn't dead and that I knew the truth. That's when you finally let me in, and we finally made this connection."

I look at her sadly as I see tears forming in her fawn-colored eyes, "Honey,

I'm so sorry."

I try to recall a time when she looked so young, so innocent. Her auburn hair curling lightly around her shoulders as I see them slightly shaking and I know she's holding back a break down. Amberly, even though she is smaller and frailer looking than most girls her age, has always been so strong, so tough. Almost like nothing ever touched her. She never seemed like a child to me. She may be a seventeen-year-old but her spirit, her mind and thought process is of someone in their fifties. She is always one step ahead, thinking independently and seeing the path in front of her like she knows how to get to the destination she wants to reach. Looking at her now and seeing that, for the first time, she is a teenager and she's scared, sad, and worried.

"I know you are but now I'm not only fighting to get to know my father for the first time but my mother as well. This version of you, you're happy and strong and different and I love it and I don't want to lose out on knowing you." She looks over at Aaron, "Either of you."

I touch her cheek lightly and she places her hand on mine as she closes her eyes. "You won't. I promise."

Finally, I can visibly see the toll using her magic has taken on her. She's past exhausted and needs some rest. Honestly, I'm surprised for her age and for it being the first time she's ever used magic this big that she's even still conscious.

Before I can voice my concern, she raises her hand to her head as her eyes close, "I think I'm going to go get a drink of water and maybe get to bed a little early. That took a lot out of me." She lowers her hand to glance in my direction, "But I want to talk more about Vladimir and the other six tomorrow and maybe try this again as you said."

I smile at her, "Sounds like a plan. Go get some rest honey; you're going to need it for tomorrow."

She nods her head as she stands and makes her way towards the door but not before Aaron stands and adds, "I also want to talk to you tomorrow about setting up some time to work with you. Train I mean, and hopefully teach you how to use your wolf senses and to shift. These things may come in handy sooner than I would care to admit," he turns his gaze to me for a moment before he continues, "and I think it's important to keep training with your mother on how to use your other powers until you get strong enough with them," returning his attention to our daughter with a smile on his face he says, "and I want you to take on sparring with the rest of the pack. It is time you learned to defend yourself. Not just with your magic or with your wolf senses but also in the physical sense." Knowing I may have a rebuttal he looks at me one last time, "She needs to be prepared. We can't always be with her and this world just got a whole lot darker for her."

All I can manage is a nod. The thought of our daughter having to fight at all, more than frightens me. It makes me angry. She's not even eighteen yet, she's still a child and she's barely begun to live. This isn't fair, isn't right. She should be happy, spending time with her friends, laughing and falling in love, not fighting for her life and worrying about the death of those she loves around her. What could Vladimir possibly want with her that would turn her life into this chaotic mess it has become?

I would do anything to protect her, shield her from this. I would, without hesitation, take this on myself, but I know, this is something she has to do herself. Her life as an innocent, carefree child is over and there's no turning back. This was a future I had always hoped to protect her from and now it's here, and it has come far too soon. I know there's nothing I can do to protect her from this and that is a hard pill to swallow. I would give anything, do anything if it meant she could continue to live her life and be normal and do things that kids should be doing at her age. I was hoping to protect her from a life that was anything like mine was growing up but now hers has become more dangerous than I had ever imagined and that thought terrifies me.

I look at them both as my daughter smiles back at me and she makes her way out the door. I look after her and for the first time, I no longer see her as my child. I see her as an adult, a warrior, a fighter and I couldn't be prouder of the woman she has become and the woman she is turning into. Without realizing it, I find myself smiling at her, and the thought of what a wonderful young woman she is, and for the first time since she told me about Vladimir, I find myself thinking we can do this, she can do this. She can win.

Chapter 6

Amberly

I want to see Julian more than anything. Well, almost anything. I need to sleep that much is clear. I can feel it in my muscles, knowing it won't be long before I pass out. I haven't seen Julian or been able to talk to him about what happened when we first arrived back at the cave. I can only imagine what's going through his mind right now. If I were in his shoes I would be freaking out and thinking the worst.

Yes, I love Logan. I've loved him for a long time and probably always will... but Julian... It's different with him. I'm different with him. He makes me feel alive. When he touches me, every cell in my body wakes up and comes alive, and I feel like I am where I was always meant to be. I lose all sense of reason when he is close to me. I can't breathe right, can't think. The only thing that creeps into my mind when he's near is being closer to him, wanting him to touch me. It's like nothing I've ever felt before. I'm still trying to understand it myself. How do you meet someone and from the first moment your eyes meet feel this pull? I felt this connection without really knowing him. The more I think about it, Julian isn't even my type, yet... I can't help myself, all I want is to be near him. I feel whole, safe, and alive when I am.

Logan's the safe choice. He's my best friend, he knows me, he understands me. He knows how I like my tea, my favorite meal, and how I pick at my cuticles when my mind is overwhelmed. He knows me like the back of his hand and it's the same for me but that's not enough, not anymore. It wasn't until I met Julian and he woke me up. He's all I want now; all I find myself thinking about. And I would be lying if I said that, in more ways than one, it didn't scare me because it does. We just met and yet I feel like I've known him as long as I've known Logan. The whole thing makes no sense to me, but I don't care to find the reason behind it because of how I feel when I'm with him and he needs to know that.

I just hope it's not too late.

I hope I can get him to understand.

To see.

We are meant to be together and we will figure it all out. I'll deal with my father and we will find a way to make this work. I need to let him know what Logan means to me, to explain everything, and let him know that it's him I want, not Logan.

He's my Clark Kent and I'm his Lois Lane.

He's my Batman and I'm his Catwoman.

He's my Barry Allen and I'm his Iris West.

We complete one another. Whether he can see that or not, I can feel it and will show him no matter how long it takes. He might not understand my metaphors, but I will find a way to get him to understand. I read too much. I laugh to myself. But right now, I'm exhausted and it is time to sleep.

Tomorrow will be the start of some exceptionally long days, and I know I need to get as much sleep as possible. I've wanted for so long to be taken seriously and be taught about our past, to learn to defend myself, and how to use all my gifts. My father has my mother's agreement to do just that. It sucks that it is under these circumstances but, hey beggars can't be choosers, right? So, the bottom line is… I can make time to see Julian tomorrow, for tonight I sleep.

* * *

Amberly

I do not know when I finally drifted off, but I know for sure I'm still asleep even though my senses make me feel otherwise as the cold night air caresses my hot skin. I can feel the cool dirt under me as I sit up and look around the pitch-black forest.

I push myself up off the ground and fold my arms around my now cold body. Looking to the sky I see the full moon through a part in the trees and I cannot help but let a smile creep up on my face. I find myself wondering what it will be like to run in the forest in my wolf form as I look to the moon and let out a howl of pure joy.

Suddenly every nerve in my body feels like it's on fire and I feel like I have been running through the forest for hours and in the next moment my body and eyes aren't my own. I'm looking through someone else's eyes, feeling someone their fear. I, they, keep running even though I can barely stand, I turn to look behind me. I'm running from something, from someone. I look over my shoulder to see if

I'm being followed, and the next thing I know I'm flying through the air as a pain shoots up my leg. Moments later the air is knocked out of my lungs as I land on the ground. As it leaves her mouth, so does my subconscious.

More than a little confused, I looked down at the girl whose body I was just In. Her long midnight lavender hair is a mess covering her face as her chest rises and falls. She's a very pretty girl, about my age would be my guess, she seems to be about my height and weight as well. Her hair has a light wave to it and as she sits up against the nearest tree it falls away from her face and back down to her shoulders where it takes up residence. She's covered from head to toe in all different-sized cuts and bruises.

"What happened to you," I ask.

She jumps and looks around at her surroundings like she heard me, and I know for sure she did when she replies in a shaky voice, "Who's there?"

A little stunned, I reply, "My name is Amberly, I live here in these woods. Are you running from someone?"

"That's none of your business." Scared, she tries to stand but falls back to the earth.

"You're exhausted, you need to rest. Let me help you."

She looks to the ground and says in a low voice, "No one can help me."

"I can if you let me. Tell me where you are, and I can come find you."

Confusion sets in as she looks around the dark forest once more, "What do you mean come find me? We are talking to each other. Where are you?"

Not sure how to answer her question, I tread lightly. "Honestly, it's a very long story but I'm not," I pause for a moment, not sure how to word my answer to her without scaring her off or worse, making her ask more questions that I can't answer right now. "physically here with you. I can explain when I get there. Tell me where you are."

I can both sense and hear the panic and fear in her voice when she replies. "I, that's the problem, I don't know where I am. I just ran and kept running until. Until I couldn't run anymore." She stammers over her words pausing every few seconds.

"Ok, then close your eyes for me and think hard about things you remember seeing right before you fell."

39

I see the resistance in her eyes before she closes them and just like that I am pulled back inside her head and I see all I need to in order to find her. She's not much further from where I woke up in the forest moments ago, the only question is... when I return to my body, where will I wake up? I decided not to give her a time frame of how long it would take me to get back to her.

"I know where you are. Don't move, I'm coming to you."

Chapter 7

Amberly

When I return to my body, I am back in my bed inside the cave. Which means I was dream walking or something of that nature. Not knowing what I am capable of, or what powers I have, is exhausting. Explaining this to someone else will be difficult. What kind of powers are manifesting inside of me? Who am I becoming?

I have never heard of anyone having anything like the power I just experienced. My mind didn't just leave my body, it ended up inside someone else's mind. How is that even possible? I know my mother said I could control people with my mind, but this was something different entirely. I was seeing through her eyes, feeling what she was feeling, as if they were my own fears, my own body aches. How am I going to explain this to everyone in the morning? Like 'Hey I just went for a run and came across someone in need of our help.'

Annoyed, I jump up faster than I ever have in my life. I throw my boots on my lanky feet, and my jacket over my frail shoulders, and make my way out of the cave entrance into the brisk dark night. I know everyone is going to kill me when I come back because I left the cave alone, but it's so late and time is of the essence. I have never felt as scared as I did when I was inside her head. And I have had plenty of fears inhabiting my subconscious the last few nights. Who or what is she so afraid of? She is running from something but what could it be? For the first time, I find myself hoping I am not making a grave error in judgment by bringing someone I don't know back to the cave. What if she is a ploy? What if she's with Vladimir and this is one of his tricks to get me out and alone? He seems to know more about me than I do about myself. Maybe he knows more about my powers than I do.

I shake my head viciously, removing all my doubt. No one could fake that kind of fear.

I run through the forest for what feels like an eternity; just as I'm getting ready to give up, thinking I went the wrong way. That's when I saw her. I slow down my pace, coming almost to a complete stop, not wanting to scare her, as I round the tree and she comes completely into view.

Softly I say, "Hello."

The unnamed girl flies off the ground faster than I thought possible from how exhausted I know she is. She looks almost like she's ready to fight with her hands in tight fists at her sides, I take a step back, trying to reassure her that I'm not a threat to her.

"It's me." I quietly whisper.

And for the first time I see relief on her face as she closes her eyes and slides back down to the cold earth floor, "I thought that was a dream."

"No, I'm really here." I make my way over to her slowly, and offer her my hand, "Here let me help you up."

She offers her hand to me without a second thought. "Thank you."

I pull her off the ground and wrap my arm around her shoulders offering her support.

"Where did you come from?" She asks me.

"Not that far, we can make it, just lean on me and keep moving one foot in front of the other."

I feel her chest vibrate off me as she gives off a little laugh, "That's not what I meant. I mean where did you come from? You're not a human."

I would be lying if I said her statement didn't surprise me. I was wondering if she was a human or a supernatural being but now, I have my answer. "You're right I'm not human."

"So, what are you? Fairy, shifter, witch?"

"I could ask you the same thing."

"I'll tell you if you tell me."

What could it hurt? "OK, but the problem is I don't know how to answer that question, in all honesty."

I can sense her suspicion as her body starts to tense, and her pace starts to slow, "What do you mean?"

"Well," not sure how to word it, I figure it's just best to blurt the words out, "My mother is a witch, and my father is a shapeshifter, so I'm kind of more than one thing." She stays silent for a while before I try to restart the conversation, "And how about you?"

"I'm a shapeshifter too."

I try to hold back my surprise when I say, "Really?"

Her chest vibrates lightly against me again as she replies with a light giggle, "Yes, really. Why do you sound so surprised?"

"Well, I didn't know there were any other shapeshifter villages around here."

Even in the dark, I can see the surprise on her face, "How is that possible?"

"Up until a few weeks ago, I didn't know much about the world outside the four walls of my home. My mom kind of hid everything from me. Everything about who I really was, until I learned about it on my own. My mom and I have a bit of a complicated relationship I could say. Or at least we did until a few days ago, now we are closer than ever and she's teaching me everything there is to know about my powers and our history."

"Wow? That's messed up. I mean awesome that you and your mom are close now and she's teaching you about your powers but what about all that time you lost? I don't know I would still kind of be pissed if it was me, but again that's just me."

Her words awaken something in me. I mean my mother and I have been doing a lot better since we got here, but I don't really know why that is though. This girl has a point. What my mother did was wrong, and I was angry with her for so many years, but after we arrived at the cave all that anger just evaporated. Am I still mad at her? I have every right and reason to be. But we are happy, we are together and for now, we are safe. She's open to me in a way she's never been and for the first time, she's not holding anything back from me. I mean the truth was out, my father was alive, and I know the truth behind who I am. I'm going to start learning all the things I've begged her to teach me all these years. So, why wouldn't I let all the anger go? Why not be in the here and now and let the past stay where it is?

"Sorry, I didn't mean to be out of line. It's just if my parents had lied to me all that time, there's no way I would be able to let it go, at least not for a long time. Knowing who you are is a big part of living in this life, and we already have such a hard time figuring out who we are as a person, but to not know who you really are, down to your core well that's extreme."

I look deeper into the forest, "Yeah, I guess it kind of is."

We walk in silence for a few minutes before it dawns on me, "Hey, I never asked you your name."

"My names, Amara, Mi for short. What's yours?"

"I guess in all the excitement you didn't register my name before but I'm Amberly. An Mi? Where does that come from? Is it somehow short for Amara?" I say with a little laugh and smile on my face.

Amara stops dead and looks up at me, "Your parents, their names wouldn't be Aaron and Jocelyn, would they?"

Confused, I answered, "Yes. But how did you…"

She looks back to the ground before cutting me off, "You're all I've been hearing about for months. I was taken by this crazy man; he killed my whole village and took me. He tortured me repeatedly, trying to get in my head, to make me one of them." She looks back up into my eyes, "You're the one they are coming for."

The realization is clear in my voice, I'm sure, when I say, "Was the man's name Vladimir?"

"He was there, yes but I'd hate to say he wasn't my main concern."

"What do you mean?"

"I mean Vladimir has a lot of people who follow him or believe in his ways. But one man stuck out more than the others." She pauses for what feels like forever and just when I think she isn't going to continue she looks at me and continues, "He's darker than the others, angrier. He was the one who tortured me and tried to get inside my head. He's Vladimir's second and he's the one you should be worried about. I've never been one to scare easily, but he terrifies me."

"Do you know who he is? Like where he comes from, I know you said that Vladimir killed your family and took you, do you think he did the same thing with this guy?"

She shakes her head, "I know his name and that's about it. I don't know where he came from or even what supernatural background he has running through his veins. But he and Vladimir talked about you and your parents and the other six a lot."

My heart skips a beat, making it hard to catch my breath when I ask, "The other six?"

"Yes, Vladimir is one of the seven…"

"Surprisingly, that's one thing I did know," I can feel my brain going to work. It takes a little longer than normal, maybe because of the hour or maybe being in my mother's head took more out of me than I thought, "So maybe you can help fill in some blanks for me. If you're OK with me asking some questions?"

"I'll help if I can, but I was in and out so much from them being in my head and trying to fight them off that I can't promise I'll be of much help."

"I understand and any blanks you can fill in will be one more than I have now."

She smiles, "True. OK, ask away."

"I'm a little curious about the other six. My mom told me that Vladimir killed them all hundreds of years ago. Is that true? What were they saying about the six that you can remember?"

"No, that's not true. Vladimir lied. He wanted everyone to be afraid and go into hiding, so he told everyone he killed them."

For the first time, I can't hide my excitement. Not only because I'm getting more answers but also because it was all a lie, he didn't kill them, at least not all of them. This could be what we need to stop him. "So, tell me the truth. Tell me what you heard. Please."

Amara seems almost as enlightened as I am as she says, "Well, I know for sure that at least two of the six are still alive," she pauses to think before she continues; "I believe he said their names were Johnathan and Aayda." She stops again, but only to return her attention to me, "I believe they are the shapeshifters and the natural."

"What did he say that made you believe they were still alive? Does he know where they are?"

Worry is written all over her face, "Yes, he knows where they are and he's going after them. He wants to finish what he started. That's how I know they are still alive." Walking is getting harder for her; I can tell because her pace slows. We only have a short distance left to travel but it's obvious she needs a moment, so I stop walking.

She continues, "He's so angry at them, for what I'm not entirely sure, but I could feel his hatred. He talked about the plan to go after them right before I escaped. I doubt I'm important for him to track down first, but he has so many followers that he could have easily sent some after me too. That's why I never stopped running," She smiles up at me before saying, "Not until I ran into you that is." She takes in a deep breath and looks up to the onyx night sky before continuing, "He has enough followers to send some after

Johnathan and Aayda as well as me," she turns her gaze back to me, "and you. He's coming for you too. He doesn't know where you are exactly, but he knows who your parents are and that you are somewhere in these woods. It's only a matter of time."

"We're going to keep you safe; I promise."

The doubt is engraved in her features as she asks, "We're?"

I almost laugh at myself for not mentioning this sooner, "Yes, sorry I forgot. We are going back to my father's cave. He's the pack leader and right now he, my mother, and some of my mother's guards are there. There are plenty of us to keep you safe."

I can see the panic forming in her eyes, "You're sweet but I only need to rest for the night, then I must keep going. I need to get as much distance between me and them as possible. I've already stopped and rested more than I should have."

"I understand, and I understand you're scared, but we can help you, we can put an end to whatever it is he's doing."

"You don't know him. You haven't seen what he's capable of." Amara closes her eyes before she continues, "There's a reason he's still around, a reason he can still do what he does to people. He's strong, stronger than anyone, no one can stop him," she opens her eyes and looks over at me, "I fear not even you."

Now it's my turn to look bewildered, "Me? What do you mean?"

"He talked about you, remember. You and your family, we just haven't gotten to that part of the conversation yet."

"What did he say about my family," I pause almost afraid to ask, "and about me?"

"Let's just say from what I heard he's afraid of you."

"Me?"

"Yes, you."

Trying to hold my sarcasm back I say, "But why?"

"Honestly, I'm not sure. He didn't divulge that information. But I could tell he was scared, and he wanted you out of the picture." She pauses for a moment, and I can tell she's unsure if she should continue, but finally, she does, "He even said 'the problem', meaning you, was supposed to be handled eighteen years ago but whoever he sent to finish the job messed it up."

I mumble, "Lurch and Onyx."

"What?"

That's a story for another day, "Sorry, nothing, it's not important. Did you happen to find out when he is coming for me?"

I can hear the tension in her voice when she replies, "As I was escaping, they were getting ready to come and find you. He wasn't a hundred percent sure where you were, but he had a general idea."

A little afraid of her answer, but I ask anyway, "How long were you running for?"

"I lost track of time, but I can tell you he's at least a few days run behind," she lifts her free arm to point to the east, "in that direction."

The fatigue is finally starting to set in, I can feel her going limp, "OK, let's get you back to the cave. We can talk more about this tomorrow, we have time."

We continue the path home and out of everything we talked about only one thing is clouding my mind right now. He is coming for me and he's coming now.

"Amberly."

Startled, I replied, "Yes."

"Thank you."

"For what?"

"For finding me."

I smile. "No thanks needed. I'm glad I could help."

I can see her mind going to work and I know there is a question, something she wants to ask but for some reason she hasn't. "What is it?"

She shakes her head. "It's nothing."

"You can ask me anything I won't bite, I promise," I say with a genuine smile.

"Really, I was only thinking about how you found me."

"Oh."

She looks down at our feet moving forward slowly. "I can't put the pieces together is all."

"It's hard to explain. Honestly, I wouldn't even know how to."

"It's fine you don't need to tell me; I understand, trust me."

I look at her sadly, "No, it's not that I don't want to tell you, I just don't understand it myself. Remember when I said I just found out about my father, that I'm half shifter, and the first of my kind."

She nods.

"Well because of that I have powers I don't understand."

"You are different, sometimes that's a nice thing," she looks at me shyly, "sometimes it's a curse. Not knowing who you are or what you're capable of, can really mess with you."

"You can say that again."

We look at each other and laugh.

With a sigh I continue, "I can dream walk if that is what you even call it. But tonight, it started as that and then somehow, I ended up inside your head. Seeing through your eyes and I felt what you were feeling."

She looks at me and I'm not sure if I'm seeing fear in her eyes or awe. "You can go into people's minds?"

"Well at least that's what my mother told me, but I never tried to do it and I still don't know how I did tonight."

She looks forward and smiles. "That's awesome as hell."

I smile as we start laughing once again while continuing to put one foot in front of the other with only one destination in mind.

Home.

Chapter 8

Julian

I know I saw her come out here.

I've already wandered a good distance from the cave, and I'm starting to panic. Why would she come out here by herself and why would she walk this far alone? I can't help but be angry with her. How am I supposed to protect her, how is anyone supposed to, when she keeps running off on her own all the time? Hasn't she learned anything?

I feel the pressure behind my eyes as I glance over the landscape in front of me. Still no sign of her. Time to try something else. I close my eyes and fill my lungs with the night brisk air as I focus on hearing deep into the forest.

I can hear a squirrel chewing on his nut high in a tree a mile away. I smirk as I continue to scan around the forest until I hear it, her voice.

My eyes shoot open.

She's with someone.

I sprinted in the direction I heard her voice coming from with only one thing in mind, finding her and yelling at her for being so careless.

* * *

Julian

I see Amberly walking in the distance with a girl. She has her arm around Amberly's feeble shoulders, and I find myself wondering what she could possibly have gotten herself into now. Only a few feet away from them I look at the new girl, the stranger. She's all beaten up. Bruises and cuts over every inch of exposed skin and her clothes are dirty with mud and blood and torn in many places.

I look from her to Amberly and back again. Seriously? How in the world did she come across this girl and who is she? Where did she come from? I look off into the distance behind them, searching for any sign of life that would be lurking in the darkness. Nothing.

When I return my gaze to the new girl, I see her long shoulder-length dark lavender hair curling around her right shoulder, unmoving, even as they continue to step forward. I use my wolf site to zoom in on the area in question and I see a deep gash take up residence on the sun-kissed skin.

Her blood had made its way into her hair and dried, making it immobile as it now sticks to her skin. What happened to this girl?

Without thinking I look at Amberly and survey her, checking every inch and taking note that her body is untouched. Thank God. The last thing I need is to take her back to the cave with cuts up and down her body like this girl. Aaron I'm sure is still upset with me after the last time Amberly went into the forest alone. I'm still angry with myself for being so reckless, and not having my eyes on her at all times. But now I know better, I watch her more closely to make sure nothing like that ever happens again.

Chapter 9

Amberly

I see Julian running towards us in the darkness, and I can't stop my heart from skipping a beat. Every time I see him it's like I'm seeing a sunset for the first time. He takes my breath away and makes my heart skip a beat just like a sunset can. Every cell in my body comes alive when he's around, he wakes me up in the best way possible. I can't help thinking back to the night before I left and the feeling of his lips on mine. I can feel the smile creeping up to take residence on my face, however, it's shortly lived.

"Are you out of your mind?"

Confused, I ask, "What?"

"How could you leave like that? After everything."

Trying not to stutter, I reply, "I'm sorry, I didn't have time to wait for anyone."

The hurt is clear in his eyes, "Wait for anyone?"

Damage control time, "I didn't mean it like that. I…Amara was in trouble and I needed to get to her as fast as I could."

His gaze turns in her direction and I can feel her stiffen against me. Julian looks positively scary when he wants to, and even when he doesn't want to. His short temper doesn't help matters any.

His tone tells me he's trying to stay neutral when he says, "You're, Amara, I presume."

Amara hesitates before answering. "Yes."

His gaze goes from Amara to me before he speaks again, "How do you two know each other?"

"Well, see, now, that's the thing." His glare makes me involuntarily take in a breath, "Up until now we've never met before."

And now the anger is clear in his voice, "You mind repeating that last part for me?"

I roll my eyes as I say. "We just met."

"You're telling me you left the safety of the cave, in the middle of the night, to come out here to find someone you've never even met before?"

"Julian, please I really don't want to argue with you."

He grinds his teeth together, "Too bad."

"Fine. If you want to fight, we can fight. But not right now."

He's acting like a crazy man. I've never seen this side of him before and I would be lying if I said I liked it. I understand him being upset with me for coming out here at this hour, and alone at that, but it's not like him to be talking to me this way. Or maybe it is, maybe I don't know him as well as I thought.

"Hate to break it to you, sweetheart, but you don't control everything. If I want to have it out now, then we are going to have it out."

Surprised I say. "I never said that I was in charge. I'm not trying to control anything I just-"

He cuts me off and his anger is starting to physically show as the veins pop out in his neck. "Just what? Thought you would leave and come back, and no one would know you ever left."

I shrug and say, "Well."

Well, he's got me there. I knew everyone was asleep, or at least I thought everyone was. I never thought Julian would still be awake at this hour and come looking for me. I thought I would come out here and find Amara and bring her back to the cave with everyone still warm in their beds. Then in the morning after my parents had their coffee, and I knew it was a good time, I would tell them how I left the cave last night to go help someone and that's when I would introduce Amara. It seemed like a good enough plan. Would people be upset with me? Yes. Would they understand why I did it? Yes. So, Julian reacting the way he is, is way over the top, even for him and it is making me feel like there is something much bigger going on. However, before I get the chance to ask, he breaks my thought process.

"Wow, you are something else. You know what, I feel bad for Logan."

Now I'm angry. "What's that supposed to mean?"

"It means the poor guy doesn't stand a chance."

"And why's that?"

He looks at me and smiles his devilish smile that I love. "Because loving you is a life sentence. You're a handful. Too much for any man to deal with in my opinion."

I feel the pressure forming in the back of my eyes and I blink hard and fast before saying, "Thank you for your kind words."

"If the shoe fits."

I take another step forward with Amara following suit. "You are unbelievable."

"Pot, meet kettle."

"Grow up."

He grins before saying, "I don't think I'm the one who needs to grow up."

"Oh really."

He flashes me his serious face. "Really."

"Ugh, you're unbelievable."

He smiles. "I'm quite sure you already said that. Is that all you got?"

I look at him and I'm sure he can feel the anger radiating off of me. "No."

"Have at it then."

What has gotten into him? He is making my blood boil and saying everything under the sun to push me over the edge. Why is he baiting me like this? Why is he being so heartless? This isn't the Julian I know; this isn't the Julian I fell in love with. He isn't the person who came to me in the woods and brought me home to my father. He isn't the man who protected me from being mauled to death or the man who was so angry with himself for letting it happen in the first place. This isn't my Julian.

"Well, I'm waiting, princess."

Through bared teeth I say. "Don't call me that!"

Sarcastically he says. "What? Princess?"

"You know very well what I meant."

He smiles. "So, what if I did."

"Ugh, you make my blood boil, you know that?"

Encouraging me with his hand, "Keep going."

"Don't tempt me."

"Don't hold back. I'm waiting. Your Highness."

And the gloves are off. "You arrogant, vicious, malicious, vindictive," he gestures to me with his hands again to keep it coming as he smiles, "self-righteous, proud, vain, controlling, know-it-all."

"Wow, is that all you got?"

I can hear the sarcasm in his voice but for a moment I swear I see hurt in his eyes, but just as quickly as I thought it, it was gone again.

I sigh before replying, "You know you're really pushing it."

He leans in close to me. So close that he makes me come to a stop, "not hard enough it seems."

"Julian," closing my eyes I release a long breath I didn't realize I was holding until now, "Can we please finish this," I open my eyes to see him looking back at me, "Whatever this is later. Amara can barely stand, nor I for that matter. Can we please get back to the cave and I'll tell you everything then?"

The annoyance is clear on his face as he reaches out to put his arm around Amara so that we can both offer her some support, "No need."

"Seriously. After all of that."

"I don't care." He flashes me a smile, "Just don't do it again."

Of all the nerve, he doesn't own me. He can't tell me what to do, or order me around! Who does he think he is? My husband or something? Even then I would never let something like this fly. He started a fight with me. What did that even accomplish? And now he wants to just let it go. Act like nothing happened, that nothing is wrong. Am I the crazy one here? Is there something I'm missing? Did I do something I'm not seeing? Because this is more than just because I left the cave alone. Yes, he is pissed about it, but it would never make him act this way towards me. I know I haven't known him that long, but I feel like I have known him my whole life and better than most people. So, the question is, what's eating him up so badly that he has to treat me this way?

Annoyed, I reply, "Julian, in case you haven't noticed I'm a grown woman and I'll do whatever I want, whenever I want."

He looks at me coldly, "Not without consequences in the future." He flashes me his teeth as he smiles, "Try me."

Not wanting to fight anymore I keep quiet and try to get a better grip on Amara but my hand grazes Julian's instead. His skin barely touches mine and starts to turn my whole body to fire. Every nerve is screaming, the warmth spreading through every inch of my body. I try to ignore it and the feelings that come with it. Before my feelings have a chance to take over my vision starts to blur. I look at Julian hard and I can barely make out the confused and worried look on his face. I feel my legs come out from under me as my body starts to plummet to the earth floor and in seconds, I'm no longer in the forest with them.

*** *

Amberly

Flames are everywhere. They are close enough that I feel the heat from their embers on my skin. I look around trying to make sense of where I am but smoke fills the air, clouding my vision. I lift my hand to the neck of my shirt and lift it up over my mouth and nose as I suppress a cough. The shirt is helping to keep more smoke from entering my lungs, but I hate to say it's not helping much. I close my eyes as tears roll down my cheeks.

If this is anything like my other trips, if I get hurt here my body is still affected in the present so I need to move fast. Hesitantly, I open my eyes back up and it's like a waterfall running down my face and the pain is only increasing. I quickly run my eyes over the landscape. At first, all I see is smoke and fire until they come to rest on two bodies to my right. I slowly make my way over to them, afraid of what I'll discover. It's difficult to make out even the color of their hair as the ash covers their bodies. However, from here I can tell it's a woman and a man, but the question is still the same, who are they? I'm five feet away when I stop dead. I'm afraid to move any closer, afraid to see who is lying on the ground in front of me.

Do I know them?

I can feel the fear starting to take hold and I know I need to act fast. I close my eyes one more time and take in a deep breath from behind my shirt. I open my eyes and take the last few steps until I'm on top of them. I crouch down and put all my weight on the front of my feet as I lean over and reach out my hand. I rest it on her shoulder for a moment before I pull back and cradle my hand to my chest. Her body feels as hot as the fire.

I baby my hand for a moment and then I reach back out and quickly turn her over. As I make out her face, I fall back to the earth my butt landing hard and my shirt falling away from my face.

It can't be.

Angela!

Even though I know she's already dead I can't help but get up and reach around her to check her for a pulse and when I don't find one, I close my eyes as more tears run down my cheeks.

"How did this happen?"

I hesitate before I turn my attention to the body next to hers. I reach over, close my eyes, and roll his body to face me. Afraid to see who it is, I sit there with my eyes closed for what feels like an eternity and then I finally open them, and my free hand finds its way to my face to cover my mouth as I stifle a sob.

"Logan!"

It can't be.

How?

How is this happening?

Grief-stricken I throw myself over him and lay my hands and head on his chest as I sobbed into him. I know there's no reason to check for a pulse, I know he's dead. I hear no heartbeat, his chest isn't rising and falling, it's still. The hotness from his body doesn't faze me, all I feel is loss and heartache. The rest of me is numb.

Before I can stop myself, I cry out as I beat on his chest begging him to wake up. And that's when I see them. Four more bodies on the ground only ten feet away from where I am with Angela and Logan's bodies. Then I look further to see more bodies behind the new ones I've come to discover. Knowing I need to get up and see who they are, I take Logan's hand in mine as I close my eyes once more and whisper, "You're not dead yet. I won't let this happen. I promise I'll find a way to stop this."

I open my eyes and lay his hand back on his chest and make my way to the next pile of bodies. Once it hits me that there are four more here and Angela and Logan are behind me, the fear becomes real in my chest, so real that I stop breathing. I fall to my knees near the only woman in the group and I forcefully pull her to face me as I scream, "MOM!!"

No, NO, NOOOOO.

Knowing who the rest are already I turn the man over next to her quickly, praying I'm wrong.

"*Aaron.*"

Then the next. Troy.

And finally.

I stop. Afraid to be right, praying I'm not. I reach out one last time as I pull him in my direction and then I can't stop.

Julian.

I cover his body with mine as I hear this loud animal-like cry, and it takes me a moment to realize it's coming from me. The pain in my chest is heavier than I could ever imagine it would have been. Lying here around me is everyone I love in this world and they are all dead.

My mother, my father, all my friends, and the two men that I love.

I look back at Julian as I feel my heart skip a beat. Losing Logan, my mother and my father was bad enough and hard enough to swallow but losing Julian, it's unbearable. I can't breathe, I can't think. And then I hear him.

"*Amberly?*"

I look down even though I know he didn't say anything, but I know it was his voice, Julian's. Then I feel it. The heat on my skin, but it's not from the fire, it's more like electricity. It's the same feeling I always get when he touches me. He has his hands on my arms. I can feel it as he calls my name again and this world, this vision leaves my mind and I return to my reality, but the question is how far off is this vision from coming true? Before everything fades away, I look around and take in what I can.

* * *

Amberly

"Amberly, open your eyes."

I can feel the electricity expanding and traveling in every direction from where Julian's hands are holding onto me. I want to see him, need to see him, need to know that he's ok. I need to let myself see he's ok. I need to know that what I just saw hasn't really happened yet. Our earlier fight is the furthest thing from my mind, all I care about is knowing I haven't lost him, really lost him. I fight to peel my eyes open. When they finally do, they come to rest upon coffee-colored hair. I can't stop the smile that forms on my face as my eyes come to rest on his and I can see all the tension evaporating into the air above him as he closes his eyes and releases a long sigh.

"What happened? Where did you go just then?"

Not entirely sure how to answer that question or even if I should, at least not right now, I look over at Amara as I say, "We need to get her back to the cave."

I can see the anger starting to form in his eyes, "Amberly."

"I'm fine, I promise."

"You don't look fine."

I smile at him weakly as I place a hand on his. "I'm sure I look like death, but I promise I'm ok."

I see the anger replaced by worry in his eyes as he says, "I think you should rest for a moment."

"I can rest when we get back to the cave and our warm beds."

And that fast the anger returns. "You were out for a few minutes. I think you need to sit here a little longer. I want to make sure you're well enough to walk."

"I just told you I am."

He looks at me sternly. "Well, no offense, but your words don't carry much weight with me lately."

"I know. But we need to get back."

"I want to know what happened, Amberly."

"We will talk back at the cave, I promise, but we need to get her there before she falls over."

He turns around to look at Amara for the first time, taking notice that she's ready to fall to the ground, "Fine but when we get back, we are talking, don't think you're getting out of that." He pauses as he turns his attention back to me, "You sure you can make it back to the cave?"

"Yes."

Reluctantly he removes his hands from my body and walks back over to Amara. It takes everything in me to stop myself from reaching back out to him. All I keep seeing is everyone I love around me dead. I can still feel the flames and my heart still hurts. I know it hasn't happened, but I know it's going to and soon. Unless I find a way to stop it. I need answers because I'll be damned if this vision is going to come true. I'm not about to lose everyone in my life, and not like this. There is one thing I do know for sure. I know their deaths are at the hands of Vladimir so it's time to get some real answers about him so I can stop him once and for all.

As I look at Julian, and Amara, the need only increases as I feel a tug at my heart. I will not lose him. I will not lose any of them.

* * *

Julian

We walk the rest of the way in silence, which is hard for me. I can see how tired Amberly is and I can tell there is something she isn't sharing with me. Something has been going on with her and I don't know what it is. A part of me wishes we could go back to the night before she left, back to being just

Julian and Amberly. Two people who never kept anything from each other and talked about everything. I could feel how close we became in such a short time, and I know it's not just me who felt it or maybe I should say feels it. I've known her longer than she's known me. I've come to know her better than I know anyone else and I've watched her grow into the woman she is today. I loved her long before she ever knew me, long before she ever spoke a word to me. That day changed everything. Being able to be close to her, have her get to know me and her liking me back was more than I ever hoped for. But when she left to return home, I knew what we had would be tainted. I know being with him changed what we had together. And now more than ever I know what I must do and that it must be done soon. Many things are holding me back, but the main thing is I know once I go through with my plan, she will hate me forever and because of that, I will lose the one thing that makes me the man I've worked so hard to become.

Her.

Amberly's voice pulls me from my thoughts as she looks at Amara, "We're almost there."

How did she find this girl? How did she know she was in trouble? What is she running from and do we have to worry about it knocking on our front door? Amberly promised me answers and I intend to get them.

"So, Amara, Amberly says until tonight you two never met, but how is it she knew you needed help and where to find you?"

Amberly glares back at me, "Julian, don't be rude."

"I'm not, I'm just asking a question. You know, one of the million that I have."

Amberly sighs, "I told you we can talk when we get home. It's only a few more steps. I don't think it will kill you to wait a few more minutes for answers."

"Well, maybe I'm tired of waiting."

"Seriously Julian. It's a few more minutes."

"No, because once we get back, I'm tucking you in, so no better time than the present to ask my questions and get some answers."

She looks at me with an annoyed look on her face. "Tuck me in, for real!"

"What? I thought that was very gentlemanly of me."

"I don't think you know what a real gentleman is."

"You didn't have any complaints before."

She looks at me and I can see the anger building in her eyes but for me, it's a game of cat and mouse. A game that I enjoy playing with her very much.

"Just because I didn't voice them to you doesn't mean there weren't any."

"Ok then shoot. Tell me."

She lets out a long sigh. "I'm not in the mood, Julian."

I laugh at her, "You're never in the mood."

"Well, I'm sorry I'm such a buzz kill."

"No apologies needed. Just answers please."

She stops walking and looks at me. "Seriously, Julian. Ten more minutes that's all I'm asking for. I think you can afford a little patience."

I smile as I reply, "I don't think you know me very well."

Something that looks like hurt makes its way across her face and now I wish I was the kind of person who thought before I opened my big mouth. Before I can say another word Amberly picks up the pace as she makes her way with Amara into the cave entrance.

Chapter 10

Amberly

My blood is boiling underneath my skin. I can feel it trying to escape its fragile home. How could he say I don't know him? I know we haven't known each other long but I feel like I know him better than I know anyone else. As for him wanting answers on what's going on with me, what do I say?

He's the one person I want to tell but he's also the one I'm most afraid of telling. I don't know what these powers mean, and they scare me, so how can I expect him not to feel the same way? What if my telling him the truth scares him away? Sadly, I know it's a risk I'm going to have to take because hiding the truth from him, lying, it's not something I can do.

As Amara and I enter the cave entrance I turn to look in her direction, "We can keep you safe here."

"Nowhere is safe, not until Vladimir is stopped," She stops walking and takes in a breath, "I know you mean well, and I appreciate everything you've done for me so far, but you need to understand the risk you are taking," she turns her gaze on me, "Especially for a stranger."

"It doesn't matter if I've known you for five minutes or seventeen years, I would still help you just the same."

I can see the confusion as well as hope on her face, "Why?"

I lightly push on her back to get us walking again, "Because that's how I was raised. You help someone if you can, plain and simple."

"But that's what I'm trying to tell you. You might not be able to this time. As much as you want to, it might not be something you can do."

Now it's my turn to stop, "Why would you think that?"

Amara stops and closes her eyes before she responds, "Because you don't know what Vladimir and Aidan are capable of," She opens her eyes as her shoes play with the dirt at her feet, "They won't stop until they get what they want, and you already have their attention and by helping me you're only making your chances worse."

"Aidan?"

"That was the name of the other man, the one who does all of Vladimir's dirty work for him."

I try to give her a reassuring smile, "I understand why you're scared and why your first instinct is to run but I promise we will do all we can to keep you safe. And you're safer here with us than out there on your own."

"Nothing is going to stop them and by me staying here it only means he will find you sooner."

I make my voice as calm as possible before I reply, "He's going to find me one way or another so for me it doesn't make much of a difference whether it's now or a few days from now."

"Ok. Do you mind if I change the subject?"

I look over at her curiously. "Sure."

"So, you and that guy."

I try to keep the annoyance out of my voice. "Julian?"

"Yeah."

I smile shyly. "What about him?"

"You two seemed very." She stops abruptly.

"Very what?"

"I don't know the right word to use."

I laugh. "Julian can be very intense."

He knows just as much about me as I do him, maybe more. He knows how to make me smile, and laugh and he knows how to make me so angry I could pull all my hair out. And to talk to me like that, fight with me, in front of Amara, a stranger on top of it. It's not like him at all. Normally, he would at least wait until we were alone. I feel bad for Amara, we've only just met and that's the first impression she gets of us.

"I guess that's one way to put it."

I look over at her. "I'm sorry you had to watch that."

"Hey, no biggie. It was actually nice."

Surprised, I ask. "Nice?"

"Well, when you're locked up and tortured for weeks and then running for your life it's nice to run into something that's so…normal, I guess would be the word, well it's nice."

"I guess I understand what you mean."

She laughs. "And I can see where for you it wasn't so nice."

I smile. "Yeah. He can really make my blood pressure rise."

"I think that's a normal thing for him."

"What do you mean?"

"When you're that good-looking and have that kind of attitude… I think he expects women to drop at his feet."

"I didn't think of it like that."

She laughs. "Girl, don't tell me you didn't realize how good-looking he is?"

"No, that I've noticed." I laugh.

"Good because I was getting worried."

We look at each other and laugh. It's nice to just laugh with someone new, someone who doesn't know everything going on with me. And it's nice that for a moment all my other worries and concerns seem to be drained from my body. Talking and laughing with another girl about normal teenage things is more of a relief then I thought it could be.

Her smile falters a little before she says. "But you shouldn't let him talk to you the way he does."

"I don't."

"It seemed to me like he was winning that argument."

"He would like to think so, I'm sure."

She glances down at our feet before continuing. "Once you start letting them treat you a certain way it gets harder to make it stop."

"So, I've heard."

"I'm sorry I don't mean to get in your business."

I smile reassuringly at her. "You're not."

"You sure?"

"Yes. It's nice talking to someone different about him."

She looks over at me, "So are you guys dating?"

How to answer that question? Before I left that answer would have easily been yes, but now. I don't know, and I think that's the hardest part about this whole thing. How can it feel so right one second and then so wrong the next? How can he be so hot and cold? Before I left, I never would have questioned how he felt about me, or what he wanted, but now. Now, I feel like I don't know anything. I know you don't talk to someone the way he was unless there is an underlying issue. I know we haven't talked about the night I left… or when I got back… or Logan… or really any of it for that matter, but could it really have changed us that much? Not knowing one hundred percent that we are together, I say the only thing I can.

"No. We aren't."

Surprised, she asks, "Really?"

I laugh. "Why do you say it like that?"

"Because I would have thought you were halfway down the aisle with the way that fight went."

"No, definitely not."

"Well, I guess that's a good and bad thing."

I stop walking. "Good and bad?"

"Yes. Good because you are a little young to be married. Bad because you already fight like a married couple."

We laugh. "Yeah, I guess I see what you're saying."

"But he is your boyfriend then?"

I don't answer right away. When I do, the only comment I can manage is, "I wouldn't classify us as a couple."

As much as I thought we were, and as much as I would love for us to be together, and find a way to make this work, I can't say we are something that I'm not sure we are.

"I'm sorry."

I look over at her. "What for?"

"For asking you about it. You seem like you... love him."

Lying not only to her, but myself, I reply. "No. I'm not in love with him."

I can see the surprise on her face at my answer and I know she's about to say something else, but then I see something out of the corner of my eye and turn my head to my right so fast I almost gave myself whiplash and to my dismay I see my mother running towards me, "Where have you been? I woke up to see how you were feeling after earlier and you were gone."

"I'm sorry, Mom, didn't mean to worry you."

She cuts me off as she throws her arms around me knocking Amara's arm clean off my shoulders. I don't think I've ever seen my mother this relieved. And for the first time, I thought about where her mind must have gone when she went to my room to find an empty bed and me nowhere to be found inside the cave. With everything going on lately I know I made her think the worst.

I try to force a reassuring smile on my face as I continue, "I can explain everything when we are alone," I gesture with my hand, "This is Amara, and she needs our help."

Amberly

"I don't think we need to go back in your head, again," I say to my mother as soon as we enter my father's room.

She looks at me, misunderstanding, "What do you mean?"

"Well, long story short, Amara was with Vladimir."

Fear masks my mother's face as she turns for the door, "We have to get…"

"Mom, I meant she escaped. He was torturing her."

She stops dead a foot from the door and turns to face me as she brings her hand to her lips, "Oh, that poor girl!" She drops her hand and steps in my direction, "Where are her parents?"

"She said Vladimir killed them, but he spared her and took her back to his village."

The skin between her eyebrows wrinkles up in a funny way, before she asks, "Why did he take her?"

"She said he was trying to get in her head, make her one of them."

I can tell she's trying to keep her tone neutral when she asks, "What does that mean? Make her one of what?"

"I don't know, we didn't have much time to get into all those details."

"Maybe you should have. That might be something we need to know."

I smile at her, "I know, Mom, but she knew other things that seemed to be a little more important. Something, I think, will help us stop him."

Intrigued she moves closer and crosses her arms over her chest and leans in close, "And that would be?"

"Well for starters she confirmed that he is alive and he's coming for me," I see the panic in her eyes, but I continue, "but she also told me that he's afraid of me. I'm a problem for him and he wants me out of the way."

Surprise takes over her facial features as she asks me, "What?"

"Mom, please if you were ever to be honest with me now is the time."

Now I can hear a hint of anger in her voice when she says, "What are you talking about?"

"Do you know why she would think Vladimir was afraid of me? I'm not even eighteen, my powers haven't even fully matured and won't for a few more weeks… and he's thousands of years old."

She closes the little bit of distance that is left between us, puts a hand on each arm and looks me in the eyes when she says, "Honey, I don't know why he would be afraid of you, that's the truth." She smiles before continuing, "If he is afraid of you there is a reason and I intend to find out what it is."

Wanting to move on to the next topic I tell her, "Mom, there was something else that Amara told me."

She walks over to her seat and plants herself in it, "What was it?"

"Two of the six, they're alive."

For the first time hope is clear on her face, "Who?"

"Amara heard him planning to go after them. It was Aayda and Johnathan, but this means there could be someone who knows how to stop him."

"If anyone knows his weaknesses or his plans, it would be one of them."

"We need to find them, but I don't know where to start."

"We will figure that out. We have time. How long till he makes it here? Did Amara say anything about his plan?"

I shake my head. "She said it was a few days run but she also said he didn't know exactly where I was."

"That's good, that means we have time."

"Time? You say it like you're talking about something other than what I think we're talking about."

She smiles at me. "It means we have time to train you, prepare you," she looks at the door, "and the others."

My vision pops back into my mind's-view. With a shaky voice I say, "Mom."

"What is it?"

"I don't want anyone to get hurt."

She places her hand on my shoulder. "I know and we are going to do our best to make sure that doesn't happen."

"How?"

"We train."

I sigh. "And what if that's not enough?"

She lightly touches my face. "It will be."

"You don't know that."

I can see recognition in her eyes. "Is there something you're not sharing with me? Is something bothering you?"

I want to tell her but I'm not ready to talk about what I saw in my vision. "No."

"Are you sure?"

"Yes. I'm fine. I'm just worried."

"I know. We will get through this and we will finally make it a safer place for everyone once we put a stop to Vladimir."

"I know we will."

I can see the wheels turning in her eyes as she turns for the door once more, "I need to go fill your father in. Will you be ok?"

"Yes." I smile.

She returns to my side and places her hands on my shoulders as she places a light kiss to my forehead. "Go eat and we will get together in a few hours."

"Sure thing."

I watch as she walks out the door, food is the last thing on my mind. I know I should eat but first I need to see Julian. We need to talk, it's time. If I'm going to share what's going on with me with anyone right now, it's him. He deserves as much. I can't expect us to work if I hold something like this back from him.

How is he going to react? Will he be afraid of me? Will he pull away? It doesn't matter, I need to start sharing what's going on with me with the people closest to me and I want to start with him. I take in a deep breath, start towards the door and hesitate.

Maybe I should eat first. I laugh to myself.

Chapter 11

Amara

My gratitude towards Amberly is miles long. Relaxing for the first time in days, getting cleaned up, and having a good meal feels so good. For the first time I caught myself wondering what she and her mother could be talking about, but I know it's about me and what I told her. I wonder what she will do when she learns her daughter is in danger?

Amberly is a rare breed for sure. Kinder than anyone I've ever known. No one I know would have taken someone like me in and put the rest of their family and friends in danger just by association. Or fed and clothed me. Her kindness makes me speechless. There aren't many people in this world like her and it will be a much darker place if she's taken from it.

"Hey, Amara, right?"

I look up to see one of the most handsome men I've ever seen looking down at me. His light chocolate eyes feel like they are looking right through me and into my soul. I drew in a slow breath as I continued to admire how his coffee-colored hair curls around his ears in just the right way.

I can see why Amberly would put up with all his bs, he is beautiful but there's something else about him. I can see in his eyes and feel that deep down he is one of the sweetest guys I'm sure I'll ever have the pleasure of getting to know. I can feel him trying to figure me out as he continues to scan me with his eyes. I feel the blood under my cheeks rushing to the surface as I nod my head and look at the ground, "And you are Julian."

I hadn't been able to get a good look at him before. It was too dark for one, but I was also so exhausted that paying attention to anything other than putting one foot in front of the other just wasn't an option. He's the kind of handsome that takes your breath away if you stare at him too long. He seems almost flawless.

"That's my name, don't wear it out."

I laugh, "So you are one of those kinds of guys, I see."

"If you mean strong and ruggedly handsome then yes you are correct."

This time I can't help but let out a full-on laugh, "I'm sorry. It's been such a long time since I've been able to laugh." Once I can stop, I look up at him, "It feels nice."

He seems a little uneasy as he sits down next to me. I can tell something is bothering him but he's hard to read. Normally, it's easy for me to pick up on what could be bothering someone, but he baffles me. Being around him though it's calming. I normally don't like new people but Amberly and Julian seem different, feel different. It almost feels like this is where I'm supposed to be, almost like this is where I belong.

Realizing he's not going to say anything I continue, "You're easy to be around and that's rare for me."

"I know the feeling." He says as he looks away.

"Really, you have a hard time being around people?" I looked away from him for the first time, "I never would have pictured that."

I can see the pain in his eyes when he says, "I'm more of a loner."

Trying to lighten the mood I say with a smile, "Now that I could picture."

"Really?"

I shrug, "Well when you talk to people the way you did Amberly earlier-"

"That was needed."

Puzzled, I ask, "Needed?"

He nods.

"How do you figure?"

He closes his eyes as he takes a deep breath and opens them again on release, "You don't know what I've been through with her. She's...a handful."

"So. I still don't see how that made it OK for you to talk to her the way you did, even if you were worried."

He looks at me amazed. "Worried. Me?"

I laugh. "You can't tell me you weren't."

He looks away from me as he says, "It's complicated."

"I can see that."

He shakes his head. "No, see, a few weeks ago she left the cave, and she was almost mauled to death by another wolf. She almost didn't make it."

I closed my mouth from the surprise. "Well, then again, I understand why you were worried about her."

He says his next words with such conviction. "I wasn't worried. She's the alpha's daughter, she will one day be alpha and it's my job to make sure she lives through the night. So, when she takes off it makes it hard to do my job. So, what you witnessed wasn't worry, it was annoyance."

The look in his eyes is telling me a different story than what he's voicing but I'm not sure what it is. Before I have the chance to call him on it, he speaks again.

"So, Amberly didn't really get around to filling me in."

Right down to the point this one. "Honestly, I don't know what answers you're looking for."

"Ok, for starters, how did she find you?"

"I don't think that's for me to answer, honestly."

"And why is that?"

I recall Amberly and my earlier conversation about her powers and I know if she wanted him to know the truth, he wouldn't need to ask me the question.

"That's just a conversation I think you should have with her and not me." I can see the confusion in his eyes, so I change the subject, "So you and Amberly, you guys are a thing, right? I asked her but her answer didn't make any sense."

For the first time, his body gets tense and his voice goes up an octave or two, "No! What would make you think that?"

"I just thought you guys were with the way you talked to each other."

Irritation is clear in his voice, "And how was that?"

"Just seemed like there was a lot of sexual tension there." I laugh.

"No, like I said before it was because she's my alpha's daughter so the tension you were seeing, or sensing was because I hate taking orders from anyone. Especially someone younger than me."

I must look away from him when I reply, "I get that."

I can see a flicker of interest in his eyes, "Why do you ask?"

"I..." Looking as far in the other direction as I can I say, "No, reason."

"The one thing I'm good at is knowing when someone isn't being honest with me."

I turn my attention back to him and he flashes a smile that makes my heart skip a beat. If Amberly and he aren't a thing, what would it matter if I'm attracted to him? I'm in a new place and it looks like I might be staying here for a while so what's the harm in getting to know him?

"I only asked because it seemed like something was going on between the two of you and I didn't want to step on anyone's toes that's all."

Surprise covers his face, "Step on anyone's toes, huh?"

I nudge his shoulder with mine, "Don't tease it's not nice."

"Just admit it, you think I'm hot." He looks away with a boyish grin masking his face.

I can't help but smile, "OK, fine since you need me to say it for the sake of your ego, yes you're not horrible to look at."

He throws his hand over his heart and falls back against the wall like he's been struck, "Oh, how you wound me."

Laughing, I say, "Hey, you wanted the truth, right?"

He smiles big enough for me to see the bottom of his two front teeth, "Yeah, but you could be nice about it."

"That was me being nice." I smile.

He places his hand on his chin and looks to the ceiling like he's thinking, "Hm, well, if that's you being nice, I'd hate to see you being anything other than that."

"Hopefully you'll never have to." I pause and look at him playfully, "just don't cross me and you should be fine."

"That's a relief."

I pause unsure if I should ask but I decide it needs to be said. "Can I give you a little advice?"

"Depends on the advice you're trying to give."

"All I was going to say is you should be nicer to her."

Confused, he asks. "Her who?"

"Amberly."

He laughs. "I'm nice enough."

"If she's your alpha's daughter you might want to try harder then."

"Why, you think she's going to tell on me?" He says sarcastically.

I shake my head. "No. I'm just saying no matter what a woman doesn't like being talked to that way or disrespected. It would go a long way if you were...nicer."

"Well thanks for the advice, I'll take it into consideration."

I look down at my hands not sure what to say now but before I think of something, he asks a question of his own.

"So. You were with Vladimir?"

"Yes."

I can see he has a lot of questions but he's unsure which are safe to ask. "Do you know why he took you?"

"Honestly, I think the only reason he takes anyone is to build up his army."

His eyes get wide. "What do you mean?"

"From what I learned he must go all around the forest and choose who he wants and the rest he," I pause not wanting to think about it much, "the rest he disposes of."

He looks to the ground for the first time. "I'm sorry."

"Not your fault."

He looks up at me again before continuing. "So, he just came and took you? And then what? Did he just expect you to follow him and be on his side after he took you from your home and loved ones?"

I whisper, "He has his ways."

"Meaning?"

I look intensely at him, "he has someone who can get in your head. Can change your memories. Make you think you joined him willingly."

I see tension forming on his face as he says, "So, everyone in his army is brainwashed."

"I think so, for the most part at least."

I can see the wheels turning in his mind. "Well, then we might have a chance."

"What do you mean?"

"If they are brainwashed there might be a way to get to them."

Surprised, I ask. "You want to save them?"

"If there is a way, we will find it. No one deserves to die for something they wanted nothing to do with."

I look down at my hands on my lap. "After being tortured like that. I don't know if there will be a way to reach them."

"Amberly."

I look up into his eyes. "What about her?"

He smiles. "She's powerful."

"I figured if a man like Vladimir is afraid of her then she must be."

"But it's more than her being strong."

80

Confused, I ask. "What do you mean?"

"I think she can get in people's minds just like Vladimir's secondhand can."

Nervously I ask. "Really?"

"I'm pretty sure it's one of her powers."

I smile. "Well, if it is then maybe those people do have a chance. From the little time I've known her I know if she can help someone she will."

I see something like admiration flash over his face and just as quickly it disappears, "That's definitely, Amberly."

"If we can take out his army, that will take his legs out from under him."

Julian looks to the doorway as he nods.

It feels wrong that I'm this attracted to him. I can't stop thinking about what it would be like to kiss him. I can't even remember the last time I kissed someone. I start to wonder if I said that out loud because the way he's looking at me now is like he's scared or unsure. But I know I didn't say it out loud. I'm not one to embarrass myself, especially around new people or someone I think is good looking. So why is he looking at me so intently and why does he look so torn?

Then, without warning, I feel his lips on mine as his hands knot themselves in my lavender onyx hair. His kiss feels hesitant but also forceful if that makes any sense. But it also feels nice. Without thinking I lift my arms to go around his neck and pull him in closer. I could get lost in his kiss, soft and his lips feel feverish to the touch. I'm starting to be drawn deeper into the kiss and his touch but then a loud bang echoes through the room and we jump apart.

I peel my eyes away from a panting Julian as I follow his gaze to the source of the noise. It's Amberly and even if I didn't take notice of the tears running down her cheeks the pain is clear on her face as she looks from me to Julian.

* * *

Julian

I can hear her thoughts as they reach out to me and I know this is my moment. Amberly will be back any minute and I know if I'm going to do this, I need to do it now. But I still can't help but be hesitant because I know once I do this there is no turning back, but I know it needs to be done. I look over at Amara both unsure and scared, knowing that my life is about to be changed forever, and not for the better. I never wanted to imagine my life without Amberly in it but I know I need to because once I do this, she is going to hate me.

I know I need to act fast before I change my mind, but my body is already fighting me, it knows what I'm not trying to admit. I force myself to ignore the feelings, and reach over and put my hand on Amara's cheek pulling her over to me almost forcefully. As our lips crash into one another I move my hands and tangle them up in her hair. She kisses me back and now I need to go through the motions. I picture Amberly and not Amara as her arms go around my neck. I sink into the kiss wanting more as my hands get lost in her hair.

I try to only imagine Amberly but it's impossible because even with my eyes closed it's so obvious it's not her. The smell, the feel of her hair, and the kiss. The kiss is so different. I feel like I could pick Amberly out of a lineup just by kissing her. I imagine her smell. I always thought she smelled of peaches and vanilla, so I try to only think of that. I imagine her thin, soft hair in between my fingers instead of this thick, rough hair and lastly, I think of her kiss. Of the electricity that would course through me at our touch.

I imagine only Amberly.

And then I'm sucked in. Wanting the kiss to be deeper. I want it to never end. But moments after I get into my character, I feel it. My heart shatters into a million pieces and that's when I come back to reality and realize it's not Amberly I'm kissing. But it's Amberly I'm feeling. Seconds later I hear a loud crash and I pull myself away from Amara and my gaze comes to rest on Amberly with tears running down her cheeks. Knowing that I'm the cause of her obvious pain shatters me in a way I never thought possible. I want to run to her, put my arms around her, and make that hurt disappear but I can't, I know I can't. This is for the best; this needs to happen. Not only because we can't be together but because we shouldn't. I'm not good enough for her and I know it. As much as I've tried to shut down those thoughts in my mind it doesn't work. She's so kind, gentle, smart, talented, and well let's face it she's just everything I'm not. She deserves someone who can give her things I can't. Someone who can love her like I can but build her up and push her towards her future.

She looks from Amara to me and back again and I can feel the pain as if it's my own, because it is. I want to comfort her, but I know that will undo everything I just did, and I remind myself I did it for a reason. However, I would be lying if I said that made this any easier.

I always thought of myself as a selfish man. Someone who could never truly put anyone above them self. I never let myself care enough about anyone else, never wanted to give a damn and I preferred it that way. The moment I would start to feel something for someone and see myself wanting to let them in, to tame me, to settle down, I would do something to make them want to run. I would always pull away, and even now I'm doing just that but it's not for the same reasons. I can see myself being happy with her, genuinely happy and in many ways that scares me, but I know she would be worth letting in, worth loving and giving my all to. But would it be fair to her? What could loving me bring her? Nothing. I would only hold her back and I need to not be selfish for once. She needs to let me go and this is the only way.

Even as her pain calls out to me from across the room, I know it's worth it and I would do it all again. I would do it because even though she is broken right now she will be better off without me. She will have less hurt this way than if we were to try to defy her father and the pack just so we could be with one another. She needs them and they need her, and I can't take that from them. For once I am not a selfish man but every part of me wishes I could be in this moment.

Amberly looks at me one more time before she turns and walks away, and I'm left with an emptiness in my heart and Amara in an awkward silence.

* * *

Amberly

I hear my stomach growling at me and I know I can't put off a meal any longer. I intend to eat a whole lot of something but not before I talk to Julian. I need to tell him everything whether I want to or not. He needs to know. I need to know that we can still move forward, that this can work.

I've loved Logan for so long that it is weird to imagine my life without him. He was the one I wanted to spend the rest of my life with but when I met Julian everything changed. He changed me, woke me up and he makes me the best versions of myself when I'm with him. I will always love Logan, but my heart is with Julian and for that reason he is the first person I need to talk to, need to tell everything to.

My heart skips a beat knowing I'm getting close to where he is and that I'll be seeing him soon. I know that being able to sense someone is a wolf trait, but I haven't really learned how to do that yet. With Julian, though it's like I feel a pull from wherever he is and when I follow it, I can tell where he is and know when I'm getting closer to him. It's something so different and so amazing.

It feels like it's been forever since I felt his hands on my skin even though it's been less than an hour. Being away from him is the hardest thing and that's another difference between him and Logan. It is more than me wanting Julian around all the time, it's more like I need him around. It's hard to explain but I feel stronger with him. It is more than just an emotion or feeling with him, it runs so much deeper. Yes, Logan and I know each other better and have been through so many life things together and he's been my best friend, my shoulder, my rock, my ear, my voice of reason and so much more throughout my life. He's been the one constant thing I've always had and the thought that I could lose that because of me choosing Julian over him is hard. But I would be living a lie if I choose Logan. I don't think I would truly be able to give him my whole heart. Not now, not after meeting Julian, knowing him, kissing him, and seeing what my life could be with him. And I know that what Logan and I share runs deeper than our feelings for each other. We are best friends, so I hope and pray that he will think that's enough and that I won't lose him in the end.

My heart skips another beat as I enter the room, the one I know he was keeping Amara company in. My eyes scan the room automatically and that's when I see them. This time my heart doesn't just skip a beat, it stops. I blink a few times to make sure I'm seeing what I think I'm seeing. And every time I open them it's the same view. Julian is kissing Amara.

Julian is kissing Amara!

I must remind myself to take a breath as the journals I had in my hands fall to the ground. Julian kissing another girl. I never thought my heart could hurt like this and I never thought he would be the one to make it hurt like this. I thought he felt what I felt. I thought this was something more, that we were something more. I look from Amara to Julian and back again as the tears roll down my face.

How can loving someone feel so right and then turn out so wrong? How can you love or care for someone and do something like this? Why is he kissing her? Her. Someone he doesn't even know. Someone who just came into our home. Someone he yelled at me for even going after in the first place.

How could he do this?

How could he do this to me?

How could he do this to us?

For a moment I blame myself, is it something I had done? Am I not enough? Did I do something wrong to make him kiss her? Is this his way of getting back at me for Logan? I push the thoughts from my mind and remind myself that two wrongs don't make a right and that even if that is why he's doing it; it doesn't make it OK. To do something to intentionally hurt me, someone he claimed to care so much about.

I was fighting tooth and nail trying to find a way for us to be together like I thought we both wanted. What was the point? I heard whispers about Julian about who he was and the things he had done to other girls in the pack. But I never thought he could or would do that to me. For some reason, I held myself to a higher standard and that's my fault. After all, a leopard can't change its spots right.

Julian looks at me and for a moment I think I see pain in his eyes, but I ignore it as I look over at Amara. Amara, who I brought here, who I promised to protect. I mentally kick myself. I look back at Julian and my heart skips a beat as I feel more tears rolling down my cheeks. Without a word, I turn my back on them and walk out of the room trying to hold the shattered pieces of my heart together with each step I take.

Chapter 12

Angela

I walk into the room and almost trip over all the journals lying on the ground. I look up to see the new girl Amara and Julian sitting in silence.

"Hey, there you are, I've been looking everywhere for you. We need to talk." I look back down at my feet, reach down, and pick one up to inspect it, "Hey, these are the journals of our ancestors, the ones about the seven, where did you find…" I trail off when I look up at Julian. "What's going on? What's wrong?"

He jumps out of his seated position and makes his way past me and out the door, as he mumbles, "I don't want to talk about it."

I turn my attention to the new girl, "I take it you don't care to talk about it either, huh."

Her cheeks turn scarlet as she looks at the ground, "I think it has to do with us kissing, and Amberly walking in on it."

Oh, crap.

"Which way did Amberly go?"

She looks up at me, "I'm not sure, but being a girl myself I would guess her room."

I'm about to take off down the hall when she grabs me lightly by the arm, before I have a chance to wonder how she reached me that fast she says, "I didn't know they were a thing, if I had, I never would have kissed him. He told me they weren't, and she said she wouldn't classify them a couple, so I figured it didn't matter," she looked away with a sad expression on her face, "She was so hurt when she walked in on us."

I turn my attention back to her, "It's not your fault. Julian, well he's going through something and it's really hard to explain. But he's a good person, he and Amberly, well they are an even bigger confusing story. But I promise you no one is mad at you. Right now, they are angry at themselves and maybe each other."

I can see she's trying to smile for my benefit but she's failing miserably, "Hey, why don't you go get something to eat I'm sure you're hungry and then get a nice shower."

"I did when I first got here but thank you."

"Well from what I've heard you've been running for a few days so I'm sure you would like to soak in a nice hot bath and being of wolf blood I know you're still hungry. All that running takes a lot out of you."

As if on cue her stomach growls and her cheeks turn that cute crimson color all over again. I see Dean walking down the hall and yell for him. He walks over to us slowly.

"Dean, this is Amara."

Amara looks at me and says, "You can call me Mi, I prefer that honestly."

Dean smiles down at her, "Mi, it is then."

I look at them and smile, "Dean, would you mind taking her for a real meal and then showing her where the tubs are, so she can enjoy a long hot soak. I have to attend to a few things."

"It would be my pleasure," he moves to the side and out of Mi's way as he gestures with his hand, "Ladies first."

Amara looks at me and steps closer so that Dean won't hear what she has to say, "If you go and talk to Amberly please let her know I didn't know. I would never have done that if I had known. She's been so nice, and she's been a life saver in every sense of the word so I would never betray her in that way."

"I know and I'm sure she knows too but I promise I will tell her when I see her. Now don't worry about it anymore, OK. Go and enjoy yourself and relax. You've been through enough and you need to enjoy your downtime."

She nods to let me know she understands and with a smile, she moves back and walks past Dean to the exit leaving him to follow her. I find myself smiling as they walk out of the room, however, it's short-lived.

Now I have to be on clean-up duty.

I wish Julian had waited. I told him I would figure it out. But Julian, being Julian acted without thinking, and now I have my work cut out for me. I just hope and pray I can fix this mess that he's created.

* * *

Angela

I figured it was smarter to track down Julian first before he does something more self-destructive than he already has. I hope there is a way to fix this because I would hate to see the version of Julian without Amberly. We thought he was bad before her but honestly, I believe he will be so much worse now that he's had and lost her.

I reach my destination, the spot where we used to hide to get away from the pack when we were kids. It's the one place that Julian and I share. Our hideout is hidden deep inside the cave, somewhere no one else in our pack has ever ventured. I make my way around the last curve to see the moonlight flickering off the midnight water below. There is a small opening in the cave ceiling that lets the light from outside shine in on the small body of water. It is also the only source of light. The walls here are smoother than one would think, and they always have bits of condensation on them. I look at the body of water in a longing way. I forgot how warm this part of the cave was. I can feel the beads of sweat starting to drip down my forehead and I lift my arm to wipe the back of my hand along my now very warm skin. When I pull it away it's covered in rivulets of sweat.

As kids, we would swim here for hours without a care in the world. The water was always the perfect temperature despite how warm the air was. We would find it cool, comforting, and refreshing. Here is where we made our pact to always have each other's backs no matter what and since that day we have always kept that promise.

I look off into the distance and see Julian's head emerge from the water down below. His usual caramel lightly curled hair looks straight and pitch black as the water drips off and lands on his bare shoulders. Even from this distance, I can make out the ginger in his tense eyes and I know this isn't going to be an easy conversation.

"Julian."

Still shoulder deep in the cool water he turns around to face me and all I see is anger in his features. I know he's mad that I followed him and even angrier that I knew where to find him. However, there is one thing more obvious in his eyes and that's pain. I can feel my heart breaking for him as it skips a beat.

"We need to talk. There's something I need to tell you." I say almost in a whisper.

"I'm sure it can wait." He says as he turns his back to me once more.

I know he wants to be alone and I do not blame him, but I know what I have to say is the one thing that will mend the broken pieces back together, "I think you might want to hear this."

Annoyance is clear in his body language as he swims swiftly over to the shoreline. He exits, leans forward, and shakes the water out of his raven-colored hair. When he stands up his hair is curled all around his face, hiding his eyes. Without realizing it my eyes start to travel from his face to his bare chest. It's been many years since I've seen him without a shirt on and he's always been pretty full. After all, it's the only thing he ever put real effort into. He always had to have the biggest muscles out of everyone in the pack. It was almost like he felt his physique is what defined him as a man. He always needed to be the biggest and the best in everything and if he wasn't, he would push himself until he was. Looking at him now, he's filled out more since then but in a good way.

A smile creeps up on his face and that's when I remember his power, "How many times do I have to tell you it's not nice to eavesdrop in someone's head?"

"Apparently, one more time."

I smile as I bend over and pick up his dirt covered shirt and throw it in his direction, "Put this on please."

He catches the sapphire shirt in his right hand as his smile grows wider, "Why, you can't talk to me without my shirt on?"

"Stop being an ass. There's something we need to talk about."

He throws the shirt over his head forcefully, "I wonder what could be so important."

"It's you and Amberly…"

The hurt is all over his face as the skin around his eyes tightens and he cuts me off, "I took care of it, it's done." He turns his back to me once more.

"No, it's not."

He stops dead only turning his head to face me, "What are you talking about?"

"I spoke to Aaron, like I promised you I would, and he told me you can be with her."

I don't think I've ever seen him move so fast. In less than a second he's standing in front of me and I can see the light returning to his chestnut eyes when he says, "What did you say?"

I smile, "You heard me right. Aaron told me you and Amberly can be together. He's given his blessing."

And just as quickly as I saw the light it was gone, "No, you must have misunderstood what he said."

"No, Julian I didn't. He said something about you and Amberly being foreordained and because of that he can't stop you from being with her."

His head shoots up to look me in the eyes. He places one hand on each of my shoulders and leans in closer, "What did you just say?"

"You need to learn some new words." I can see now is not the time to mess with him as I feel the anger growing in him once again as his hands lightly squeeze the skin of my shoulders. "The part about you and Amberly being able to be together or the part about you two being foreordained?"

"The foreordained part. Are you sure that's what he said," I nod at him and he continues, "How is that possible? That hasn't happened in hundreds of years."

"Wait, you know about this?"

He nods his head.

"But how? Aaron, said it was only passed down Alpha to Alpha?" I see a deeper pain forming in the base of his eyes. "Julian?"

"I..."

Not wanting to push but something tells me I should. "Julian!"

He turns away and places his hand on his right elbow. "My father told me about it, and many other things when I was very young."

"But how would you know?"

92

Julian stays quiet, too quiet and that's when it dawns on me. "Unless…"

He turns around and I can see a fire blazing in his eyes. "Yes. He was an alpha."

"Why did you never tell me?"

"What would it have mattered?"

I place a hand lightly on his hand that rests on his elbow, "It matters. It means you would have been the Alpha of your pack. You have alpha blood running through your veins."

"Even if I do. Aaron is alpha and I would never challenge that."

"I'm not saying you would."

His voice becomes very firm with his next words. "If the pack knew another member was from an alpha bloodline… well nothing good would have come from it."

I realize now what he's saying. He was worried either they would have him overthrow Aaron so Julian could have been alpha, or they would have killed him so that he wouldn't challenge their alpha when he got old enough to do so, and knowing our pack it would have been the latter.

"Aaron would have protected you."

"I know."

Confused, I ask. "Then why?"

"I had my reasons."

"And now?"

He looks at me sadly. "What good would it do for anyone to know now?"

"Well, even though this foreordained thing has come to light, you are of an Alpha bloodline so by all pack rights you would have been with Amberly to begin with. So, I'm a little confused on why you didn't say anything before."

"I don't know." He takes a step towards the waterline, "But what exactly did Aaron say to you?"

Knowing he isn't going to shed any more light on the subject, I sigh. "I told him about the pull you felt that led you to her all those years ago and that you can communicate with her when you're both in human form, even though she doesn't have your power to hear people's thoughts and that's when he told me you two were able to be together. He said he couldn't do anything about it."

"Did he seem ok with it, with us?"

I nod. "He wasn't too happy with thinking of his little girl with any guy honestly, but I think he was happy it was you."

The smile grows on his face as he pulls me in his arms and swings me around in a circle and then lowers me back down to the dirt earth. "This is great, so he really said we have his blessing?" I only nod, afraid to say, "I need to find Amberly."

He starts to walk off, so much happy energy radiating off him and then suddenly it's gone as he stops dead. "Amberly." He lowers his head, almost in shame before he continues, "Angela, I think it might be too late."

He turns to face me once more and I can see the hurt forming in his eyes as it breaks him down. In the next moment, he's on his knees, hands on the dirt ground in front of him. He takes a handful as he forms a fist and I see his body begin to shake violently as he holds in a scream.

Chapter 13

Logan

Walking into her room I know something isn't right long before I see her. She's curled up on her bed and I can hear her crying from the doorway. I say her name just loud enough for her to hear. She doesn't move an inch, so I slowly make my way over to the bed and lay down next to her.

I put my hand on her shoulder as I say in the softest tone I can, "Amberly, what's wrong, talk to me."

Without a word, her sobs get louder as if my words reminded her of the very thing she was crying about in the first place. Without warning she rolls over and buries her face in my chest. I brush her tangled mess of auburn hair out of her face and then place my hand on her back trying to comfort her. I can feel the anger growing inside me as her body shakes against my hand. I continue to beat it down. I've known Amberly her whole life and I can count on one hand how many times I've seen her cry, so I know whatever happened it's nothing small and for that reason alone I am angry. However, now is not the time to act on my anger.

I look down at her and move a strand of her tear-soaked hair away from her face once more, "Please, tell me what happened."

Through her sobs, she manages to get out one word, "Julian."

Not needing to know anything else I pull her closer to me as her sobs continue to grow louder and all I can think about is beating his face in until there's nothing nice left about it. I want to do it so bad but right now this is where I need to be. She needs me, and her needs always come first. So, I hold her in my arms rocking her back and forth as I let her cry out and wishing I could take the pain from her.

The thought that someone could hurt her this much kills me. Anyone who gets to know Amberly would never intentionally hurt her because she's just too good of a person. I can feel my anger for Julian reaching a boiling point and for the first time I find myself mad that she loves him, mad that it wasn't me because I know in my heart if she had chosen me there is nothing that could ever make me turn my back on her, nothing that I could ever do that would put her in this situation.

The first thing I noticed when we arrived here was the cave. It was grand, tall, almost half the size of the pine trees all around it. The entrance wasn't something you noticed, you had to really look for it. If you didn't know there was one there, I honestly don't think you would find it. For this reason, the cave just looks like a huge mess of boulders. And the trip coming here was no joke either. Your shoes kicked up dirt in the air with every step making the air around you sometimes uncomfortable and everywhere you looked it looked the same as the last place you just passed. Same trees, dirt, and rocks everywhere.

The second thing was Julian. I knew the moment he walked up to us that something had happened between him and Amberly and I knew then I had lost her. The way she stared at him and the sadness in her eyes that mimicked his own when he saw us together. I knew she loved him.

Amberly's sob pulls me from my thoughts and brings me back to her and the brisk room. As I looked down at her I realized there is one thing I do know for sure and that's that you can't help who you fall in love with, no matter how much you may try to. Your heart wants what it wants. So, I can't blame Amberly for anything that's happened these past few weeks. I can only blame myself for not showing or telling her how I felt sooner, then this could have all been avoided.

And now I'm angry with myself. Troy and Amberly have always been the two constant things in my life and I promised to look after them. But this time I failed, and I failed big time. I was too afraid of crossing that line. I was too afraid of worrying that maybe she couldn't love me and if she could that maybe she could never love me the way I love her. I was afraid of us failing and because of that I never let myself cross that line with her and that fear has now brought us to this place. A place where she loves another man and I'm sure she loves him more than she loves me. A place where she lays on my chest shaking from her sobs. And all because I couldn't get up enough balls to just tell her how I felt.

I find myself thinking that maybe if I had told her about my feelings that maybe we would have been together this whole time and maybe, just maybe, she never would have gotten feelings for Julian and she wouldn't be sitting here crying.

I have no one to blame but myself for my cowardliness.

* * *

Logan

We spent hours lying together until she cried herself to sleep. Once I knew she was going to be passed out for a while, I covered her up and snuck out of the room to track down Julian. I've been looking all over for him, for what feels like forever, and just when I'm ready to give up and head back to check on Amberly, I see him.

Without a word, in a few short strides, I reach his side. I place my hand on his shoulder turn him around with force and punch him as hard as I can in the face. I can feel a lot of the anger that built up, leaving my body as my fist connects with his face. I look down at him on the ground.

I see Amberly crying.

Feel her in my arms as she shakes from the sobs.

Feel her falling asleep as she continues to cry.

And the rage only grows. I don't need to know what he did all I know is whatever he did it hurt her.

I want to beat him half to death, but I know that won't make her feel any better, but I would be lying if I said it wouldn't make me feel better. I smile down at him on the ground as I fight with myself and what my next move will be.

Should I let my instincts take over?

Should I walk away?

I know whatever I do to him will only make her feel worse. One thing I always promised myself is, I would never be the reason behind her hurt. I look down at Julian as he sits on the floor cradling his bloody lip and I know if Amberly was here this would only hurt her more.

Could I do it?

Can I walk away?

Ever since I laid eyes on him, I didn't like him. I could tell there was something off about him and him being a wolf didn't have anything to do

98

with it. There was a darkness in him, I could feel it. Guys like him. They don't care about anyone but themselves. Hurting others is something that gets them high, so they do it over and over.

I look down at him as I say sternly. "Stay away from her. This is your warning."

Chapter 14

Julian

I'm on the ground holding my chin in my hand. I feel the blood drip down my chin onto my hand as I look up to see Logan looming over me, and I can't say I'm at all surprised. He caught me off guard but that won't happen a second time. I don't need to ask why he punched me in the face or what he's even doing here. I know because I would have done the same thing. Yet, another reason why I don't like him is because I know we are more alike than I care to admit, and I can tell from his punch how much he loves her and what he would do to protect her. I can't help but in some way like him, which is going to make this next part even harder.

He looks down at me with an angry fire in his eyes. "Stay away from her. This is your warning."

I put my hands in the air, palms facing out toward him and stand up, "Listen, you had every right to punch me, however, that's it, you only get one free shot at me, so I would think carefully before you make your next move."

He looks interested in my offer as the smile on his face grows, "I don't need to think about anything. And I don't need any answers, whatever you did that was bad enough to make her cry like that is reason enough for me to kick your ass."

My smile disappears, "She's crying?"

"Don't even act like you care."

I can feel the fire starting to build in my chest, "Don't you dare presume to know how I feel about her."

He throws his arms wide, "Then please enlighten me," he puts one hand on his chest over his heart, "Because I would never do that to her. I would never make her cry that way."

I turn my head away from him and whisper, "That you know of."

"What's that supposed to mean?"

I turn my graze back in his direction, "She told me all about you, just left out the part about her feelings for you."

He crosses his arms over his chest as he buries his shoes further into the earth, "OK, so she told you about me but what does that have to do with the fact that I would never make her cry? I could never hurt her like that."

"You think she's never cried over you mate? Because if so then you're living in your own reality somewhere far, far away."

He returns his arms to his sides as his hands turn into fists, "Amberly, tells me everything, if I ever made her feel anything close to how she's feeling now she would have talked to me about it."

"Don't be naive."

"OK, since you know everything about her then why was she crying, what did I do to make her cry?"

I know my smile shouldn't be growing on my face right now but I can't help but be happy that there's something about her he doesn't know that I do and that she shared it with me, "She cried over you because you were her best friend and she felt like she couldn't even talk to you about what was going on with her," I put my hand to my chin and look to the sky like I'm thinking, "But then again now it all makes sense," I return my gaze to him, "She must have cried over how she felt about you for all those years. Seeing you with other girls wasn't easy I'm sure. Not when she loved you like she did."

I can feel an inferno radiating off him, "You know nothing about her, and you know even less about me so don't act like you know why she cries because you don't. I've known her our whole lives, I've always been there for her. You just came into the picture, MATE," I can tell he's mocking me, but I only smile at him as he continues, "And you are already on your way out from the looks of it."

Now it's my turn. I smile as I punch him square in the jaw with all the power I can. He doesn't see it coming. As my fist connects with his jaw he stumbles and seconds later finds himself on the ground, just like I was only moments before.

I point a finger angrily in his direction, "You would love that wouldn't you, but I hate to break it to you brother, but I'm not going anywhere. If she wants me, I'm always going to be here, however, she may want or need me, I'll always be here in your face for you to see."

"Not for long from the looks of it."

"You know nothing about what happened. She may not be able to forgive me but that's her choice, no one else's, and even if she doesn't want to be with me it doesn't mean I won't be around for her."

He smiles devilishly at me, "You won't get within five feet of her."

"Really? Who's going to stop me?" I flash him my pearly whites.

His smile grows. "No one will have to do a thing. If I know Amberly as well as I know I do, she will handle it herself."

"I think you underestimate what we've grown together these last few weeks."

His smile fades away and it is replaced with a flaming anger, "No, I think you're underestimating what you thought you had with her."

"I know what we have, the question is do you?"

Uncertainty takes place on his face. "What's that supposed to mean?"

"It means, my friend, maybe you are yesterday's news to her. Maybe she outgrew you or maybe you just waited too long to show her you cared for her."

He gets in my face and it takes everything in me not to push him, "None of that matters, either way, she'll never want you; she never did. She was only substituting you for the real thing she felt she couldn't have."

Now the fuse is lit. I grab him by the shirt and punch him in the face, hard. I pull my fist back repeatedly and every time it connects with his face. The anger is like a fire being blasted with gasoline. All the hurt, anger, and loss I've felt throughout my life is being thrown into my punches and I can't stop.

The loss of my family.

Punch.

Growing up in an unknown place.

Punch.

Feeling alone.

Punch.

Feeling like I'm not enough.

Punch.

Feeling like I'm never good enough.

Punch.

I feel his nose break under my fingers, but I can't stop myself from continuing to bring him back to me and punching him again and again until I see her. She feels as clear as anything in my head, like she's right there with us, even though I know she's not. I can see the hurt on her face, and I know I put it there and I know he had every right to come here and to even say the things he's been saying. I know what I'm doing right now will only cause her more pain. Without a second thought, I release his shirt and he drops to the ground.

I don't look at him, I don't speak a word as I turn and begin to walk away. I hear him coming in my direction, but I don't do anything as he collides with me and takes me to the ground.

For a moment I find myself wondering how he could have possibly gotten up so fast. After the beating I just put on him no one would have gotten up from that. And for a moment I realized he might be like me in more ways than just having good taste in women.

He's on top of me now and I can see the punch coming from a mile away, but I do nothing to stop his fist from colliding with my face. Not the first one, not the second, not even when I lose count.

I think of her.

Nothing else but her.

Her smile, the way it touches her eyes.

The way her eyes shine no matter how dark a room can be.

The way her hands feel on my skin.

Her lips.

The electricity.

The fire.

I long for her in more ways than I realize. I know now she's my reason. The reason I didn't die with my family all those years ago. The reason Aaron found me. The reason I found her. I was always meant to find her. I can feel it now.

I can taste the blood in my mouth as I start to choke on it, and I don't even care. I deserve everything I'm getting so I continue to lay there as the blows keep coming. I can feel myself starting to fade but I fight it.

I did this.

I messed up, again.

I pushed her away and all because I didn't want to fight. Didn't want to fight for her. But there's no better fight. Nothing is worth it more than the love of a good woman. Someone you know will always be there, always have your back, always love you. Someone who's love wakes you up and makes you not only want to be better, but you actually are better. There's no one else like her, she's one of a kind and what I feel for her is something that can't be explained in words.

I can hear someone yelling in the distance, but the punches never stop. And a huge part of me doesn't want them to because for each punch I see clearer. Now I know no matter what the future holds. Whether she can forgive me or not. If she goes with Logan. It doesn't matter, I will find a way to make this right. I will find a way to be with her because there is no doubt in my mind, we were made for each other. And when I get her back, I will never let her down again. I will never be so foolish. I will fight for her, for us, and what we have with my last breath.

Aaron

Pulling Logan off Julian, I must admit I'm a little surprised. Not to say that Logan couldn't take on a few rounds with someone, but I have never known Julian to end up on the bottom of a fight. Not unless he wanted to get his ass kicked. I look from Logan to Julian and back again and that's when it hits me, Julian must have gone through with his crazy plan after all. I was really hoping that Angela would have found him before he had the chance to mess things up like he always does.

I try to make my tone as neutral as possible, "What's going on this time?"

To my surprise it's Logan who speaks first, "I'll let him fill you in."

He looks at Julian and then turns and walks away. Julian is still laying on the ground propped up on his elbows. I look over at him as he looks away from me. Logan isn't my charge or my responsibility. However, unfortunately for him, Julian is.

"Julian?"

He lifts his right hand to wipe the blood from his chin, "I have nothing to say."

"You may have nothing to say but as your Alpha I would like to know what that was about."

He rolls over and onto his feet, "What else would it be about? It's always the same thing, or should I say the same person."

He starts to walk away but my words stop him, "You did it didn't you?"

"I'm sorry to say that Angela got the news to me too late," he turns around to face me and I can see an ocean starting to form in his eyes.

It takes me by surprise. Julian has always been a rock, never showing any emotion. That was until my daughter came along. He always told me a man isn't supposed to cry.

He blinks a few times, pushing back the angry tears and continues, "She'll never forgive me, and I can't say I blame her. I will never be able to make this right and even if I could she will never be able to trust me again. Whenever I tell her how much I love her and how I will never hurt her she won't be able to believe it, not after today." He lifts his hand to his face to rub at his eyes feverishly.

"She already knew what she meant to me and in me doing what I did she will either think I've lied to her this whole time about my feelings and never trust my word again or worse she will know how I feel about her but always think she can't trust me, and, in the end, she will always get hurt. So, bottom line it's a lose-lose situation and there's nothing I can do to fix this."

"Julian, I don't know what happened and I don't think I want to, but I also don't think you're giving her enough credit here."

For the first time I can see a little hope in his eyes but just as fast as it was there it is gone again, "After what he told me," he shakes his head from side to side, "I wish you were right but this time I'm afraid you might be wrong, and I have no one to blame but myself."

"I think you still have a lot to learn about love."

He lifts his head to meet my gaze, "She doesn't love me," he points a thumb up over his shoulder in the direction Logan left, "She loves him. That much I do know. And I can't say I blame her. She thinks she loves me, but she can't, she doesn't even know me. But I love her, more than I've ever loved anything or anyone and that's something I plan to fight for."

"A woman does not cry over someone she does not love. I learned that the hard way many years ago." I say with a small smile on my face, trying to reassure him. "And you should fight. The only thing in this world that is worth a fight is love. The love of someone or to protect someone you love. Those are the only time's I will ever raise a hand."

I can see the light coming back into his eyes slowly, "How did you know she was crying? And you fight," he scoffs, "now I know you're lying."

"I would say something smart like I'm her father, so I know but you know me better than that," I release a small laugh which he returns with a small smile, "I walked past her room on my way here and I heard her crying. I thought I should check in on her, but I thought it was best to leave her be for the time being. And I'll have you know when I was your age, I was the one always being found in a fight." Surprise takes hold of his face. "My father was always finding me in some kind of scrape."

"But how did you know it had to do with me? Amberly, crying I mean." He pauses. "I can't really picture you in a fight."

I look from him to the direction Logan left in and I raise my eyebrows, "Come on I'm not that slow, Julian."

This time he releases a real laugh as his hand ruffles the hair on the back of his head, "Yea, I guess it was pretty obvious."

"Especially since you were letting him beat the crap out of you, that's when it became a no brainer."

He returns his hand to his side and smiles, "Yea, we both know he would never get a punch in otherwise."

"Well, I didn't say that."

We lock eyes and laugh at the same time. I've always been closest to Angela and him in the pack, they were the closest things I had to children, but in all the years he's been with us I've never had this kind of connection with him. He's different, open, carefree even and I know it's all because of my daughter and I hate that, before now I was so closed off to his feelings for her and all because of his rank. Well, that and because she's my daughter and the thought of her with any guy can send me to my knees. I know my daughter loves him and he clearly loves her, and he's changed for the better for her. How could I want anything less for my child?

"As for you not being able to picture me in a fight, let's hope the day never comes when you have to see me in action."

He flashes me his teeth. "Why, you think you could take me?"

"I know I could take you; And you know it too." I smile back.

"Care to make a bet on it?"

I shake my head at him with a wide smile. "I don't think that's a good idea."

"Why not?"

"Because I know you Julian and I know if we place a wager on it that you will be egging me on for a fight."

We looked at each other and burst into laughter.

"You're right, I would."

My smile is ripped from my face before I say, "Julian, you need to talk to

Amberly."

He looks off in the direction of her room, "I don't think that's the best idea."

"The longer you wait the harder it will be and the less likely she will listen to you, trust me on that."

"I know you're right. I'm just worried that nothing I will say is going to matter and the fear of that is crippling."

"Women can be more forgiving than we realize. That doesn't mean we should put them in a place where we need forgiveness."

He slides his hands into his pockets. "I would never have hurt her intentionally. I mean I'm good at it, but I don't mean to do it. This time, it was different. I felt like I had no choice."

"We always have a choice."

He looks at me and I can see in his eyes how lost he feels. I wish there were something more that I could do, other than a pep talk. But knowing my daughter, I know Julian can get through to her. He just needs to not give up so easily.

"It's time to fight for what you want."

He nods his head.

"Show her what she means to you. Words are just that, words. They are not action. You need to show her you care and that you were wrong. Make her understand your reasoning behind doing what you did and promise her it will never happen again. And then prove it to her. Every day."

"Was that your whole 'actions speak louder than words' talk?"

I smile. "Yea, I guess it was."

"I know you're right. It's just a conversation I'm not quite ready to have."

"I'm sure she wasn't ready either. To see whatever it is she saw you doing."

I can see the guilt taking hold of his features. "How did you-"

"I know everything Julian. When will you realize I see everything?"

"I didn't know what else to do."

I sigh. "I know."

I can hear the panic in his voice. "I don't think you do. I know I had to do something big or else she would never have walked away from me and I needed her to. I knew we could not be together. I could not let you or the pack down. I couldn't be selfish. I knew if I told her why we couldn't be together she would have fought with me. She would have fought with you," he looks at me, pleading with me to understand. "She might have left the pack and I couldn't change that."

"That's the thing though. You didn't give her a chance."

He shakes his head back and forth viciously. "You know as well as I do that, she never would have walked away from me."

I sigh. "I know."

"So please tell me what else I could have or should have done?"

I release a long slow breath. "You should have given her a choice. Because now, you have to pray she will be willing to listen to you."

I see the question in his flaming eyes long before he asks it. "And what if she doesn't?"

"Then you keep fighting until she does."

Chapter 15

Jocelyn

I return to Aaron's room and there sitting on the bed is Amberly and I can see in her posture that something is wrong.

"Amberly?"

She turns around and I can see the tears in her eyes from across the room.

"Mom." She says through sobs as she gets off the bed and runs across the room and throws her arms around me.

I am in shock that it takes me a second to react. I hug her tight. I lean back and reach up to move her tear-soaked hair out of her eyes. "Honey, what's wrong?"

"Everything. There is too much going on at once I barely have a second to breathe before something else happens. I was trying so hard to be strong, to hold it all together. To not be afraid, not show fear, and to keep pushing forward."

I pull back further so I can see her whole face, "What happened? What are you talking about? I know this is about more than Vladimir."

She looks to the ground, "You're right Vladimir is a part of it but it's also my power, Julian." She looks up into my eyes and for the first time in her life I can see fear in hers, "Mom, I'm scared."

"Oh, honey."

"I shouldn't be able to do the things I'm doing. No one else in our village has ever had the powers that I have."

Trying to calm her I brush my hand against her cheek, "They may not have in the last few hundred years but before that many of our ancestors were able to travel in time in their sleep and even read minds."

"It's more than that. I found Amara because I jumped into her mind when I was sleeping. I was seeing through her eyes and feeling what she felt." She closes her eyes as she shakes her head from side to side forcefully, "That's not normal, I know it's not."

"Maybe for someone like me or even Logan and Troy that wouldn't be normal," she opens her eyes before I continue, "But for someone as special as you, it's more than normal." I remove my hand from her face and take her hand in mine, "I know it's scary, but you'll get the hang of your powers, I promise. It will take some time and practice, but it will come naturally to you soon enough."

She moves away from me and back over to the bed. She stands there quietly with her back towards me, "I saw something."

I take a step towards her, "What?"

She hesitates so I don't push her. She continues to stay silent, so I make my way across the room to stand behind her. I lift my hand and put it on her shoulder. She takes my hand in hers and turns around to look me in the eyes, "I saw you, I saw dad," she takes a deep breath, trying to calm herself, "I saw everyone in this cave," she uses her free hand to wipe away the tears running down her face, "You were all dead."

I reach up with my free hand to move her matted hair from her face and lay my hand on her wet cheek, "Honey, it was only a dream."

I can see the seriousness in her eyes, "No, Mom it wasn't a dream. I was touching Amara and then Julian was touching her at the same time and I jumped again or something like that. I was completely awake."

"That's not possible." I turn away from her trying to collect my thoughts, "You're telling me you were still awake here as you jumped into this," I pause unsure what to call it, "vision?"

"Yes, my eyes were open and everything. Julian was holding me and calling out my name and I heard him while I was in the vision," I can see hurt in her eyes, and I know it's about more than this vision, "He's what got me out of it."

"Your powers are already advancing so fast. As a witch our powers start at a young age and then progress through our lives until we turn eighteen," I move past her and sit on the bed, "But your powers never really matured and now they are all coming so fast and growing and changing," I look up at her, "I don't know how your powers will work being half witch and half wolf."

"Mom, I always wanted you to teach me about them and train me but now, I'm not so sure. They are so out of control and they keep growing and I keep seeing things I don't want to see."

I can tell there's something more going on but first I need to tell her something that's been weighing on my mind, "Honey, there's so much to teach you and so much to tell you but the most important thing right now, that you need to know is we will get through this. We can teach you how to control your powers." It's time she knows what I know, "Your great, great, great aunt. She had some of the same powers you're now starting to manifest," I can see the interest in her eyes, so I continue, "She was the closest thing to a full descendant of Philomena."

"The original witch?"

I nod my head, "Yes. Over the years all of Philomena's gifts were lost to her descendants up until your aunt." Trying to remember everything I pat the empty spot on the bed next to me, "Your aunt was able to travel in time, but she would always look like she was asleep when she did. She could also read minds and control someone for a short while." She sits down next to me and I take her hand in mine, "However, she never learned how to use her powers the right way and because of that they turned on her."

"What do you mean?"

I close my eyes, afraid of the rest of the conversation, "When you're a witch you have to learn about your powers sooner rather than later so that you can learn how to use them because the stronger you are as a witch the stronger your mind must be," I open my eyes and look over at my daughter, "If your mind isn't strong enough your powers can corrupt you and turn you from good magic to evil; it can even kill you." I see the fear in her eyes, so I continue quickly, "However, you are showing more powers that are almost the same as Philomena's. She was the only witch who was able to do what you told me you did."

"What does that mean?"

"It means somehow her direct blood runs through your veins," confusion is written all over her face, "Which means if you're anything like her then things are going to keep progressing. She started out just like you, with being asleep and time traveling, and then she was awake but not really, kind of like what you said happened to you today but later it progressed to where she could astral project her mind into another time and still be present here."

"How is that possible?"

"I don't know but it hasn't been studied for thousands of years because no one has had the power since Philomena and your aunt." I smile at her, "If you have this power already, I'm sure many more of hers will come and I know you're strong enough to control them." I place my hand on her cheek, "This is why Vladimir is afraid of you honey because he knows how strong you are. You are cut from the same cloth as the original witch and that may just mean you can stop him."

She jumps off the bed faster than I can react, "Mom, I'm barely eighteen, this is a thousand-year-old crazy dude we are talking about here."

I stood a little surprised, "Honey, what's going on, I've never seen you like this before. Nothing ever scares you."

I can see the guilt in her eyes and now I wish I never said it, "Mom, I know nothing about my powers, my past, nothing about my wolf side, this crazy psycho wants to kill me because he knows I'm the only one who can put an end to his crazy ass and then there's everything with Julian..."

She just stops talking almost as if she just realized what she said, "What happened with Julian?"

I can feel the hurt radiating off her as her shoulders start to tense up, "Nothing."

"Amberly."

She practically screams at me, "I saw him and Amara kissing, OK!"

"Oh, honey."

She turns away from me, "I don't want to talk about it, there are a million other things we can and should be talking about right now and he is not one of them."

I know she is serious but at the same time, I want to talk to her about it because I can see how broken she is from what happened. I thought I knew what was best for her, who was best for her. I thought Logan was it, that they would one day end up married with children of their own but after seeing her and Julian together, and now seeing how hurt she is I know. It's Julian, and it will always be Julian for her. I can see she is trying to hold in a cry as her shoulders begin to tremble slightly.

"You don't have to talk about it if you don't want to."

Sternly she replies, "Good."

I smile lightly, "but if there comes a time you do want to."

She looks up at me. "I know Mom."

"I just wanted to make sure you did."

She nods.

"I know I haven't been the kind of mother in the past where you felt like you could talk to me about things, but I hope you feel like you can now."

"I do Mom. It's just."

The silence that lingers between us is deafening. I can feel the anger, sadness, and tension in the air around us as it takes my breath away. She has so many emotions running through her and with good reason. I only wish I could take some of this weight, this burden off her shoulders. Like she said she's barely eighteen and the fate of the world is weighing on her shoulders. She should not have to worry about such things. It's hard enough being a teenager and coming of age, trying to find out who you are and finding your place in this world. Add that to your growing powers and learning to control them and then a whirlwind of emotions as you try to find the right person to share your life with. All those things are expected in life and are hard enough to cipher through so adding anything else on top of that almost feels cruel.

She knots her fists up in the hem of her maroon t-shirt and for the first time, I notice how fragile and frail she looks. The shirt barely rests on her shoulders, almost as if it has gotten too big for her. I can see her hands going to work under her shirt.

I sigh. "Talk to me, please."

A tear escapes and trails down her cheek. "It's too hard right now."

I rub my wrist feverishly as I reply, "I understand."

"I just can't wrap my head around it. Why would he do that?"

"That's something you need to ask him, honey."

She shakes her head. "I can't."

"Maybe not right now, but sleep on it."

"I don't think sleep is going to change how I feel Mom."

I place my hand on hers. "It may or it may not, but you want to have a clearer mind before you see him."

"I know. You're right."

"Just promise me something."

She looks up at me alert. "Anything."

"Before you talk to him make sure you know."

Confused, she asks. "Know what?"

"What you really want. Or I should say, who?"

I can see her thoughts running away with her as beads of sweat start to form on her forehead, and I find myself mentally checking the temperature. It's cool here. Everything is getting to be too much for her, and she needs a time-out. I only wish there was something she could afford right now.

She looks back at the ground before answering back in a low voice. "I thought I knew."

I don't need to ask her what she meant because I already know the pain she's going through. She thought she loved Logan, and she did and probably still does but then she found Julian and found a completely different love. She fell for Julian in all the ways she never did for Logan and it was a love that consumed her in every way. She thought she knew who she wanted, and needed and tonight that reality was shattered for her.

Men.

"Just take some time. Rest. Refresh. Think. This isn't something you need to rush. Picking the right person to be with, it's important."

"I know."

I smile as reassuringly as I can. "I know you do. Whoever you choose is the one you want next to you when the world comes crashing in around you. He needs to be the one who calms you in the storm as well as gives you something to fight for. It's a hard choice and a fine line."

I can see uncertainty in her eyes. "How do you know who's the right choice?"

"It's something you feel. It sneaks up on you in a way you can't explain."

I can see in her eyes she knows the feeling I am speaking of and I know she knows in her heart who she needs to choose. The question is will she be able to admit it to herself?

Logan

I am dreading going back to Amberly. I know once she sees my face, she is going to ask what happened and she's going to be mad at me. I also know the subject of Julian is the last thing she will want or needs to talk about.

I reach my destination and stop. I stare at her bedroom door, my hand hesitating on the brass, harsh doorknob. I find myself wondering how they turned the inside of this cave into these living quarters. Running bathrooms, kitchen and many rooms with actual doors. Yet I have never seen any pipes visible and I know there's no way they got them inside the rock walls. So how do they have running water, or electricity for that matter? Unless…maybe they had a witch, help them? Maybe, they used spells. Aaron was with Jocelyn for many years, maybe she taught him how to do it.

It has been a few hours now since Julian and I went a few rounds, so I'm hoping she's still asleep. I close my eyes and let out a low sigh as I push the door open. When I look up, I see her sitting up in her bed with her arms wrapped around her knees and her chin resting on them. I can tell she is deep in thought and hasn't realized I walked in yet.

Not ready to have her look at me and see the damage inflicted on my face I look around her room for what feels like the first time. It's a nice size. At least twelve by twelve in dimensions and the ceiling is at least fifteen feet high. The walls are all smooth with a light precipitation on them. The ceiling isn't smooth like the rest of the walls, it holds a lot of sharp edges. In her room she has a queen size bed, with lavender color bedding and her bed is covered in all size pillows and I find myself wondering what she needs them all for.

Along the walls are two seven-foot-high bookshelves packed with books of all different colors and shapes. An eight-foot-long dresser and a nightstand next to her bed with a lamp. All the furniture in the room is the same color, brown and looks like they were made from the wood of the trees outside. All hand made.

I release a slow breath as my eyes come back to rest on her, "Hey, you."

At the sound of my voice, she turns her attention to the doorway and smiles. "Hey, I was wondering where you were, I wanted to talk to you."

I fidget with the sweat filled hair on the back of my head. This move must be something we guys do when we are nervous and I hate the thought that he and I have anything in common. I find myself hesitating to move any closer to her, not ready for her to tell me how stupid I've been or how mad she is at me for my actions. I can see her many questions running through the changing expressions on her face, "Sorry, I went for a walk."

She gets off the bed and starts to walk towards me and my heart stops when I see the smile leave her face. Her hand flies over her mouth as she comes to a stop in front of me. She stands there in silence for what feels like an eternity. When she finally removes her hand from her face it's only to add it to mine. She moves my face from side to side so she can inspect the damage.

With her hands on her hips she asks, "What did you do?"

Sarcastically I say, "I fell down some stairs. You know me."

She doesn't look amused when she says, "Logan."

I shrug, "What?"

"Come on. I know you didn't fall down any stairs, we don't even have stairs."

Crap I forgot about that. Not like she wouldn't have seen through my lie anyway. "Ok, you caught me but why does it always have to be me that did something?"

She crosses her arms over her chest, "Logan."

I put my hands up in the air in a surrendering gesture, "Fine, fine you caught me, ok."

Her hands return to her sides, "What happened, Logan?"

"I went to teach someone how to treat a lady."

With fear in her eyes she says, "Oh, please tell me you didn't."

I walk towards the bed putting my back towards her, "If I did, I would be lying."

I can hear the anger in her voice, "Why? Why did you have to go and do a crazy, stupid thing like that?"

I say it low but loud enough, so she can hear me, "Because I love you and because I can't stand to see you hurt."

She's quiet for a moment and then she asks in a low voice of her own, "What did you say?"

I turn around slowly, "I said, I love you."

I can see the tears starting to form in her eyes as she looks away from me for the first time since I re-entered the room. I walk over to her slowly until I'm standing in front of her. I raise my hand to put my finger under her chin to make her look up at me, "Why does that make you sad?"

"It's not what you said, at least not really."

I remove my hand and return it to my side, "Then what is it?"

"Well, for starters I've waited to hear you say that for what feels like forever," she turns her gaze to her bedroom door, "and the fact that the first time you say them to me is after you go and get into a fight with the only other man I've ever loved," she looks back at me, "so I'm sure you can see the problem."

I admit hearing her say she loves Julian made my heart skip a beat, but I would be lying if I said I didn't understand why she loved him. The main question on my mind is does she still love me? Or does she love us both?

"What did you want to talk about?"

The smile returns to her face, "Don't think I don't notice what you're trying to do," I grin back at her and take her by the hand as she continues, "but I'll let it go," she starts to walk over to the bed pulling me by the hand with her, "for now."

We reach the bed, and she sits down first, "There's a lot I need to tell you and I don't know how you're going to feel about it, but I need to be honest with you."

I can see something heavier than Julian is weighing her down, so I sit next to her and lean in close. As our shoulders touch lightly, I say, "I'm all ears."

*　*　*

Logan

We talked for hours as she told me everything. How she had been traveling in time to the past and as of last night even the future. She told me about the vision she had of everyone dead and about the conversation she had with her mom and how this is only the beginning for her powers. She also told me how she's not only afraid of what will happen with Vladimir but she's more afraid of her powers and of herself.

Not knowing what you're capable of can be very scary but for Amberly I can see where it's worse. She was never really taught anything about her powers or how to use them, not until now. I promised her long ago that I would always be here and that I would help her find out everything there was to know about her past and about herself and that's as true now as it was then.

I can see she's getting sleepy and I don't want to upset her but there is one subject we haven't talked about that I feel I need to before I can move forward or decide what is best to do next.

"Amberly?"

She rolls over in bed to look at me, "Yes."

"I know you might not want to talk about this, but I really need us to and I'm sorry that it's after such a long crappy day, but I need you to tell me about Julian."

I don't have to be looking at her to know that the sound of his name returned tears to her eyes.

She rolls onto her back and takes in a deep breath, "What do you want to know?"

"You said you loved him earlier," she turns her head to the side till our eyes meet, "do you still? Love him I mean."

She looks away from me again, "I don't think I could ever stop loving him," and with those words our eyes lock again, "Just like I could never stop loving you. No matter what you'll both always be in my heart and I can't change that, and I don't think I ever want to."

"So, that was my next question. Does that mean you still love me?"

She smiles, and my heart skips a beat, "Yes, I still love you, goofball." She looks back at the ceiling, "Why are you asking such weird questions?"

"Because I needed to know if there was still a place for me in your heart."

She smiles. "Always."

"I know, I just needed to know if it was more than in the friend capacity."

"I'm always going to love you more than I would a normal friend. I don't see there ever being anything that could change that."

I grin from ear to ear. "Don't think Julian will be too happy to hear that."

"I don't care." I can see the anger flaring up in her eyes when she looks over at me, "There is something you need to understand. What I feel for you I also feel for him. Despite what he's done, just like you, there will always be a place in my heart for him, too. No matter how much I wish otherwise."

I nod. "I understand."

"Do you?" I can hear the seriousness of her question in her tone.

"Yes. I wouldn't expect less."

"I don't understand it myself. I wish I could forget him, pull him from my heart and scatter that love in the breeze," she looks at her bookshelves. "Why can't life be simpler? Like a book. Cut and dry."

"They aren't all that way."

She smiles. "True."

"Plus, what fun is a life that is bland? Yes, having your heart broken sucks but it's how we learn and how we grow. We learn to find the people in life that are worth our hurt, but pray that they will never inflict it upon us."

"That's the hard part."

I nod. "Yes. Trusting someone with your heart isn't a simple task."

I see her out of the corner of my eye as she slowly lifts her hand and wipes away a tear that was trailing down her cheek and I wonder if now is really the time? But I need to know. I can't mess this up, not again.

"Talk about a serious conversation before breakfast, huh." She laughs.

"I'm sorry I didn't mean to upset you."

She shakes her head as she places a hand on mine. "You didn't. However, I am wondering something."

"What?"

"Why did you ask me those questions?"

I pause unsure if I should continue or not, "I needed to hear your answers. I needed to know."

"But why now?"

I close my eyes and focus on her hand on mine, her touch, it feels like home. I open my eyes slowly letting the light seep in as her face comes into view, I say in a whisper, "so that I could decide whether or not to do this."

I lean over and put one arm on either side of her head. I look down at her surprised expression before I start to lean down slowly. When she doesn't stop me, I continue my movement until our lips touch. I kiss her slowly as I notice her hesitation. Unsure if I should push further or pull away but in the next moment, I can feel her lips moving with mine and feel her hesitation lessening.

I take this as a sign to let go.

I stop holding back and my kiss turns into one of longing and becomes fast and almost forceful. This is something I've wanted to do for weeks now ever since we arrived, I felt a need to kiss her again. But I never wanted to push her into making any decisions. Not while she was already dealing with so many other changes in her life. I didn't want to be something for her to stress over. But now, here in this moment, nothing has ever felt more right. Kissing her feels normal, like it's something I've been doing all along.

She begins to feel tense under my lips once more and I'm unsure if it's because I took her by surprise or if it's for another reason. I press on hoping to get an answer. I slowly lean on my left side so that I can touch her face with my right. Moments later I move it to her hip to turn her on her side and pull her body in closer to mine. I feel her body relax as I move my hand under the hem of her shirt and place it on the skin of her back. I apply pressure there to move her body as close to mine as it can. Something must have clicked for her because now she is really kissing me back. Her lips are hot and hard on mine as she throws her arm around my neck to pull me closer and I wonder why I never did this sooner and how I could have lived before this moment. There's nothing like loving someone who is your friend first. Building that structure first makes all the difference in where the relationship can go.

***

Amberly

Kissing Logan feels wrong this time. Every fiber of me is saying to push him away and I'm having a lot of trouble understanding why. It was less than a week ago when we kissed, and it felt nothing like this. It's Julian. I know it is. As his hand reaches my face his touch doesn't feel wrong, it feels familiar and confusing at the same time. I feel torn and I don't know whether I should continue to kiss him or push him away. The last thing I want to do is hurt him like I'm hurting. I don't know yet what the future holds for me and Julian, or if anything at all. After what he did but I owe it to Logan to figure that out before we take the next step, don't I? However, before I can decide his hand finds its way to my hip as he pulls me closer to him, seconds later his hand is under my shirt and on the skin of my back urging my body closer to his.

A few weeks ago, this is the only thing I could think about, Logan and me. Him kissing me, him telling me he loves me too. I try to remember that feeling, that need for him to want me the same way I wanted him. I try to forget that I ever met Julian. After all he's with her so there's no reason I can't be happy with Logan, right? I mean Logan made me happy once before so why can't he now? I know I still love him, I can feel it, but I still can't help but wonder if that will be enough. Will he be able to push Julian from my mind, from my heart enough for me to really give this a shot? I know it's possible to love two people at once but what happens when you love one a little more and you can't be with that person? Is it fair or right to try to be happy with the other? If you know in your heart that they would be your second choice given the option, is it fair to act like they were your first when they weren't? He's my best friend and for that reason alone I know we could make it work between us.

I reach up and wrap my hand around his neck and pull him in closer, as I finally allow myself to get into our kiss. Soon it feels right, being here in his arms, the one place I had dreamt of being for longer than I can remember. I push his body with mine until he's on his back and I'm laying over top of him. Our legs get tangled together and with his hands on my back he sits up and moves me to take up residence on his lap. I reach up to put my arms back around his neck and I can feel his smile mimicking my own under our lips as his hands become firmer on my back and squeeze my love handles. His kiss becomes more passionate as one hand makes its way to my hair and gets lost in it.

Logan

I can see her starting to stir, so I quickly grab the cupcake off the table next to me and light the candle. Last night was by far the best night of my life and

I'm happy I took the risk, and the timing couldn't have been more perfect. Being able to spend her eighteenth birthday with her but on a different level than just her best friend, is more than I could have ever asked for.

She's cute when she sleeps but it has nothing on when she stretches as she first wakes up. She smiles as she rolls over, her mess of auburn hair covering most of her face. Her smile is ripped from her expression as her eyes come to rest on the cupcake in my hand.

"What's that?" She says as she looks at the object in question with hate.

I look down at the cupcake in my hand a little confused, "It's a cupcake."

She sits up in bed faster than I've ever seen her move before, "I know that but why do you have it?"

"It's your birthday that's why."

She closes her eyes, "Logan, you know how much I hate my birthday."

"Yea, but that was before you had your dad here to celebrate it with you and before you had so many people to celebrate it with."

She opens her eyes and looks at me with a fake smile on her face and I can tell she's trying only for my benefit, "I've always had people to celebrate it with, it's just I never wanted to. Yes, partly because of my father but also because something always feels like it's missing."

I turn and put the cupcake on the stand next to the bed before I turn back to her, "I always thought that maybe what you felt like you were missing was your father. Are you telling me you still don't feel different today?"

"Honestly, no I don't. It's hard to explain but something still feels like it's missing, but I don't know what it is. I just don't feel up to celebrating, I'm sorry. I hope you can understand."

I wish there was something more I could do to help her get over this hating her birthday thing. Ever since we were kids, I would try to get her to celebrate it but every year she would only get madder at me when I tried. A few years ago, she started tuning out that her birthday was coming up and she would tell everyone not to bring it up when the time came.

I mean today is a big day, it's her eighteenth birthday and she has her father with her. I really thought this was one she would want to celebrate. This is also the year when her magic is at its peak and I thought for that reason alone she would want to celebrate but I don't want to push it. We have been in such a good place since last night and I don't want her to push me away again.

I smile at her before saying, "Ok, then we won't celebrate. What do you want to do today?"

I can see the determination in her eyes, "I want to train."

"Amberly, come on, not today. I'll agree not to celebrate today but at the same time we aren't going to train."

I can see the disappointment on her face but it's only there for a moment and then it's replaced with the devilish grin that I always liked. She reaches over and grabs me by the shirt and pulls me down to her and I can't help but smile as our lips touch.

* * *

Logan

I could tell Amberly was still tired, from being up so late with me last night. As I left the room, I told her to get some rest and I would get her up in a few hours. I wanted to find Troy. I have been wandering the cave looking for him for a while now and I'm about to give up hope when I hear his loud laugh just around the corner. I can't help but smile as I shake my head from side to side. I turn the corner and see him and Angela laughing together.

"Hey, guys, what's so funny?"

Troy looks from me to Angela and shrugs his shoulders, "Nothing, just talking is all."

Curious, I ask, "Where have you been all this time? Haven't seen or heard from you for a long time." I grin at him.

He smiles back as he looks at Angela, "Angela's just been showing me around and telling me a little about herself and what it's like to be a shifter."

Can't say I'm not intrigued, "Maybe she could have that conversation with Amberly. I know she's been very eager to learn about that side of herself and she's been even more eager to train."

"Speaking of the birthday girl, where is she hiding today?"

Angela's eyes get brighter as she claps her hands together with a smile on her face, "Oh, my God today's her birthday?" She pauses long enough to slap Troy in the chest, "Why didn't you say anything?"

Stung Troy's smile fades as he rubs at the spot on his chest, "Sorry, didn't think it was something to really share."

Angela puts her hands on her hips, "Seriously? Her father has never met her, let alone been able to celebrate a birthday with her and today is her eighteenth. That's a big deal in our world."

I look at Angela as I say, "It's a big one in ours as well, however…"

I can't help but trail off, I mean how do I tell her not to tell Aaron and that Amberly hates her birthday and she still doesn't want to celebrate it, even with her father.

Confusion is plain on her face when she asks, "However, what?"

Before I get the chance to come up with something to say Troy beats me to it, "Amberly, doesn't really celebrate her birthday. More like she hates it actually."

"What? Why?"

"Don't know honestly, she never really told me the reason." Troy says as he turns his attention back to me.

"It's not my place to really say why but the point is she still doesn't want to celebrate it and I think we should honor her wishes."

Angela's face crinkles up in disgust, "Honor her wishes? Who are you man? Forget that, she never had someone like me planning her birthday. She's going to love it," she looks over at me for what feels like the first time, "what in the world happened?"

Troy turns his gaze on me then and adds, "Yeah, man what happened to your face? I mean it's uglier than normal."

Angela shoots him a look and slaps him on the chest again.

131

I looked away before answering, "Had to take care of something."

Troy laughs, "With your face?"

I turned to him, "Yes, with my face. Now drop it."

The realization is clear in Angela's eyes before she turns to face Troy once more and she leans over and to my surprise, as well as Troy's from the looks of things, gives him a kiss on the cheek before heading further into the cave, "Come find me in an hour."

She leaves us both looking at each other in confusion, as I hear her giggle her way down the hall.

Chapter 16

Julian

Coming around the corner I can hear Logan and Troy talking. I hear one of them mention that it's Amberly's birthday today and before I can stop myself, I look at Troy and ask, "Today's Amberly's birthday?"

I take notice at Logan's hands turning into fists at his sides, "Not, that it's any of your business but yes, it is."

I know it's not going to be a pleasant conversation, but I know it has to be done. I look at Logan again before I close my eyes, "I need to talk to you."

He walks closer to me till he's in my face, "I have nothing more to say to you," he turns around to look over at Troy, "I'll meet you and Angela in an hour."

He hits my shoulder with his as he makes his way past me and without hesitation, I turn around and lightly grab him by the arm, "I know you don't, and I don't expect you to listen, but I really do need to talk to you." I look over at Troy as his body gets stiff like he's waiting for a sign. I turn my attention back to Logan, "Please, I just need a few minutes of your time and then I promise to never bother you again."

I can tell he's intrigued by the idea, so he turns around to face me as he folds his arms over his chest, and I realize this is going to be harder than I thought. All I want to do is punch him in the face repeatedly. But from the look of it, I don't think it could take many more hits. I can already see light purple and green marks forming around his right eye, the left corner of his lip as well as his nose and I remember I broke it. It looks too good to have been broken however, and I find myself wondering if he did a healing spell on himself or something. But if he did, why not take care of the rest of his face too?

He turns his attention to Troy as he says, "Go find Angela and see if she needs any help. I'll catch up with you in about an hour."

Troy relaxes a bit, "You sure?"

Logan nods his head in Troy's direction and then turns back to me, "You have five minutes."

* * *

Julian

I tell him everything. And when I say everything, I mean everything. After filling him in I tell him how everything has changed now and that I need to talk to Amberly.

I can't tell if it's hatred or annoyance on his face but either way, I know it's not good. I wouldn't blame him if he hit me again but that would defeat the purpose of this talk. I want him and me to be on good terms, I need us to be because I know it's important to Amberly and I can see in his eyes he knows the same.

"I can't stop you from talking to her, but I can't promise you that she will."

I look to the ground as I release a sigh, "I wouldn't blame her if she didn't listen, but I still have to try."

I can see something like uncertainty in his eyes when he says, "Well, I think there's something you need to know before you do."

"There's nothing you can tell me that will stop me from talking to her."

He smiles. "I know that but that's not why I think you need to know. I don't care if you talk to her."

I roll my eyes, trying to hold together my composer. "What is it?"

I can tell that whatever he's about to say isn't something I'm going to want to hear. "Well, things changed between me and Amberly last night."

Afraid of the answer I ask. "Meaning?"

"I spent the night with her."

"And."

He looks at me unsure of what to say next, "We slept in the same bed all night."

My heart stops, but I don't let it show. I laugh, "Is that all?"

I see anger flare in his eyes. "That might be nothing to you, I'm sure you've done that with plenty of women. But Amberly isn't just some woman."

My smile disappears, "I know that."

"So, then don't act like that's a normal thing for her because it isn't."

I sigh. "Anything else I need to know?"

He pauses, almost unsure if he should continue. I wait in silence until I can't take it anymore.

"Well."

"Maybe I should let her tell you."

I shrug. "Doesn't matter to me one way or the other."

"I don't think you'll think that once you see her."

I can feel the heat rising to the surface. "Nothing could have changed that much since last night."

"You mean other than you kissing the new girl?"

I sigh. "I explained that already."

"Doesn't make it OK."

I almost scream, "I didn't say it did and I'm beating myself up for it believe me."

He mumbles, "Not enough if you ask me."

The fuse is light, "No one asked you!"

I turned my back on him not wanting to hear anymore. I take a few steps in the direction of Amberly's room as I hear him call after me.

"We kissed and she admitted to loving me too Julian. Thought you should know."

Amberly

Despite what Julian did and how much I'm hurting, I can't seem to let him go. The way he makes me feel is something I've never experienced before. Even though seeing him would make my heart ache and not in a good way, I still want to. When I'm around him everything feels right, calm but at the same time, he can make my heart race. I feel like I'm inside an inferno when I'm around him. I don't think there is anything he could ever really do to make me forget him or to stop loving him the way I do.

I know I need to let him go, after what he did. I can't let him back in, just so he can do it all again. If I forgive him now, he will think it's ok and that he continues to mess up and it won't matter because I'll always take him back and then I'll be the one hurting.

No, Logan is the safer answer. Safer choice. I can't stop thinking about him. About his lips on mine. What does this mean? Am I ready to take this step and let Julian go and move on with Logan? He's a good man and a great friend and I know he loves me. But is it fair to him? Fair that he's not my first choice. I need to talk to him, and I have to do it today before things get more messed up than they already are.

I hear a knock at my door, but I don't feel like getting out of bed, so I yell, "Come in."

No one enters.

A little annoyed I repeated myself and again nothing. Just when I start to think maybe I was hearing things, the door starts to open, slowly. My heart falls into my stomach as he enters the room, looks me in the eyes for half a second, and then looks to the ground.

He's gorgeous.

Broken.

His all-dark attire certainly showcases all his best features. The top three buttons of his shirt are open, exposing some of his chest and I find myself sucking in a breath. His coffee-colored hair never looked more beautiful with the tangerine just noticeable and his light chocolate eyes shine in the dim light in a way I've never seen before. Had he been crying? No, not Julian.

"I need to talk to you."

I can't reply, I'm frozen. My heart hurts so much from just looking at him, more than I thought it would. And without wanting to, as if it is a reflex of some kind, I go back to walking in on him and Amara kissing and suddenly the hurt is overshadowed with so much anger.

I look at the wall before I respond, "I don't want to talk to you. I thought you were Logan." I don't know why but I look over at him and when I see the hurt on his face, I feel a little better and then I become angry with myself, "please leave."

I can tell he wants to go yet he continues to stand there. He places his hands in his pockets as he says, "I can't."

"The hell you can't. It's called "turn around and put one foot in front of the other until the door hits you on the ass on the way out.""

I can see a small grin forming on his face and my heart skips a beat and I'm mad at myself all over again. He hurt me, no he more than hurt me, he shattered me and yet he stands there and expects me to talk to him like nothing happened? And my heart continues to react to his smiles and charms and I just won't have it. I try to think about what my mom said last night. To make sure I know who I want before we speak, and I thought I did. I wanted him… since the day I first saw him in his human form… I wanted to be his… but, after what he did, I don't know what I want anymore. The only thing I know for sure is I won't be hurt like that again.

He runs his fingers through the back of his hair, "I promise I'll leave but first I need to talk to you, I need to explain, and I need to tell you something that your father told…"

He wants to explain to me why he kissed her? I think not. I cut him off angrily, "I don't care what you have to say. There is nothing I want to hear, nothing you can tell me that will change how I am feeling or what I'm thinking. Nothing that will change what I saw and what you did." I make sure to put much force behind my next word, so he understands me and what I'm saying, even though I'm not too sure myself. "Nothing."

For the first time he really looks at me and as much as I've been trying to hide it, I can tell by the look on his face that he can see the hurt all over me, "I'm so sorry Amberly, the last thing I ever wanted to do was hurt you, but I felt like it was the only way-"

I laugh trying to hide all my other emotions as I cut him off and say, "Hurt me, don't flatter yourself."

"You can act like what I did, didn't affect you in some way, and I wouldn't blame you for that, but I know you better than you think I do, and I can see how much I hurt you in doing what I did." he pauses as he takes in a deep breath, "There's no excuse but I need you to know I didn't do it for the reasons you may be thinking I did."

"I don't care what your reasons were. We never said we were together, you're allowed to do whatever you want, just like I am."

I can see the pain in his eyes before he looks away, "If you're referring to you and Logan and last night then yea, you're right." He looks back in my direction before he continues, "I can't tell you who you can and cannot be with and that's not what I'm here to do. I just want to tell you why I did what I did so you understand."

Logan must have told him about last night. And now I find myself both mad and annoyed at him. He had no right to say something to Julian because I know the only reason he did say anything is because for him it was like he won or something, and I'm not ok with that. I'll deal with Logan later but for right now I turn my attention back to Julian and say, "And again, I don't care to understand, and you don't owe me an explanation."

He lets out a long-annoyed sigh before he replies, "Ok, fine you may not think you need one, but I need to give it to you so you're going to sit there and listen to what I have to say, and then I will leave you alone if that's what you want."

A little surprised, I close my mouth and cross my arms over my chest ready to hear whatever comes out of his mouth next.

"Thank you."

I smirk as I say, "You're not welcome."

He can't help but smile back before continuing, "Please, just let me get this out without you saying anything. I want to say what I have to and then I'll leave."

I nod my head in agreement and then he continues, "What I did wasn't right and what I'm about to tell you isn't so that you forgive me or to justify it, it's just facts. First, is something that we've talked about before. With you being the alpha's daughter, we aren't allowed to be together, no one would approve of us and they have every right not to. I'm not good enough for you, I never have been and never will be. I knew it all those years ago when I found you in the woods. I knew I could never be half the man you deserved but every day I went back because I wanted to be close to you, wanted to get to know you. Even if I could never have you."

He takes in a deep breath before he continues, "That still hasn't changed, if anything, it's truer now than it's ever been," his gaze comes to rest on me once again, "what I did tonight I did for those reasons. I knew we could never walk away from each other, not with the way we feel, or felt, maybe now in your case," he can see I'm about to say something, so he raises a hand to stop me, "You promised." I nod to encourage him to continue, "I thought the best thing I could do for you was walk away in hope you find someone who was right for you in every way. But I knew there was no way I would convince you to walk away, so instead, I came up with this plan." He closes his eyes and turns his back to me, "I had to make you hate me, it was the only way I knew you would walk away from us." He draws in a deep breath before turning to face me again, "So when Amara asked if we were a thing, I lied. I saw an opportunity to make you do just that, hate me. And it killed me, you may not believe me, but it did, and then when Angela came to me to tell me she spoke to your father about us…"

Now I can't help it, "Wait what? You've been talking to Angela about us? About this insane plan of yours and she's been talking to my father, are you kidding me, Julian?"

He lifts his hands to cup his face and as he pulls his hands down his lips pull away from his mouth and it takes everything in me not to laugh at him.

He returns his hands to his sides saying, "Amberly, you promised."

"I know I did but you shouldn't have been talking to Angela or my father about things in our relationship and your worries and concerns. You should have been talking to me. After all that's how a relationship is supposed to work but I guess you don't understand that."

"It's different in a pack, I guess. I'm sure you, Troy, and Logan have talked about each other's relationships. It is what friends are supposed to do. They are there for every part of your life. To listen, to help, and give advice when they can. So yes, I went to them for help because you were the biggest choice I've ever made in my life."

I can only get out two words. "You're crazy."

"I'm surprised you're just now seeing that."

I roll my eyes, "Nope, I've always known that."

"I just need you to understand," he slowly walks over to the bed and hesitantly takes my hand in his, "What I did I did for you, I know that sounds stupid, and I don't blame you if you don't believe me, or never want to see me again, but it's the truth. What I did. It is unforgivable. I understand that, but I don't want you thinking I did it because I didn't mean everything, I've said to you. I love you; I have never stopped loving you and it's because of that, I did what I did. I'm telling you the truth now, because if you could somehow find it in your heart to forgive me for being the stupid boy I was for that one minute tonight, then maybe, just maybe, we may still have a chance at a future."

I am not sure what to address first; how I'm feeling, the apology, the fact that I'm pretty sure he just told me he loves me for the first time, or the fact that he just mentioned we may have a future together.

"Please, say something."

"I have nothing to say."

He looks down at his hands. "I know you well enough to know you always have something to say."

I let out a long breath. "Ok, well maybe I don't know what to say."

"Can you at least tell me you understand why I did what I did."

"Understand?"

He looks at me sadly.

"Julian, you're asking for a lot more than I can give right now."

"I know, and it's not fair of me, but I need you Amberly. I need to know we can fix this."

"Well, maybe you should have come to me first before kissing the first girl that crossed your path."

He places his head in his hands. "I know."

"You acted without thinking."

"I know."

"And what you did. It broke me Julian."

His words come out almost as a cry. "I know."

"I don't know if this is something I can forget."

He looks up at me and I can see the sadness in every line of his face. "I'm not asking you to forget."

"To forgive you I would have to forget."

"Don't say that."

I almost scream, "It's the truth."

"I know I hurt.."

I cut him off. "You know nothing. Until you walk in on me kissing someone else when you thought you meant everything to me, until you feel your heart break in your chest as my lips are entangled with someone else's, you will never know. Never understand."

"I couldn't imagine."

I cut him off again. "You're right you can't and be happy you can't."

"I will find a way to fix this, fix us."

"I don't think we can. At least not right now. There are a million other things we need to be focusing on right now."

Impending doom being the biggest thing. But he needs to understand this isn't going to correct itself in a day. I need time to think, to heal, to forgive. But most importantly I need to decide if I want to be with him after what he's done or if I want to give me and Logan a shot.

"I know and we will, but I promise you I will find a way to repair the threads between us, if it's the last thing I do."

I close my eyes exhausted.

"You're everything to me, Amberly."

"Could have fooled me."

"I know. I promise to make it up to you and to prove how much I care for you."

I sigh as the last of my energy leaves my body. "Julian, just let it go. Maybe this is how it needs to be."

"Don't say that."

I can feel the anger boiling over as I yell, "Don't say what, the truth."

"It's not true, it can't be. The way I feel for you, I know you feel it too. The heat, the electricity, you can't deny it."

"I didn't."

"So, how can you for a second think this is how it's supposed to be?"

"Because that's what I need right now."

He lets out a long sigh. "Then for right now I'll back off. I'll give you space, and let you do what you need to do. Just promise me you won't let us die, not before we've had a real shot at this."

I try to find my voice, but nothing comes out. I'm struck speechless and that feeling intensifies when he leans in and takes my face in his hands and our lips meet. It's nothing like when Logan and I kiss, it's so much better. This feeling, if someone asked me to describe it, I would fail miserably. Every cell, every nerve in my body is reacting to him. The heat builds so much faster this time than ever before. The electricity moves from my lips down to the tips of my toes and I find myself wondering if this is normal. Does my mother feel this when she kisses my father? When you find someone you love, is this what it's supposed to feel like? If so, why don't I feel this when I kiss Logan?

Part of me wants to feel it, feel him, the electricity, the connection. Then the other part wants to push him away, yell, and hit him and demand that he leaves. He must sense something is off because he pulls away and takes in a deep breath, like he's been underwater for too long. He brushes the loose piece of hair out of my face and tucks it behind my ear as he smiles. He leans down to kiss me on the forehead, longer than someone would normally.

He turns away from me and heads over to the door, turning back to say,

"I'm sorry. I had to do that at least one more time."

I can see the sadness in his eyes as he fights with himself. I know he doesn't want to walk out the door, but he knows it's what I need, what I asked for. For the first time I find myself not wanting him to go. Furiously, I push the thought back down, deep down in my gut, hoping, praying it won't surface again.

"Don't forget what we had. Don't let that fire burn out."

And with those words he's gone again.

Leaving me....

Angry.

Frustrated.

Sad.

Wanting.

I look at the door wanting to run after him, but command my feet to stay where they are. Do I really want to run after him? Do I want to forgive him?

Yes.

Ok, fine. I do, but I can't. I can't let what he did seem like it was a small thing. I can't let him know I miss him, his touch, his kiss, his presence. He needs to know what it's like to feel my absence. To know what his life would be like without me there. He needs to know for sure what he feels is real, and that I'm what he wants.

If not,

Then he needs to let me go.

And I...

Need to move on.

Chapter 17

Amara

"This place is amazing."

Dean smiles at me as I continue to look around. "It's home."

I look down and try not to sound as sad as I feel, "You're lucky. I would give anything to have a place like this."

I can see something that looks a little like excitement in his eyes. "You could stay here with us."

"I wish I could, but sadly sitting in one place for too long isn't my thing."

Dean looks away from me for a moment before saying, "It might not have been your thing, but maybe now it could be."

For, not the first time, I catch myself entertaining that idea. Anyone would be crazy not to. To have a pack as close as this one. To have your own room again with no expectations of you, other than to be part of the pack. To be surrounded by people who genuinely care and want to help. It's what any sane person would want. It's what I've craved, even when I lived with my pack. I never felt like I fit in. But here. It's a different story. But by staying, I would be putting everyone here at risk, and even though I've only been here a short while I've come to care for them, and I can't be selfish.

"It's not safe for anyone if I stay, and Amberly shouldn't either."

"I never said it would be safe. You and Amberly are safer here. There is strength in numbers and your odds are better here with us than without."

"I know you're right. But I can't let anyone be in danger because of me."

I can see the wheels turning in his head and I take the moment to really admire him. Are all the men in this pack so good-looking? His long raven hair is pulled back tight in a ponytail. He looks like a preppy, pretty boy. He looms over me by almost a foot, easily, and I find myself wondering if he had to kiss someone as short as me. How awkward that would be. Can't be easy on the back. However, with his muscles, he could easily pick up any girl, no matter their size, without breaking a sweat. And a girl could easily get lost in his deep chocolate eyes.

"If you don't mind, I was kind of wondering, what happened to you? To your pack, and why does this guy Vladimir want you?"

I looked away from him before answering, "That's a long story."

"I have plenty of time. I'm here to listen." he pauses and looks at me with interest, "If you want?"

"I wouldn't even know where to start." I look away from him, unsure if this is a subject I want to talk about.

"Maybe the beginning, or wherever you're most comfortable. Knowing more about you might make it easier for us to help."

I smile at him; the thought is nice. To be around my people again, people like me, shifters. To feel like I have a home, a safe place to rest my head. It's a nice thought, but one I won't focus on much. I remind myself not to get too close to anyone here because just like my village they could all be gone in the blink of an eye, and I promised myself after that day that I would never get close enough to anyone. To feel that kind of hurt, that kind of loss is not something I think I can go through again.

Maybe I should tell him my story, not because he's asking, not because he thinks it could help them protect me. Maybe it will help him to understand why I'm so reserved, why I don't stay in one place too long and also what could await them if Amberly and I stay here.

"OK, well, have a seat because this story isn't a short one."

I take in a deep breath, "About a year ago, I think, I lost track of time when I was being tortured, but anyway that's when Vladimir's men came to my village. They killed everyone but me and one other kid who was a few years younger than me. There weren't many kids in my village, but I don't think it would have mattered if there were, because they only seemed to have interest in the two of us. The rest of them didn't look at it twice and I still don't understand why."

"They killed everyone, even the children?"

"I didn't see them but I'm assuming they did since I never saw them at their village but there is no real way to know for sure."

He looks down and moves his head side to side, "I'm so sorry you went through that."

"It feels like forever ago." I shrug it off.

He turns to look at me once more and I can see the hurt for me there in his eyes, "It doesn't matter how long ago it happened or how strong you are trying to be, no one should have to go through something like that."

Now it's my turn to look down. He's right. I do try to be strong and act like it doesn't hurt or bother me that I saw everyone I knew, loved, and grew up with die before my eyes. I couldn't do anything to stop it. "Thank you."

"You don't need to thank me, but just know I'm here to talk about anything, whenever you think you need someone to talk to."

I look back at him and continue wanting to get this retelling over with and move on, "So, after they killed everyone, they beat me pretty bad and took me back to his village. There they tortured me, asking me the whereabouts of Amberly and when they knew I didn't know who they were talking about they still beat me until they thought I would be weak enough. That's when Aidan, Vladimir's second, tried to get in my head over and over again. He continued to beat me down, hoping in time he would be able to get in. I heard others talking about how they really break you. They change your memories and make you a part of their army."

I can hear the surprise in his voice, "So, everyone who is following Vladimir isn't doing it willingly?"

"I don't know if there was any truth to what they were saying. They were there just like I was so maybe it's something they overheard a guard talking about, or maybe it's something they came up with on their own to make them feel a little better about the situation we were all in."

He nods his head trying to not interrupt again, I guess.

"Aidan tried to enter my mind more times than I can remember but he never could. I could tell he was getting mad about it. He mentioned how it never happened to him before. So, a few nights ago I was able to escape while everyone was planning to leave the camps and go on their missions."

"Their missions." I can hear the interest in his voice.

"Before I got away, I heard the guards talking about Amberly, and how they knew she was somewhere to the west in the woods and they were coming to look for her. They were also talking about how Vladimir learned about where a few of the other seven were hiding out."

I can feel the nervousness radiating off him. "Did they say which ones?"

"From what I overheard it was the shifter, natural, and healer that they heard were all together somewhere."

Dean stands up for the first time in a while and I find myself standing with him and wonder when I did.

"We need to tell Aaron. Maybe we can find them first. Maybe with them, we have a chance."

"I wish it were that easy."

"Why wouldn't it be?"

I look down at my feet, "Just because they think they are alive, doesn't mean they are. If they are then they have known where they are for days now and I'm sure they have found them by now," I look back up at him, "So even if they were, I'm sure they are dead by now and if not then worse. Plus, I already told Amberly about it, so I'm sure she told her parents by now."

"What could be worse than being dead?"

"Being back at the camp with Vladimir. Trust me that would be worse than death for anyone, especially someone who he thinks betrayed him."

Chapter 18

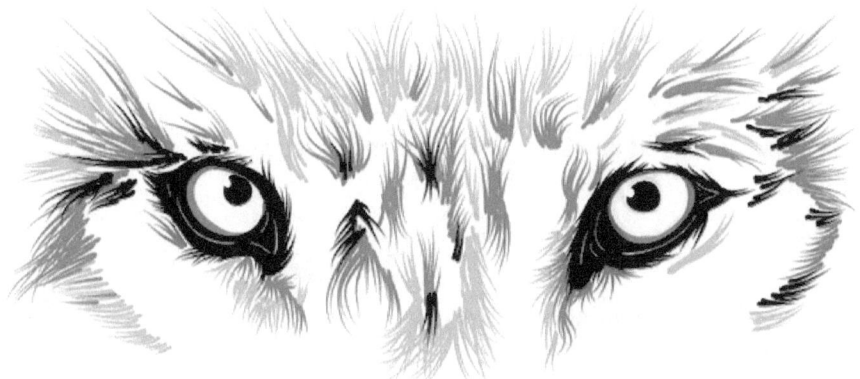

Aaron

I can't help looking at my daughter with joy. I may not have been around for her first eighteen years of life, but she has become such an amazing young woman. So strong, smart and beautiful. She's been begging me since the beginning to train her. But when she found me this afternoon, I could sense she needed something else to focus on, and after seeing Julian I knew it was a good idea.

I see Angela out of the corner of my eye, and I turn to look at her and I can tell there is something she needs to talk to me about. I look back at Amberly and John sparring. "I'll be right back, continue to teach her the defensive moves, they are more important right now."

I reach Angela in a few short strides, "What's wrong?"

"Nothing's wrong, just need to talk to you."

"OK."

She looks over at Amberly, "But not here."

She gestures for me to follow her. I smile and let her lead the way, hoping there isn't another situation I need to defuse. When we were another ten feet away from where I was watching Amberly and John, she stops and turns around to face me with a smile on her face.

"Did you know today is Amberly's eighteenth birthday?"

I turn around to face Amberly's direction to see her still sparring.

"No, I didn't." I turn back around to Angela, "But then we need to get on teaching her to shift and fast." I turn to head back towards her, but Angela stops me.

"Aaron."

"Yes."

I can tell she is debating whether to continue.

"Angela, what is it?"

She looks up at me and smiles, "It's her birthday."

And then I realize what she's been trying to say. It's my first birthday with my daughter, and it's her eighteenth.

"We need to do something for her."

Her smile grows, "I agree but Logan and Troy told me she hates her birthday."

I turn to face her in surprise, "Hates her birthday?"

"Yes, they said she always has."

"Well, she might have in the past, but this year is different and it's special. Can you plan something out for her with her mother, and friends, while I keep her busy here and train her some more?"

"That was the plan."

I smile back at her before heading back. I yell over to Amberly, "Ok, that's enough of that. It's time to teach you the really important stuff."

I can make out her smile from here and I pick up my pace.

* * *

Aaron

Learning to use your senses and to shift for the first time is a big deal, and it's also very hard on your mind and body. I try to take it as slow as possible, so we can get a few things out of the way in her training and enjoy the rest of the day.

"So, I want you to close your eyes and take in a deep breath and focus hard."

"Okay."

She closes her eyes and I see her take in a big deep breath and let it out slowly.

"Now I want you to focus and see if you can hear what I'm hearing off in the distance, if so tell me what it is."

The skin at the top of her nose starts to wrinkle up and I know she's trying hard. You can do it, focus.

Her eyes open fast, "It's a deer. About two hundred yards to the east."

I smile. I couldn't be prouder. Learning even the easiest of our powers takes hours, sometimes days for most, and she got it in under an hour. I can barely hide the happy father feelings.

"This is amazing, Dad. I can't believe what I was missing."

"You haven't even scratched the surface," I say with a smile.

"I've heard Angela and Julian talk about their powers, even seen them use them, but I never thought this is what it was like."

"Being a witch is something I'll never know, but a shapeshifter, I know the feeling. The way the back of your eyes sting as you reach out enhancing your sight. The way your ears feel waterlogged before you hear into the distance. But the shift, that's when the real fun begins."

She smiles at me and then looks away, "What's next?"

"Let's try your sight," I say with a smile.

* * *

Amberly

I'm starting to wonder if it's supposed to be this easy. I picked up on that deer in no time at all. But then I remembered how I used it back with Lurch and Onyx, and I guess it would technically be my second time trying to use it, but still not bad.

As I try to focus in on the eagle at the top of the highest tree, I can feel a pressure forming behind my eyes just like my father mentioned. It's not painful, it's more uncomfortable than anything. But again, it only takes me a minute or two before my vision zooms in on it and I can make out every feature.

"This is incredible."

I can hear the smile in my father's reply, "It really is. There's nothing like it in the world."

I closed my eyes once more, releasing my site. As I open them, I turn to my father anxiously. "Is it time now?"

I can see the uneasiness on his face, "To shift?"

"Yes."

"I don't know if you're quite there yet."

154

He turns to walk away from me, and I run over and stand in front of him. "Then when? I need to be able to use all my powers if I'm going to defeat him."

"Amberly, you shouldn't have to. You are only a kid. That is what me and your mother are here for, and the pack. We are here to protect you."

"You can't always be there," I say thinking about the time I was mauled by the wolf, and I suppress a shudder.

"I know that, but you've been training all day and it takes a toll. Let's wait until tomorrow's training."

I stand up straight, "But I'm not tired, I can keep going."

He laughs, "I don't doubt that you could."

"Dad. Please."

He looks at me with sadness in his eyes. "Fine, we will try it. But only once. Then you should get something to eat, and rest for an hour before meeting with your mother for her training."

"Deal." I can't hide my excitement.

"Close your eyes again," He looks at me and I do, "Now take in another deep breath and focus."

I do.

"I want you to feel your body, every nerve, every muscle and I want you to think, imagine the shift."

I focus hard, harder than I ever have, and I can feel pain starting to spread through my muscles, but I don't stop.

"Imagine your body changing, molding, shifting."

I can hear him circling me as he guides me on what to do next.

"See your hands shift. See your nails growing, your hands turning to paws as the fur starts to form on them."

The pain gets stronger with each second and I don't know how much more I can take but I'm determined to get this part of my training down, it's the most important one I need to learn from my dad.

"Can you see it?"

I nod my head in response not wanting to break my concentration.

"Now see your back starting to arch as the spine starts to shift."

I can't help but wince and I can hear my father starting to walk towards me, "I'm fine, Dad, keep going."

"Amberly."

"I'm fine please, Dad."

He releases a sigh. "Think about the dirt shifting, moving under your feet, your hands as they start to shift into paws. Feel the dirt attaching itself to your now-changing body. Do you see it?"

I nod again.

I'm trying so hard to focus but the pain is becoming too much, and I can start to feel the sweat forming on my face. I feel lightheaded and like I am wobbling.

"Amberly, that's enough."

I can hear the urgency in my father's voice, but I don't want to stop.

"Amberly, I said that's enough." Then I feel his hands on my arms but only for a moment. As he pulls them back fast and I hear him suck in a breath.

I open my eyes to look at him cradling his one hand in his other. "Are you OK?" I slur.

"I'm fine. But are you?"

"I'm good, Dad."

I try to stand, but the world around me turns black as I fall back down to the earth.

Amberly

I can hear my mother and father talking, more like arguing, not too far from me. I peel my eyes open and peer up at them. I've never seen my mom so worked up, which is saying something because she was always mad at me growing up.

"What's going on?"

They turn their attention towards me as all the anger is wiped from their faces and replaced with what seems to be an uneasiness but relief at the same time. My mom makes it to my side faster than I can blink. She removes a strand of sweat filled hair that was stuck against my forehead and tucks it behind my ear.

"How are you feeling?"

I don't feel lightheaded anymore, and the pain in my joints and muscles has disappeared altogether. I sigh with relief. "Honestly, fine. Just a little tired, but not as tired as I would have thought."

She turns around to look at my father who turns his attention to me. "Are you sure you're feeling ok?"

"Yes, I'm fine."

I stand up slowly, testing out my body for aches and pains and to my relief finding none. I place my arms out, only far enough for me to check for any marks. Once I'm satisfied, I smile and look over at them. I place my arms far out in front of me to show them for inspection.

"See, not a scratch."

My mother releases an emotion filled sigh, "That's not what we were talking about and you know it. You overdid it today, Amberly."

"There's no such thing, not now. I need to be ready, and I can't take months, or even weeks to learn what I need to."

She closes her eyes, "I know that honey, but you can't kill yourself in the process."

"I'm not. I'm just pushing myself."

Aaron speaks next. "Which can be one in the same."

I turned my attention to him, "What do you mean?"

"I mean that if you push your body or mind too far and too fast then that's it. There's some things that you can't come back from."

"I know that, but I think you're underestimating me."

My mother looks at me. "I don't think he is."

"Mom?"

"Honey, you're very strong and very determined, and I love you for that, but sometimes I think you don't know your own limitations and I'm worried you're going to push yourself too far."

I look away before I reply, "I understand you worrying about me, but if I don't get this all down and soon," I look back at them, "It won't make a difference whether or not I pushed myself too far."

Their faces mimic each other with concern.

"So, how about this? I'll grab something to eat, and I'll take it easy the rest of the day, but only if we continue tomorrow."

They look at each other and with just a look they know what the other is thinking. It's scary how well they know each other sometimes.

It's my father who answers. "Fine, but it will be light training tomorrow."

Annoyed but I don't push it because I still got what I wanted. I need to train and as long as I continue, even just a little, then I'm stronger than I was.

* * *

Angela

"Julian."

He turns around slowly. "Hey."

"Where have you been?"

I can see the hesitation in his eyes, "I was talking to Amberly."

I try to hide the excitement I'm feeling, but when he doesn't say anything more, I have to ask, "And?"

He releases an exhausted sigh, "I kissed her."

I can feel the smile form on my face before I can stop it. "And?"

"And nothing."

I roll my eyes, "Julian, what did she say?"

He shakes his head back and forth, "She didn't say anything. I kissed her and walked out."

"Why?"

I can see the sadness that lingers on his face, "I was too afraid of what she would say."

"But what if she forgave you? What if she wants to be with you? Did you tell her about what her father said?"

He looks at me and I can see the moisture forming in his eyes, "I told her everything, but she was still so angry I don't think it made much difference. But I can't say I blame her."

I place my hand on his shoulder before saying, "She loves you Julian, she will forgive you just give it some time."

He turns away from me, "I don't deserve her forgiveness."

"You were only trying to do what was best for her and our pack. You knew that she could not walk away from you, and you knew it would tear her and her father apart if he told her she couldn't be with you. You did it for her, Julian."

"She kissed Logan."

His words almost knock me over.

"What?"

He looks at me and I can see the hurt growing in his eyes. "She kissed him." He chokes out the words and then falls to the ground, and I fall with him, putting my arms around him and I know I'm the only thing holding him together. I fear letting him go. Knowing no matter what happens things will never be the same with them again. And suddenly my heart hurts.

To lose a love so strong and pure as theirs, one that takes hold of you. Every cell. It's something that most people don't recover from, and looking now at Julian in my arms I know this is something he won't be able to live with. Fear fills me. He will never be the same again.

I brush his coffee-colored hair out of his eyes as I place my chin on the top of his head and whisper to him reassuringly. "It will be ok."

Through a sob I barely make out his next words. "It won't be. I knew she loved him, and my fear was she loved him more than me, and I would lose her because of it. But now..."

He is silent for a while and I don't want to make him think or feel more than he already is, but I know he needs to let this out. "But now."

He peers at me from behind his curling locks, "I pushed her to him. She's with him because of what I did."

"Julian, yes she cares for Logan, and I'm sure she loves him, but she loves you too."

"Maybe. But it might now be enough."

I feel his body calming under my arms as I say, "Only time will tell. Just have faith and give her the time she needs, but always continue to be there for her and show her that you're not going anywhere, and that what happened will never happen again."

"What if it's too late? What if she's with Logan now?"

I close my eyes, "Then you'll have to let her go. If it's meant to be, she will find her way back to you."

"That's what I was afraid of."

I smile as I lay my cheek against the top of his head. "I have a feeling you two are meant to be, Julian. Just let it play out, and focus on other things right now."

He laughs. "Easier said than done."

I move back and look at him. "We will do it together. I'll get you through it. Ok?"

"You're always there for me."

"And I always will be. You're my brother, who else would I be there for, if not you."

He flashes me a weak smile. "Thank you."

"What is family for?"

He sighs. "I was hoping to never need someone for something like this."

"I know."

I release him and lean back as he wipes at his face angrily with the back of his arm. Julian was never one to show emotion or look weak, as he would call it. I find my heart aching for him, but I also feel deep down in my bones that this is going to work out. I honestly believe he and Amberly are meant to be with each other. But for now, we need to focus on more important things. Vladimir is coming, and we need to be ready. We also need to read the journals that Amberly found, maybe there's something in them to help us defeat him.

I stand and reach out my hand to him, "Now, on your feet soldier, we have work to do."

He flashes me his warrior smile and takes my hand.

Chapter 19

Amara

Every nerve in me is buzzy with nervousness, as Dean and I walk down the hall in search of Aaron. Since I've been here, I haven't needed to talk to him yet, and I don't know why but the idea is making me feel a little uneasy.

I follow Dean through the cave until they come into view. Amberly and her parents are huddled together and talking about something serious from the look of it.

Dean walks up to them and apologizes for interrupting, and Aaron says something about them being finished and asks what's going on. Dean tells him how we should all talk in private, so we make our way into a separate room away from the rest of the pack and that's when Dean looks at me.

Guess that's my queue.

"I, um, was talking with Dean and filling him in on my adventures I guess you could say, and there was something he said we should tell you."

Aaron looks at me and I can tell he's waiting for me to continue but for some reason I get choked up.

Dean steps forward, "She said that Vladimir knew where three of the seven were hiding and they were going to find them."

Jocelyn talks for the first time, "Three, I thought it was two?"

Dean looks over to where she is standing, next to Aaron now, "Yes. Three of them, I believe she said it was the shifter, healer and natural."

Aaron and Jocelyn look at each other and she says, "Three of them is definitely better than two, especially if it's those three. They were known to be the strongest out of the group." She pauses but only for a moment to look back in my direction, "Did you happen to hear them say where they might be hiding? Amberly filled me in on most of your conversation, but she didn't know whether you overheard where they were hiding or not."

"I didn't get much more than what I already told you, unfortunately."

She returns her attention to Aaron, "We need to go and look for them. Maybe Amberly can get a read on where they are."

I realize, for what feels like the first time, that Amberly is in the room with us. She's been so quiet, standing in the very back of the room, that her presence wasn't noticed until her mother brought her up. As I look back at her, I can tell by the way she's standing that she wants to leave but it's like she knows she can't.

Without looking in our direction she says, "I can do it."

Her parents look back at her and Aaron says, "Tomorrow, you still need your rest."

Amberly looks at me and then quickly turns her gaze to her father,

"Tomorrow, then." And she's gone.

I look back at Dean and her parents and give them an apologetic look, and then I walk out after her. I look down the hall and don't see her anywhere. I run to the end of the hall and see her in the common room getting ready to head down the hallway to her room.

"Amberly, wait!"

She stops dead but doesn't turn around.

"Can we talk for a minute?"

Still nothing.

"Please."

She doesn't turn but her head in my direction, "Follow me."

I walk down the hall for what feels like forever until we reach what I can only assume is her room. I knew it was down this way, but I didn't know which room was hers. She pushes the door open and gestures for me to follow her inside. Once the door clicks closed behind me, she turns to face me, as she crosses her arms over her chest.

I can hear the anger in her voice when she says, "You wanted to talk, so talk."

Hesitantly, I look to the ground before I open my mouth. "I'm sorry."

She almost laughs the words out, "You're sorry?"

I turn my attention back to her and I can see all the hurt she's been hiding as it starts to take form on her face threw her smile, "Yes. I didn't know you and Julian were involved. If I had, I never would have let him kiss me. It happened so fast I didn't even realize what was going on."

I can see fury starting to replace the hurt on her face, and I know I'm not choosing the right words. So, I try again, "You brought me here, gave me somewhere safe to rest my head, a nice meal and so much more. I would never intentionally do anything to mess that up or to hurt you."

She lowers her arms to her side, and I can see her starting to let her guard down.

I look to the ground again, "You've given me more than you will ever know or understand."

I strain my ears to hear the next words that come out of her mouth, "I

165

don't blame you."

I look back at her as she sits on her bed and wraps her arms around herself, almost like she's trying to hold herself together. I make my way over to her and look down, unsure if I can sit down. She looks up, smiles, and nods to the spot on the bed next to her.

I sit down unsure if I should say what I'm about to. "You know. I could tell in some way he was holding back. Almost like he didn't really want to kiss me."

She looks at me unsure. "He said he did it for me."

Confused, I ask, "What do you mean?"

"He said that he knew he wasn't right for me, not good enough and we weren't allowed to be together because of the laws of the pack, or something like that."

"Even if that's true, he didn't need to do what he did. I swear men don't think before they act. They are always so quick to mess a good thing up."

I see a small smile starting to form on her face for the first time, "You can say that again."

"I may not be much older than you, but one of the things I've come to notice over my years is that a lot of men are the same. They never seem to know what they have until it's gone. So, most of the time, they do something stupid and mess it up and that's when they learn to appreciate what they have." I pause to look over at her once more, "Sometimes they change because of the mistake they made and sometimes they don't. It depends on the man and has nothing to do with us."

She looks hard at me like she's trying to register what I'm saying, "Sounds like you have some experience in the area?"

"I hate to say it, but yeah, I kind of do."

"I don't understand why they always have to mess up a good thing. If it's good why break it? You don't need to fix something if it works and you're happy. And if you're happy, why mess it up in the first place?"

I suppress a laugh. "No one ever said men were smart."

"And they say we are the more complicated sex."

We both look at each other and laugh. We sit in silence for a few moments before I see the pain returning to her face.

"He told me that he made a mistake and that things have changed, and we can be together now. He said they will be different."

"Do you believe him?"

She lowers her head. "I don't know."

I pause before asking, "Do you love him?"

She turns to look at me, and the pain is clear in every feature of not only her face but her entire body. I don't think I've ever seen anyone love someone as much as she does. It's obvious to me now.

"More than I should."

I look away as I release a sigh, hoping I'm about to give the right advice since it's not my strong suit. "Then maybe you should talk to him. I'm not saying what he did was right or to let him off the hook or anything. He needs to know what he did was wrong, and that something like that won't be forgiven again."

She looks over at a book resting on her nightstand, "I think it's too late for that."

"It's your choice, but if you love him then you owe it to yourself, not to him, but to yourself, to talk to him and see if there is anything left to fight for. I haven't known you very long, but I know that love is the one thing that is worth the fight. It's the only thing in this life that is worth the battle. When you find it, if you have faith in it, and believe that this person is your person, then you need to fight for it until you can't anymore. Until it hurts too much to keep fighting." I pause and take in a deep breath. "If your feelings are real for someone it's going to hurt, and there are times when it will hurt so much that you find it hard to breathe, but if the happy times and the way the person makes you feel is stronger then that hurt, then you need to keep trying. Some people are worth the battle, you just need to make sure you're fighting for the right one."

She turns to me again, "It's not that. I would fight for him, for us. I have."

"Then what?"

"I kissed Logan."

I'm sure the surprise is clear on my face before I say, "Wow. Well, you definitely have some good taste, that's for sure."

We both let out a little laugh before she continued, "I've loved Logan for years, but up until a few weeks ago, I never knew he felt the same way."

"What changed?"

"Julian."

I smile, "Of course. Typical male. They either want what they can't have, want more than they have and take it for granted, or they don't act like they want something until they are about to lose it."

"I think in Logan's case it was more of the fear of losing our friendship if I didn't feel the same, or if we tried and it didn't work."

"Yea, that too but to me that's just an excuse. If you feel something for someone then you tell them. You act on it because if you don't, then you lose whatever you could have had with them because you let the fear win. That person could have been your someone and you let them slip through your fingers because you were too chicken to pull the trigger."

She looks at me in a funny way that I start to laugh, and I say, "Sorry. I can be a little blunt and wordy sometimes."

She nods her head in agreement as she smiles back. "No, you're right, but I did the same thing. I never told him how I felt."

"Well, then you both screwed up." My smile widens.

She sits in silence for a while before she replies. "I don't know what to do."

"It's a tough choice, but what you need to ask yourself is who can't you live without?"

"It's more than that now."

"It's not going to be an easy choice, but it's one you need to make and soon if you hope to keep any kind of friendship with the one you don't end up with."

When she looks over at me, I can see the tears starting to form in her eyes. "I know but I can't see myself losing either of them. One way or another, someone is going to get hurt. I've made such a mess of my life."

"That's how we learn. You're going to make many more mistakes in your life, but that's how you move forward because you learn from them, and you understand which way to go the next time."

She looks over to the door, almost like she's begging for them to walk through it. "I don't know how to choose. Logan has been my whole life, my best friend. He knows me better than anyone."

She pauses so I take that as her answer. "Seems you made up your mind then?"

"No. Logan has been all those things to me, yes, but Julian. I don't know how to explain it. He makes me feel something I've never felt before. He makes me feel awake. I have something with him I've never had with Logan."

I can see the wheels turning in her head as I say, "Who do you want to be with, Amberly?"

"I wish there was a simple answer to that question."

"There is."

She looks almost hurt when she says, "There's not. Not anymore. Logan and I kissed, and I feel like if I don't give it a chance, I'll lose him altogether. And the thought alone leaves an emptiness in my heart. And then there's Julian. I haven't known him more than a few weeks but it's like I'm drawn to him. I feel like I'm a part of him and he's a part of me. So, no matter who I choose, I feel like I'm losing in the end."

"Well, I can tell you something like that only comes around once in a lifetime."

The sadness is back. "I know, but he hurt me. I've never been that hurt before."

"That's how you know it's real."

I can see the tears starting to roll down her face, "But how can I trust him not to hurt me like that again?"

Her question leaves me speechless.

Chapter 20

Angela

"Everyone ready?"

I look around to see everyone taking their places. I sent Troy to go get Amberly from her room and bring her to the common room in the cave where everyone else was waiting.

I know she doesn't like her birthday, but today is a big day, and she needs to celebrate it with everyone who loves her. I haven't known her very long, but I feel like we've always been with each other. Like we were always meant to meet. It is something I've felt since the day she entered this cave, for the first time, and I've been trying to understand it ever since that day, but nothing makes sense. She feels like a sister to me, and in more ways than I can explain I feel closer to her then more than half my pack, who I've known over half my life. I never knew someone could come to mean so much to you in such a short time.

Just when I thought I was done learning the important life lessons she shows up and continues to teach me every day. I'm happy Aaron has finally met his daughter and he has his family back, a family he thought he had lost forever, but more than that I'm happy for everyone in the pack to have Amberly. Having her around has awakened us and made us all stronger and closer. She's been a light in the darkness that we never knew was surrounding us, until she showed up. Aaron has changed so much since she came to the cave and in a good way. So have I, but the one who has changed the most is Julian, and I couldn't be happier for him.

I worried about him so much growing up. I never thought he would find someone who could beat down the walls that formed around his heart but somehow, she did, and I couldn't be happier. She has made him a new person entirely. Someone I'm proud to call a brother. He's become the person I always knew he could be and that's all because of her. And because of that, I have to do the one thing I always swore I never would. I need to intervene in his love life, and fix what he messed up and just pray it's not too late to run damage control.

I can hear voices coming from down the hall and I turn to look at everyone, so they know to get ready. Everyone scatters to their designated area and I take mine by the light switch. I find myself smiling knowing that this birthday is a huge deal and I'm so happy we all get to share it with her. Whether she likes her birthday or not, after tonight, I'm hoping that will change. I wanted to make tonight as special as she is to all of us and looking around at all the happy and anticipating faces around me, I feel like I have.

All that matters now is that she likes what we did here, and she feels like part of the pack and has a great night because she more than deserves it. I could never give her what she's given us, but I hope this at least shows her how much she really means to us, and despite everything coming our way we wouldn't trade her or her friendship for anything.

I hear the voices getting close, so I sink down to the floor not wanting to be seen when they make it to the threshold.

I smile and wait.

* * *

Amberly

"So, Logan told me what happened," Troy says.

I look over to see him smiling, and it's enough to make me want to punch him, but then again with Troy, it doesn't take much for me to want to inflict bodily harm on him. Maybe that's the brother-sister thing we have going on, who knows.

I grin. "And?"

"Well, are you gonna give the guy a shot or what?"

A bit annoyed, not sure if it's really his question or if it's just from the day I've had, I sigh, "I don't see how that's any of your business."

"Well, I think it is if my two best friends are about to be all couple-like around me."

"Even if we are dating, I would promise to keep that to a minimum," I say with a smile.

"So, you are dating then?"

The smile fades, "I didn't say that, Troy."

"But you didn't not say it either."

The smile returns to my face, "You're incorrigible."

He flashes me his pearly whites, "Well you love him, and he loves you, so

172

I don't see why not."

"It's more complicated than that, Troy."

He looks away from me for the first time, as his smile fades. "I know it is. I just don't want to see either of you hurt."

I close my eyes trying to keep all the stress from the day locked away inside. "That's what I'm trying to avoid."

He grabs me by the arm lightly and makes us come to a stop. "Just promise me you will think and think long and hard before you decide between Logan and Julian because once you do, I don't think there will be any going back."

I touch his hand on my arm. "Trust me that's all I've been doing."

He smiles at me and we start walking again.

"Why is the common room so dark?"

I turn to see Troy still smiling but he doesn't say anything. I try to find the switch on the wall and turn it on. But before my hand can locate it the lights turn on and the room is filled with a blinding white light.

I hear people shouting throughout the room.

"Surprise!"

"Happy birthday!"

I fight back the urge to turn around and run, but then I feel Troy's hands on my back pushing me forward. He knows me too well. I force a smile as I look around the room to see all the decorations, beautiful purples and blues. The tables are covered in cloth material I've never seen and there are balloons everywhere.

As I wonder where they could have been hiding all these things, my eyes come to rest on a table on the far-left side of the room. I feel the pressure forming behind my eyes as I use my wolf senses to heighten my sight. I see the table is overflowing with all different-sized boxes.

Presents.

Directly next to it is another table and on it rests the cake.

It's beautiful.

It's five tiers in height, decorated in a lavender frosting. There are trees all around and in the center is a wolf. Around the wolf's neck is what can only be my amulet and below the wolf it says, 'Happy 18th Birthday Amberly.' I can't help but smile as I know this was all of Angela's doing.

I look around at everyone until my eyes come to rest on Angela who's talking with Logan on the other side of the room. As if she can sense me looking at her, she turns around to face me with a smile that reaches her eyes. I smile back and mouth 'thank you' and she replies with 'you're welcome'. I keep looking around the room to see everyone's here. Everyone but one person.

Where's Julian?

* * *

Julian

I want to be in the common room with everyone to celebrate Amberly's birthday, but I feel like maybe I shouldn't. Maybe she doesn't want me there. Today is her day, and I've already messed up enough, I won't mess up tonight for her.

I hate myself for hurting her like I did. I can't believe I did something so stupid. And I don't blame her if she never forgives me. She should be with Logan; he would treat her better. As much as I don't like the guy, I know he would take care of her and treat her better than I have or probably could.

Once all this craziness is over, she should be happy every day. Like they say, trust is a hard thing to earn, but once it is lost it's almost impossible to get back, and I destroyed all the trust she had in me and then some.

I never thought I could meet someone who would mean as much to me as she does, I never really cared enough to change and not make a mess of things. That's all I've ever done in my life. I would act and not care about the consequences because I never let myself care enough about anyone to give a damn whether they stuck around or not. I did whatever I felt like doing at the moment.

There was one time where someone almost got in, but I made sure she didn't stick around. I could not let myself care because I knew what caring would mean. It would make me weak; I would give in to something that could hurt me all over again. I didn't treat her the best, and we went round and round as she tried her hardest to not give up on me until I pushed her hard enough to where she was out the door for good. This was around the time I first saw Amberly in the woods, and I didn't want to feel anything for either of them, so I kind of used each of them as a distraction from the other. Then once Jesse was completely out of the picture, I found myself falling into Amberly. In a way, she was the one to pick up the little pieces of me that had been affected by the loss from my other relationship.

I never planned on letting Amberly get nearly as close as Jesse did because that was it for me, I didn't want to take any more risks in exposing myself. I didn't want to have any hurt after what I was dealing with now that Jesse was out of the picture. Somehow over the years, she crept in and these last few months she knocked down every wall I had standing around me.

My thoughts are ripped from my mind when I sense someone outside the cave, maybe 100 feet to the west. They are coming in this direction and fast. I've never smelled anyone like this before, and I've never sensed such power.

I turn back to the cave knowing there isn't much time. I run inside, hating that I'm about to ruin her night but I know I can't take on whoever they are by myself.

I just keep finding ways to let her down.

Chapter 21

Aaron

"How's it feel to finally be eighteen?"

She smiles up at me, but I can tell there is something deeper in her smile, "Feels the same as every other year. Other than finally having my father here with me to celebrate."

I can't stop the smile from forming on my face, or from looking down at her with pride. She's come such a long way these last few weeks, and she continues to push herself every day to be better than she already is.

I would be lying if I didn't say I was worried about her. Not only about her pushing herself as hard as she is but of what is to come. From everything we have heard and learned, for some reason Vladimir wants her out of the picture. I only just got my daughter back and I'll be damned if I let anyone take her away from me again. I look over at Jocelyn's smiling face. I'll be damned if I let anyone take her from us.

This is something I've dreamed about for longer than I can remember. My family, together, smiling, happy, and safe. When I knew we were pregnant it was the happiest I had ever been in my life. Up until Jocelyn I never even thought about kids, but I knew one day I wanted a family with her and then as quickly as that day came it was ripped away from me. Now after eighteen long years I finally have it, everything I've ever wanted without knowing I wanted it in the first place. And it's so much more than I thought it could ever be. The love I had for her back then is nothing compared to the love I feel for her now.

I'm torn from my thoughts as I hear Julian running through the cave, fast. I turn in the direction of the common room entrance knowing he will be there in moments with how fast he runs.

Something is wrong.

He appears at the entrance and scans the room until his eyes find me and once they do, I can read in them. It was all I needed to know.

Danger.

So much for the safe part. I knew it was only a matter of time before they showed up at our door, but I was hoping I could enjoy this one night with my daughter, and that for once she could enjoy her birthday. I was hoping we could have a few more weeks to train the pack and her people and friends and her most of all. I look over to see her smiling face as mine fades. I know she's not ready to go up against someone like Vladimir, and I'm not ready to let her. As a parent you're meant to do everything you can to protect your child. From the big and little things but knowing that there's something you can't protect them from, no matter how hard you try, is hard to accept.

I look over at Julian. Matters of the heart are something you can never protect your children from. You can teach them about what love is, and who people are, and how to hopefully choose the right person for them, but at the end of the day it's not something you have control over. Just like Vladimir. It's difficult for me to admit to myself but I know I would never be a match for him. I look around the cave at everyone. None of us would stand a chance. I look at my daughter. So how is she supposed to?

* * *

Amberly

As I smile up at my father, I am realizing for the first time that this is the first birthday I've had with him, but yet something still feels like it's missing. I push the feeling deep down and try to ignore it.

I normally hate to celebrate my birthday, but this feels different. All these people, some new and some I've known my whole life, and they are all here wanting to celebrate with me. Who knew life could change in the blink of an eye and that I would be missing something I never knew I wanted?

Since I found my father, it's been a whirlwind of emotions and obstacles. But I wouldn't trade finding him for anything. Learning who I am and all the uncertainty to go along with it and my future. It's all worth it for this moment, here with everyone I love.

I can sense something is wrong before I look at my father and see it plain on his face, something's up. I follow his gaze to the entrance and standing there is the one person I've been wanting to see all night.

Julian.

He starts to walk in our direction, and I feel a tug at my heart as I remember the events that took place not too long ago. I try to look at him, but it hurts too much. As much as I love him, and as much as I wish I could forgive him, and let this go, it's harder than I thought it would be. I kept trying to tell myself it was only a kiss and nothing more. I tell myself he did it for a good reason, but it doesn't matter. How am I supposed to be with him when my heart won't let me forgive him?

Growing up you don't really think about a boyfriend until you hit a certain age, and then it kind of consumes you. You start to look at boys differently, start to think they are cute and look for things that you like about them. But you're never taught that liking someone could lead to loving them, and that love can lead to hurt. Yes, love can also be uplifting, an awakening, fire in your belly but it can also be your destruction.

I recall different conversations with my parents and other people, and them telling me that you need to find the person worth hurting for. But why would you want to hurt at all? Why would someone who cares about you want to hurt you in the first place?

The heart is a fragile thing, and that is why we protect it so fiercely.

My heart has been torn and ripped to shreds these last few weeks then in my whole life, and I'm tired. I just want my life to go back to normal, whatever that is. I want to be done fighting for my life and my heart.

I want to be a teenager.

I want to be an eighteen-year-old girl and nothing more.

I want...

What I can't have.

* * *

Julian

I walk over to where Aaron, Jocelyn, and Amberly are standing, even as everything in me is telling me to walk the other way. Amberly looks at me for a moment but then turns away. After a few moments, I see her get lost in a conversation with Angela. Part of me is happy she does because the hurt on her face when she looks at me is too much to take, but the other part of me wishes she would never look away.

I reach Aaron and try to tell him in a whisper that we have visitors.

"The good or the bad kind?"

"Not sure yet. The only thing I know for sure is that they are strong."

I can feel the uneasiness emanating from him, "how many?"

"Three."

I can see him relax a little with my answer before he asks his next question, "How long do we have?"

"Minutes."

He closes his eyes and releases a gust of air. When he finishes, he opens his eyes again and looks around the room, "I don't think three people should be a problem for all of us, do you?"

I remember the wave of power that hit me, and I look away before I answer, "Aaron, they are strong. I've never sensed anyone with that kind of power. I honestly don't know if we can take them or not."

He looks uncertain, "Three of them against all of us?" He looks around the room again at the pack and Amberly's guards, coming to a total of about seventy people and he smiles unsure at me, "Are you sure we won't be enough?" He turns to look at his daughter who is still in a conversation with Angela thankfully.

"I honestly don't know."

He stands tall before replying, "Then let us get ready to meet our visitors."

Chapter 22

Johnathan

I can feel their powers calling out to me and I know I've reached my destination and just in time. It's almost midnight which means Amberly will be eighteen in a few short hours and that's when the fun begins.

We make our way inside the cave and I trust my power to guide me to them. I wanted to be here weeks ago so that we would have more time, but unforeseen complications arose. I lift my head once more to the surge of energy I feel coming to me from a short distance away.

They are close.

* * *

Aaron

Julian and I start to make our way out of the common room but Amberly stops me as she grabs my arm and asks where we are going.

"I'm only going to step outside for a moment."

"OK, then I'll come with you."

"No," I say a little too fast, and I can see she knows something is going on. "You need to stay here and enjoy your party."

She crosses her arms over her chest, just like her mother and a smile tugs at my lips. "If you're leaving then I'm going with you, this is the first birthday I've had with you, and I would like to spend the last few hours of it with you, if you don't mind."

Well, she knows how to hit it where it hurts. "Amberly, I just need to talk with Julian for a moment and then I will return, I promise."

"Something tells me that's not entirely the truth."

I smile at her lightly.

"Dad, what's going on?"

"Nothing we can't handle."

She closes her eyes for a moment. "Why doesn't that reassure me?"

"Please, go enjoy the rest of your party."

Before she can say anything Julian leans in and whispers, "It's too late, they are here."

I turn around to look at him, "In the cave?"

He nods his head, "They are headed this way."

My daughter looks up at me concerned. "Who's here?"

For the first time, Julian answers her, "Visitors."

She turns on him with annoyance, "Yea, I got that already."

Julian smiles. "Just making sure you're paying attention."

She ignores him and directs her next statement in my direction. "You were just going outside to talk with Julian, huh?"

I smile sheepishly at her. "Please, go back with your mother."

She crosses her arms over her chest.

"Amberly, please."

She shakes her head no.

"You're as stubborn as your mother."

She smiles. "That's not the first time I've heard that."

I smile down at her. "And I'm sure it won't be the last."

"Probably not."

I see Julian's body go rigid as he looks to the entrance and whispers, "They're here."

I look down at Amberly wanting to get her to safety, but I know she won't leave, not without everyone else. I reach out with my mind to the rest of the pack. In seconds they are all around us and take position in front of me and my daughter and I do the same, placing her behind me.

I turn around to look at her once more now, seeing concern on her face as she looks from me to Julian and then to the entrance of the room as three figures emerge from the darkness.

I hear her whisper to Julian. "Nothing was going on. You are a terrible liar."

"Talk about it later."

"More like argue."

I can hear a smile in his words when he says, "Whatever you want, princess."

"What did I tell you about calling me that?"

"Sorry, I'm a little busy right now."

I can hear her scoff as she says. "Whatever you say."

They're already fighting like a married couple.

* * *

Julian

I turn my attention from Amberly to the entrance as our guests walk in and I take a fighting stance ready for anything. I don't care who they are, all I know is I will die before they get to my alpha or Amberly.

I look over to see Angela and the others all standing together and even from this distance I can see the tension on their bodies. As they look on at the newcomers, I can see they are ready for anything.

I return my attention to the three intruders, one male, and two females, as they come to a complete stop. Something about them feels familiar but old. Like they aren't from this time. Their clothes are all matching in color. A deep gray.

The woman to his left, closest to him, is wearing a dress that trails to her knees in length and the top just covers the area between her neck and shoulders. She is a thicker woman with many curves but is very captivating. Her golden hair is pulled back into a bun on the back of her head, not one strand out of place. Her dark brown eyes are scanning over the room.

The woman to his right is wearing tight pants with a short-sleeved shirt that looks two sizes too big for her smaller frame. Her deep auburn hair runs to her shoulders in length and her eyes seem to be gray, matching her clothes. She also looks much older than the other two.

The male, from his place among the three, I would assume he is the leader. He has short almost buzzed blonde hair and deep greenish-blue eyes that are stuck on Amberly. I feel my lips pull back as I release a low snarl from deep in my belly. He's very broad, a big man and just from looking at him you can tell he's a strong man.

* * *

Amberly

First, the room grows quiet as the unknown man and the women behind him walk in. Seconds later everyone forms a line of bodies in front of me and my parents to keep the strangers away from us.

Something feels familiar about this man who now stands in front of me. I lean to the side to look past everyone. I feel like I know him somehow. I know I've never seen this man before, but yet something is telling me otherwise. He doesn't feel like a threat and I can't sense anything evil coming from him. I'm sure the confusion is written all over my face when he turns his attention to me. I swear a smile creeps onto his face a moment before the woman in the dress to the left of him touches him lightly on the wrist. Then his eyes reluctantly leave me and find their way to my father.

* * *

Johnathan

I look around the room to see the tension forming. Everyone seems to be on guard. I turn to my companions and with a look they know to stop. I return my attention to the group in front of us. First, I rest my eyes on who

I know is the one we came for, Amberly, but only for a moment before my companion reaches out her hand to remind me why we are here. Then I turn my attention to who I am sure is her father, Aaron.

"We mean you no harm," I can see the uncertainty on all their faces as I continue, "You may have heard of us. I'm Johnathan," I pause to turn around to gesture to the women behind me, "This is Aadya and Serenity." I turn my attention back to the crowd.

It's Amberly who speaks first, "You're Johnathan? The original shapeshifter?"

Everyone turns their attention to her as she starts to step forward and just as quickly her father Aaron places his arm out in front of her to stop her where she stands.

"Yes. We've come a long way to find you."

It's Aaron who speaks, "And how do we know you are who you say you are? Everyone knows the story about the original seven."

I smile, "Just as I know who you are, you should be able to sense who I am if you try hard enough. It is after all one of our many gifts."

I can see the uneasiness in him as he looks at his daughter, "I want you to go with your mother."

She shoots him an annoyed look before saying, "I'm not going anywhere. Do you really think if these were Vladimir's men we would still be sitting here talking? Come on, Dad, don't be so dense."

From the mouths of babes.

Aaron looks down at his daughter and then to her mother and back to me. "Why have you come?"

"We want to help you fight Vladimir. Together I believe we can put an end to his terror. This isn't how the world was intended to be."

"How was it meant to be then?"

Knowing we don't have time to waste on these kinds of questions, at least not right now, I try to hold back my annoyance, but I know if we are going to get anywhere, I need to answer his questions first. "We were meant to be together." I look around the room at the witch village people and the pack, "all of us. We were meant to live in peace and to protect the forest and the humans who live in this world."

"So how did Vladimir get so off track?"

I can't help but look back at Aayda. "He wanted something that wasn't his to have." I look back at Aaron before I continue. "And because he couldn't have what he wanted he turned on everyone including himself and his reason for being."

I see Aaron look over at her as well and I can see him relax but I know it's not enough.

Amberly's mother speaks for the first time. "She fell in love with you, didn't she?"

I only nod my head in agreement.

Aayda speaks for the first time. "I was not something to be won or earned. No one is."

"I understand," Jocelyn replies.

With everyone talking, I catch the movement at the last moment. Aaron looks over to one of his pack members and with one look he picks Amberly up in his arms and makes a run for the back exit. She kicks and hits him as they go, and I can't help but smile at her stubbornness.

Aaron turns his attention back towards me, "You want to talk let's talk."

Chapter 23

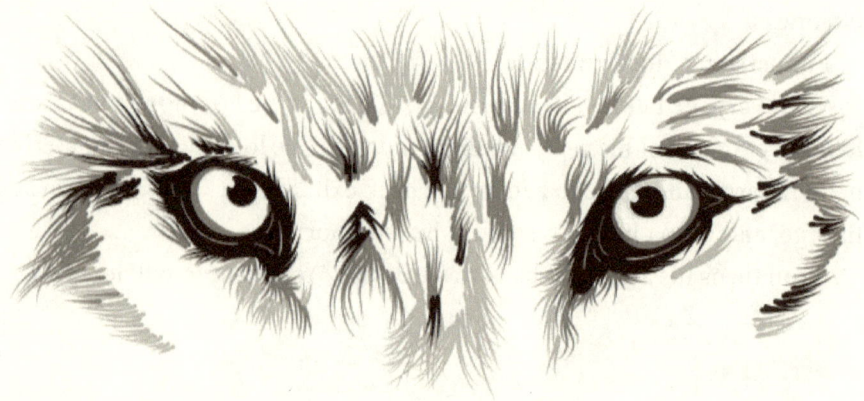

Amberly

"Put me down!" I scream.

Seconds later he places me down on the cold dirt floor. I don't know how far he took me, but I know the cave is a good distance away. I've never seen him run that fast before, everything was blurred around us. I couldn't tell which way was up and which was down. I remember Angela's telling me once that he was the fastest in the pack but until now, I never really knew what it meant to be fast, in the shifter sense.

I turn around to face him with anger clear on my face. The anger I'm feeling is so apparent that he takes a step back in retreat and raises his hands, palms out, to show me he surrenders.

"I needed to get you to safety."

"I don't care."

I turn around and start walking back in the direction that I believe the cave is in. I take three steps before Julian is there in front of me. I glare at him and then start to make my way around him, but he keeps stepping back in front of me.

Now I'm fuming. "Move!"

"No."

"Julian!"

He smiles for the first time and my heart reluctantly skips a beat as he says, "That's my name, don't wear it out."

I roll my eyes in irritation. "This isn't the time for your stupid puns."

His smile falters. "You think they are stupid?"

"I hate to be the bearer of bad news, but you're not cute." I look away from him and fold my arms over my chest, "and your little phrases aren't either."

I can hear the hurt in his voice when he replies, "I can't let you go back to the cave, not until he gives me the go-ahead. So, I'm sorry to say you are kind of stuck with me for the time being."

"Like hell I am."

Before I get the chance to walk away again, he grabs my arm lightly and when I turn towards him the feeling of wanting to scream at him is pulled from me entirely as I can see his eyes pleading with me. They look sadder than I've ever seen before, and suddenly the urge to fight is gone.

"Please, just wait a little longer. I promise I'm staying tuned in and if there is danger, I promise we will go and help but under one condition."

"And what's that?"

"That you listen to me, and let me protect you."

I'm sure the surprise is clear on my face as I nod my head in agreement.

He starts to play with the hair on the back of his neck and I can tell he's thinking hard about something.

"What is it?" I ask.

"It's just I don't understand something."

I wait for him to continue but when he doesn't, I ask, "What's that?"

"If these were some of his men," he pauses and turns to look at me, "Vladimir's men, why would they want to talk? Wouldn't they have just attacked?"

"Good question sherlock. Man, why didn't I think of that?"

"No need to be mean about it."

I throw my hands in the air as I place my back towards him. He can make my blood boil over so easily. He can read my mind so I'm sure he knew I was thinking the same thing, and that the man felt familiar, and I didn't sense any danger. But does anyone believe me, nope. Instead, he has to say what he knows I was already putting out.

I sigh. "I'm going back to figure out who our visitors are."

"We can't go back. Not yet."

"I know you want to keep me safe, and you can whether we are here or there."

He shakes his head. "I'm not chancing it."

"Everyone we love is in there."

I can see the anger in his eyes when he replies. "Don't you think I know that!"

"Then help me, let's go back."

"No."

Annoyed, I scream, "Why not?"

I see fire in his eyes when he yells, "Because you're more important!"

"No, I'm not."

He looks away from me as he says at almost a whisper. "You're more important to me."

"More important than your alpha, your pack?"

Lower he replies, "Yes."

The silence between us grows along with the tension. I can feel the truth in his words, but it doesn't change anything. Doesn't change how I feel or where we are in this tangle of emotions. Does it? It can't, not right now. I need to focus on the moment at hand, and before I even consider following the rabbit down the rabbit hole again, I need to figure out some other things in my life first.

"I won't take a chance not when it comes to you."

I close my eyes, "I know."

He looks at me sadly. "So, please don't ask me to."

I release a long breath. "I'm only asking you to trust me."

Hurt, and surprised he says, "I do."

"Apparently, not enough."

I can see the seriousness in his eyes when he replies. "I trust you with my life."

"Then take me back."

"I-"

I cut him off. "I need to go back, Julian."

"We can't."

"I didn't sense any danger, and I know if you focus enough you will sense the same thing."

He closes his eyes. "If something goes wrong…"

"It won't."

He looks at me. "You don't know that."

I hesitate before I place a hand on his arm. "I feel it."

He looks from my hand to my eyes. "If something happened to you, I could never forgive myself."

I place my hand on his cheek lightly and he covers it with his own. "It won't, you won't lose me, not tonight."

He sighs.

"Let my father know we are coming back."

He nods hesitantly.

* * *

Johnathan

"Amberly and Julian are on their way," Aaron tells me.

"Good. Time is short, and we have a lot to talk about, and even more to teach her."

I can see all the questions forming in his eyes, as well as everyone around us.

He looks at me and asks, "I don't quite understand, how did you know where to find us, and why were you looking for my daughter in the first place?"

"One of my other powers is to be able to sense other people with abilities. I can sense their power level, and I can track them based on that. That is how I found you and that is how I know who each of you are. Your powers have a unique tracker. It's as singular as DNA or a fingerprint. As for Amberly, other than her being the first of her kind, among many other things, she is also the only person I believe can put an end to Vladimir and his madness."

I can see fear in his eyes for the first time since his daughter left the cave. "Amberly?"

"Yes. It's a long story and one I would like to share with her first, I hope you can understand."

I can see the annoyance that lies in his eyes, but his concern isn't something I care to immerse myself with. There is so much to do and so little time. I need to tell Amberly everything I know, and I need to train her. I look back at Aadya and Serenity. There is so much we all need to teach her.

"Time is shorter than I would care to admit. Vladimir will find us in a few short weeks and in that time, we need to train your daughter, as well as everyone here. We all need to be at our best for this fight, if any of us want to survive."

Aaron turns to his pack for the first time to fill them all in. Moments later I sense Amberly and Julian re-enter the cave and I sigh in relief.

* * *

Amberly

"Amberly, it's nice to finally meet you. I was hoping we could talk."

No wonder he felt familiar. I look to my parents to let them know it's OK, and that I'm going to go talk with him for a bit. I'm more than interested in what he has to say.

"It's nice to finally meet you, I've heard so much about you, but at the same time not enough." I release a little laugh.

He grins at me as we take a seat. "I'm sure most of what you heard is a story made up along the way."

"Maybe."

We sit in silence, both waiting for the other to speak first, or maybe not sure where to start.

"Amberly, do you know why I came to find you?"

"Someone did tell me that Vladimir is afraid of me, so I'm guessing it has something to do with that."

He smiles at me, but this smile is one of admiration, and I would hate to admit that that makes me more than a little uneasy.

"That's one of the many reasons I came to find you. But I fear you don't understand your true power yet."

I can't help but lean forward as if being closer to him will make me hear something else in his words.

"You're like no one else in this forest, but I'm sure you already know that."

"Yes. I know I'm the firstborn of two different villages."

"It's more than that Amberly."

"Meaning?"

"You are so much more. I'm sure you were brought up with the story of the seven," he turns to Serenity and Aadya before continuing, "Our story."

Not caring to go into detail about when I first heard the story, which was only recently, so I nod as I reply, "Yes."

He turns his attention back to me, "But have you ever told the story about the originals?"

"No?"

I can tell he's trying to suppress a laugh as he answers, "They came before the seven. They are the ones who chose us and marked us with what you call a birthmark or scar, they are also the ones who made our laws, taught us that we need to keep the balance and to protect the forest, humans and animals that live here."

"But I thought that was you guys?"

He chuckles and his body responds to the action with a movement of its own. "Who gave you that idea? Never mind, like I said, our story has been over-exaggerated. You are not the only descendant from us, but you are a direct descendant of them, the first one in hundreds of years."

"What does that mean?"

"It means if you learn to use your powers correctly you are stronger than any of us," he gestures with his hand to everyone in the cave including the three of them, "all of us put together. Meaning you are stronger than Vladimir and he knows it."

"Why me? I mean why am I the first direct descendant and how?"

"Your mother is from one line and your father is from the other, so you are a product of both the lines and that has never happened before you. Mainly because we never mixed, we always stuck to our kind."

I look from him to Aadya, "You two didn't."

He looks at her as the right side of his facelifts to expose a half-lopsided smile, "You would be correct, but we never had any children," he returns his gaze to me, "Your parents had you." He pauses and looks back at the women, almost like he's unsure if he should continue.

"What?"

"Nothing. That is a story for another day. Right now, we need to fill you in on a few more details, and then we are going to start your training."

Intrigued and curious about what it is he wanted to say, I want to push the subject to get more answers, but I know now is not the time, so I bury the questions deep down, and ask him another one that has been weighing on my mind. "You mentioned the birthmarks."

"Yes."

"Can you tell me more about them? Please."

His smile grows, "Yes. Well, I'm sure just like our story your mother told you the story about the birthmarks, and how there are seven born with it that are from good and seven that are born from evil."

I nod my head not wanting to speak.

"Did she tell you that the seven good and the seven evil are always reborn at the same time, and always meant to grow up to battle for the fate over good and evil?"

I shake my head, letting him know this is new information to me.

"So far every time the good has won, and we continue to live in peace and protect the humans and everything in these woods. But I fear the scales have been tipped this time. But that is a story for another time as well. All you need to know is you and the others that were born with this mark are stronger than anyone else, and that you are either for the light or the dark, and you are stronger together. The ones who wear the mark always end up pairing up, kind of like they are predestined. They are strongest when they are united. Separate, they are only at half their strength." He turns back to Aadya again as if there is something, some key factor he isn't sharing yet. "Once they are to join, nothing can stop them."

"Meaning?"

"Other than their powers becoming doubled together they also became almost immortal on some level. That is how Aadya and I are still alive today."

Confused, I ask, "You're immortal?"

"No. We can just heal better than most and we live ten generations to most people's one."

"That's incredible."

"That is why we still look around your parents' age. We even look better than Vlad." His half-lopsided smile returns to his face.

I smile with him at the thought. I find myself really looking at them for the first time. Jonathon looks almost normal to me compared to the rest of my pack. He has short almost buzzed blonde hair and deep greenish sapphire eyes. He's very broad, a big man. Aayda is beautiful. When they first arrived here her hair was pinned up into a bun on top of her head, but now her long golden hair runs straight along her body, down the length of her arms, and rests at her elbows, but unlike Johnathan, her eyes are dark, a deep chocolate color. She is a thicker girl with beautiful curves. And then there is Serenity. She stands out from the other two, her deep auburn hair is only shoulder length and is laced with gray and her eyes seem to be gray as well. She also looks much older than the other two and it makes me wonder if that's because of the pairing thing that Johnathan mentioned, or if it has to do with something else. For the first time, Serenity notices me looking at her and she shifts in her seat looking uneasy. I look away feeling bad about making her feel uncomfortable.

I turn my attention back to Johnathan and ask. "So, I know with your power you're able to sense certain things. Can you sense who has the marks and who's meant to be with who?"

He only nods his head to let me know he can, but also lets me know that that is something he can't share with me, not right now. I have more questions than I realized I would, and it makes me feel a little uneasy. I hadn't realized there was still so much I didn't know about myself. He did just lay a big one on me, saying how I'm a direct descendant of the originals, and that's definitely big news.

"I know you said I was the first direct descendant of the originals but do my parents even know they are descendants of them?"

"I don't believe they do. The generations kind of got lost down the line."

"Then how did you know?"

He looks over at Aayda. "We have books that get passed down with each generation of the new seven. In them there is much knowledge, and one thing is the direct descendent lines."

"That's pretty cool. What else is in the books?"

"A lot."

I sigh. "So, I take it that's something else you can't share with me?"

He smiles. "Not yet. There is much we need to cover and the rest you can learn after we finish training you."

"Well, training is something I'm always up for."

He looks over at his companions and laughs. "We can see that."

"When do we start?"

He turns his attention back to me. "Now. If you're up for it."

"Heck yeah, I have a few hours to kill."

We all look at each other and laugh.

Chapter 24

Amberly

After some training time with Johnathan and the others, I walk into my mother's room with so much on my mind that I don't even know where to begin. She's sitting on her bed doing some thinking of her own from the look of things.

"Amberly?"

"Sorry to bother you."

She smiles at me, "You're not bothering me. Did you need something, honey?"

"I was wondering if I could talk to you?"

She stands and walks over to my side, "You never have to ask. What's on your mind?"

"More like what isn't."

Her smile, as fake as it is, helps my unease, "Well Johnathan told me a lot tonight. A lot about myself and my place in everything that's going on. He raised a lot more questions for me. We also got in a little light training which was awesome." I pause for a moment and look at her, "Mom, did you ever love anyone else besides dad?"

I can see my question take her by surprise, but she answers it without a second thought, "No, it was always your father."

The way she's looking at me I know she can tell that hasn't helped me any.

"Your father and I pretty much grew up together, kind of like you, Logan, and Troy. We may not have lived in the same village but once we met, we saw each other every day. He was my best friend until he wasn't. Somewhere along the way, he became more...we became more to each other."

"Mom, do you think it's possible to love more than one person at a time?"

She replies, "Yes."

I sigh and take a seat on the bed.

"Is this about Logan and Julian?"

I look up at her and nod as she comes and takes a seat on the bed next to me.

"I can't help you make that choice, honey. Only you can."

"I know. I just don't know what to do."

I can see the hurt in her eyes for me as she places her hand on mine, "You need to make this decision based on you, and what you want, and no one else. Who makes you happy, who can you count on?"

"I know, but that's the problem."

I can see the confusion in the lines of her face. "I love them both, they both make me happy, and I feel I can count on them too." I pause to look hard at her, "So what do you do when you love two people the same?"

"I don't know, honey, but you need to find out. You owe it to yourself to be happy, but also to make this choice before they go crazy." She says with a smile.

"Mom," I say with a smile.

"What I needed to see you smile. I haven't seen it too much lately."

I look to the ground, "I know."

"But at the end of the day, you can love two people at the same time, but I also know you always love one more than the other."

I look at the ground, not sure what to say. I can barely think.

"All I can say is choose the person you feel deserves the chance, someone who has never let you down and someone who makes your heart skip a beat."

* * *

Amberly

The journey to my room never felt so long. I reach out and run my hand along the wall and the cold condensation is like a welcoming friend. This cave has come to be more of a home to me than the place I grew up. I miss everyone, but this place, it's comforting in all the ways my home wasn't. There were so many times it felt like a prison, and here, here, I feel I can be myself and I have grown into the person I was always meant to be.

Thoughts of home make my heart ache in the slightest way. It is where you come from that turns you into who you are. I know that better than anyone. But in some ways, I come from here too. My dad grew up here, so doesn't that make this just as much my home as our village? Will we ever go back again? I find myself surprisingly ok with the thought that we might never return.

Turning the last corner to reach my hallway, I raise my head and see him standing there waiting for me. I lower my hand from the wall and rub the moisture onto my pant leg. Without thinking I walk over to him and take his hand in mine as I smile up at him.

"I choose you. If you still want to give this a try?"

The fine lines on both sides of Logan's lips curl up to form a smile as he peers down at me and it's the biggest one I've seen on him in weeks.

"I think you need to give me a little more than that."

I laugh. "I want to give us a chance."

"You mean?"

I smile at him. "Yes."

"You and me."

My chest vibrates from the force of my laughter. "Yes, didn't I already say that?"

"I just wanted to make sure I was hearing you correctly."

My smile falters. "If you don't want..."

He cuts me off. "No. I want to. Believe me."

"Then what's wrong?"

"Nothing."

I fold my hands over my chest. "Logan, I know you well enough to know when something is on your mind. Spill."

"I was just thinking about..."

I sigh, "Julian."

He looks at me hard in the eyes. "Yes."

"What do you want to know about him?"

I can see the uncertainty in his eyes. He's unsure if he wants to walk down this path, and ask these questions, I can see that much. "I mean you two were..."

I squeeze his hand lightly, "Were, as in past tense."

He closes his eyes. "I don't want to get in the way."

"The way of what?"

He moves slowly closer, closing the space between us. "I know you well enough to know that when you love, you love hard."

I scowl, "And?"

"So, you don't just let things go, Am."

I smile at his uneasiness. "I have."

"Forgive me if that's hard to believe."

"I know when I didn't tell you about him…"

He cuts me off. "It's not about that."

"Even if it's not, I should have told you."

"Why? We weren't anything at that time."

I look at him sadly. "True, but you were always my best friend."

He touches my cheek lightly. "And I always will be."

"But the question here is do you want more?"

He closes his eyes and releases a long-awaited breath. "I've always wanted more." He opens his eyes, and I can see all the love in them, and I can feel their embrace like a caress against my skin. "I've always wanted you. It's always been you."

I sigh in relief.

"But."

Short-lived relief. "No, but."

He smiles. "I need to know that you're in this completely before we cross that bridge."

"I told you I was."

"Are you sure? Really sure?"

I think about Julian, and I know I still love him, but I can't be with him, not after what he did to me. Logan has always been there, never letting me down. I know I can trust him with everything. Like my mother said, I need to choose the one who deserves it, and Logan does.

I nod.

"And you're not only doing this because of what happened?"

I look up at him, the hurt is clear in my eyes. "I'm doing this because I've loved you for a long time Logan, and we never had a chance to see if this," I gesture with my hands to both of us, "if we could be anything more than friends."

"And you're willing to risk it."

Confused, I ask. "Risk what?

"Our friendship."

I go silent.

"Because if for some reason this doesn't work."

I look up at him. "It will."

"But if it doesn't?"

I place my hand lightly on his cheek and he falls in against it, "It will but if it doesn't, you'll always have me."

"And you'll always have me."

"Promise."

He nods. "Forever."

Without a word, he kisses me, and his arms go around my back. Without breaking our kiss, he lifts me off the ground and I can feel his smile against my lips. I would be lying if I said this was an easy choice because it was not. It doesn't mean I don't love Julian, because I do, and I'm pretty sure a part of me always will, but I know I owe it to myself to try this with Logan. We never really had a chance to see if this is something.

People always tell you the best way to keep a relationship is to be friends first, and I think they might be right. After all, who would know you better than a friend? When you start out friends and it becomes something more, that foundation is already there.

Logan lowers me back down and as my feet find the floor our lips separate, and he leans his forehead against mine.

We stand in silence smiling at one another.

Chapter 25

Amberly

I look around frantically at my surroundings, but nothing looks familiar. No flames in sight, or cave for that matter. Hearing voices in the distance, I slowly track them until I see two people talking in the dark. Unsure of who they are or where I am, I decide to keep my distance.

This feels a little like what happened with Amara in the woods, but on some level, it feels different. I don't know how to explain it. And the one thing I don't *like is the uncertainty my new powers are bringing to the table.*

"Aidan, we are getting closer, I picked up Amara's trail five miles ahead. But I also picked up another one too."

In a matter-of-fact tone, he replies, "It was, Amberly."

His voice sends a hot electric current running through my body. I try to focus harder on him, not sure why my body reacted the way it did. Other than Julian, my body has never had this kind of reaction to anyone before. But as I look at him, I don't sense anything more than what I first did when I saw him.

He's strong and familiar in some way. And not the 'you heard about him before' kind of familiar. I can't quite put my finger on it. My thoughts are pushed down when I hear the other guy start to talk again.

"Yes. It seemed to be her. I believe they are together."

I see something that looks like a smile creep up on his face. "That doesn't surprise me."

The man looks confused or maybe it's a surprise. I am not too sure, "Sir."

"She's always trying to help out people when she should be more concerned about herself. She should have left the girl for dead."

My heart skips a beat at his words.

How can someone be so closed, so cold? And more importantly, how does he know anything about me?

"We should find them sooner now because of it."

He glances back in the unknown man's direction, "Yes, it was her mistake to take her in."

With those words, Aidan proceeds to walk forward and the man follows at a slow pace behind him.

"We will send out a search party first thing in the morning."

"Don't bother, they are still a few weeks away. I can sense her now. Just lead us to that spot tomorrow and we will continue from there."

"You can sense her, sir?"

I can hear the annoyance in his voice when he answers, "Yes. Why do you sound surprised?"

"I just didn't know that was possible."

"You should know by now why it is. After all, we are the same."

The tone in his voice when he speaks those words makes my skin crawl. The same. Is he talking about him and the man? I feel like he was talking about something else, someone else and I have a feeling it's me. But how could we be the same, in what way?

He turns his attention in my direction and my body reacts before my mind gets the chance to tell it to move.

"We aren't alone."

"Sir?"

"Someone is here with us."

Amara was not kidding about this guy being scary but also about how strong his powers were. I start to feel lightheaded and then I feel a sharp pain in my head. That's when I remember she told me he tried to get in hers. It's time to get the heck out of here.

I try to focus on the pain I'm feeling. It takes me some time but finally, just as I hear his voice, maybe five feet from where I'm hiding, I imagine my bed and my body lying asleep in it. I imagine the warmth and I can feel my body starting to disappear. In seconds I'm gone and he's standing staring at the spot my body was only moments before.

* * *

Amberly

I wake up to find Logan's arm is still around me, the pressure around my hips is comforting. I take in a slow easy breath, happy to be back in my bed with him. However, now I'm left with more questions and my life is starting to feel like that's all it is. A bunch of unanswered questions. I thought once I knew the truth about my father and my life that things would make sense, and get easier. That life would be easier, but I was gravely mistaken.

"Do you think this guy is for real?" Logan's voice sounds so far away.

I keep my eyes closed when I ask back confused, "Who?"

"Johnathan."

After my dream, I have Aidan on the brain. I replied hoping he didn't notice my delayed reaction, "I think he is."

I feel Logan shift in the bed to lean over me and I open my eyes to look up at him. His emerald eyes shine as they gaze down at me. "I'm scared for you. I would be lying if I said I wasn't."

I place my hand on his cheek which is warm to the touch, "You don't need to be. Between my mom, dad, the pack, and Johnathan all training me, I'm sure I'll be all powered up in no time."

I can hear the anger hiding in his voice, "It's more than that."

I sigh as I reply, "I know it is."

"Then please don't act like this is nothing."

I shift to get more comfortable because I know this is going to be a longer conversation than I first thought. "Logan. I can't just run away."

"Why can't you?" I know he doesn't mean it, but I can't help but give him a questionable look which makes him shrug in response, "Hey, I had to say it."

I lean up on my hands to give him a fast kiss. When I return to the bed I whisper, "I know."

He moves a tangled piece of hair from my face before he speaks again. "I want to train with you."

"I know you do, and I think you should. There were a few things I wanted to talk to you about."

He grins. "I'm all ears."

"Well, Johnathan shared a lot more with me than I originally let on."

Confusion lines his face. "Like what?"

"He told me more about the seven. Like I told you what my mom said, about there being seven more born every generation and they are born with a distinctive mark." I pause and he nods to let me know he's following where I'm going with this. "So, you're one of the new seven, as are Julian and Angela."

"I think Johnathan got his lines crossed with the rest of us. You, yes but the rest of us, I don't think so." He says with a chuckle.

"The mark on your back. Remember we talked about it a few weeks ago back in our village before we came here."

"Yeah, I remember."

"Well, Johnathan and my mother said that's how you know who the new seven are every generation."

I can see the intrigue all over his face. "What does this mean?"

"Well, nothing good."

Logan shifts again, but this time it's to get closer to me.

I smiled at him. "After we defeat Vladimir, I fear there are only more battles for us to fight."

"You mean the other seven?"

My words get lodged in my throat, so I nod my head instead.

"No matter what happens we will be fine because we are together. I won't let anything happen to you."

Before I can reply, he leans down and presses his lips against mine. First, they are soft, reassuring, calm and then I can feel the hunger in them, in Logan, that I have never felt before. He shifts himself until he is completely on top of me and every inch of our bodies are touching. His hands get lost in my birds' nest of hair as his kiss continues to intensify sending chills down my spine. It seems like his hands and lips stay lost in that spot, in that moment forever, until he moves his hand and places it on my hip as he starts to roll to his side and guides me to do the same. His hands become harder on my body. Roaming. Until they come to my shorts. He slowly guides his hand over the top of them and starts to pull them off slowly, like he's waiting for me to stop him. Part of me isn't sure what to do. I chose to be with Logan, and I love him and want to be with him but I'm not sure if I'm ready. We've known each other forever and wanted this for so long. So, what's wrong with it?

He gets my shorts over my hips and his lips leave mine as he starts to trail kisses down my body as he takes my shorts off. He sits up on his knees, looks down at me and smiles as he lifts his raven shirt over his head and discards it to the end of the bed. For the first time, I really looked at him. He's just as flawless as, nope don't even. My thoughts return to this moment as Logan lowers his body to me.

I'm now lying on my back as his lips meet mine. He grabs me around the hips and without breaking our kiss has me sit up on his lap. He starts to kiss my neck as his hands find the hem of my shirt and they slide underneath to touch the skin of my stomach, testing the waters. When I don't stop him, they go higher and higher until his hand comes to rest on my breast and I have to suck in a breath. His hand doesn't move but he looks at me and for the first time he speaks.

"Is this OK?" His voice is husky from our current events.

I nod my head and smile, but I can tell he's unsure as he starts to move his hand away. Without a second thought, I place my hand on top of his, over my shirt, and I move his hand to cup my breast firmly and then I grab him and kiss him passionately as I pull him back to the bed with me. A small moan escapes his lips as he falls back to the bed with me.

At this moment I find myself happier than I thought would be possible. I never really gave much thought to anything other than kissing Logan but now I know I was missing out. I smile underneath his lips and I know he can feel it because I feel him start to smile too. If someone had told me a few months ago that this is where I would be today, I would have told them they were crazy. But I'm happy, at this moment, with him. And the rest of the world falls away.

Chapter 26

Amberly

I wake up to see Logan still asleep. After a long and crazy night, I don't want to wake him but I'm so hungry I could eat a cow. So quietly I get up out of bed and put my pants back on. I head to the door but look back to see him still sleeping before I walk out with a smile on my face.

Bam.

"Sorry, I wasn't looking where…"

I look up to see I bumped into Julian and suddenly I'm reminded how only moments before I had no pants on and I feel exposed.

"No, it was my fault. I was coming to find you; didn't think you would be up yet."

"Normally I wouldn't be but I'm starving."

I move past him and start to walk in the direction of the kitchen only to find he's walking with me.

"Do you mind if I join you?"

"Honestly, yes."

I mean what could we possibly have to talk about this early in the morning? And all I'm going to be able to think about is what happened last night, and I really don't want to feel awkward or like I need to tell him. So, no, I would rather eat alone. I mean I have no reason to feel the way I am right now, after all he did what he did, he set this whole thing in motion and now because of it I'm with Logan and he has himself to blame for it.

"I'm sure you would rather be alone or have breakfast with anyone other than me, but I really wanted to talk to you about training today."

I turned around to look at him for the first time since I started walking. "What about it?"

"Well, your dad kind of put me in charge of teaching you today since he will be busy with Johnathan and his company."

I let out a sigh. "Of course, he did."

I can hear the pain in his voice when he says, "I mean you could wait until tomorrow to continue training if you want. But I figured you would rather deal with me today instead," he pauses to rub at his eyes, "But I guess I was wrong."

Seeing the pain he is in makes me want to please him in the only way I know I can, so I say. "No, it's fine. But I want to eat first and go back to my room and get dressed. I'll meet you in a few hours, OK?"

"You are sure."

I smile lightly, "Yes."

"OK."

I place a lot of meaning in my next word, "OK."

I walk away from him and almost find myself running down the hall to the kitchen. It's not until I reach for a plate that I realize Julian has followed me. I sigh but continue my way around the kitchen. I place a moist blueberry muffin, two granola bars, half a plate of mixed fruit and a cheese danish on my plate. I turn to the drinks section and grab a water bottle and then head to the nearest table. Doesn't matter which one I pick since we are the only two in the whole room.

Moments after I sit Julian is hovering over me. He looks down at my plate of food and I sigh. "What is it?"

I hear his stomach growl. He smiles embarrassed. "Guess I'm a little hungry myself."

"Well, there are plenty of tables."

I can see the hurt on his face when he asks. "You're really going to make me eat at another table?"

I smile unpleasantly as I reply, "Yup."

"Come on Amberly, don't be like that."

"Don't be like what," I say as I rip off a piece of my muffin and shove it in my salivating mouth.

"Shut off."

I look over at him. "What do you expect?"

He smirks as he says, "I was hoping you would forgive me by now."

"Sorry, but that's not going to happen anytime soon."

"OK, then I was hoping we could at least be civil with one another."

I smile. "I am being civil."

He raises an eyebrow. "You call this civil."

I nod.

"Well, this is the opposite of that."

I glare at him. "It could be worse."

"How so."

"I could not talk to you at all."

He sighs.

"Or I could remove myself from ever being in your presence."

"OK. OK. I get it."

I look back at my plate. "Now if you don't mind."

I can tell he doesn't want to go yet, but I don't give him the choice when I stand and start walking in the direction of the kitchen again, leaving him behind, speechless.

* * *

Logan

I wake up to see Amberly isn't in the bed with me. I quickly get dressed and head for the kitchen, knowing that's more than likely where she ended up. I reach my destination and there she is sitting at a table by herself and more than enjoying her breakfast from the looks of it.

"Hey, you."

She practically jumps out of her skin as the food falls out of her mouth and her eyes come to rest on me. I can't help but smile.

She smiles back and finishes swallowing what's left in her mouth before she replies, "You should know better than to sneak up on a girl like that."

"But you're my girl so I'm allowed." I bend over to kiss her on the cheek. My girl. I more than like the sound of that.

"Is that so?"

"I say it is." I take a seat next to her.

She finishes another mouthful, "Sorry I was so hungry and didn't want to wake you."

"It's fine, I understand."

"Are you hungry?"

I look around the kitchen and realize that no one else is up yet. "No, I'll grab something later."

"I can get you something, it's not a problem."

Just another reminder of how well she knows me. Since no one is here, I don't want to just go in the kitchen and help myself to what they have. This isn't my home, it's just a place I currently find myself.

"It's fine. I'll just take some of yours." I say as I reach over and grab a grape off her plate.

"Hey." She playfully swats at my hand.

I grab her hand and pull her close, look into her eyes, and kiss her softly. Seconds later her hands wrap themselves around the back of my neck and I feel more than happy, I feel like I'm in utopia. I never thought it possible to be this happy, or that I would be this happy with her. I never in a million years thought she would choose to be with me. She was always so much more than the average girl in our village, and I never felt like I would be worthy of her, so the thought of her choosing to be with me never crossed my mind.

I hear someone clear their throat from above us and I pull back just enough to look up and see Julian standing there.

"Can we help you?"

Ignoring me entirely, he looks down at Amberly, "You almost ready?"

She clears her throat and looks at him with annoyance covering her face. "For real? Did I, or did I not, tell you I would meet you in a few hours?"

"You did, but then I saw you over here locking faces with him," he threw a thumb in my direction, "So I figured you weren't too busy."

"Well, you thought wrong." I can hear the annoyance rising in her voice, and from knowing her all these years I know it's almost time to take cover.

"So, you don't want to train?"

If looks could kill he would have dropped dead right here with the way she is looking at him.

"Not right now." She says drawing bared teeth.

He looks at me and then back at Amberly and walks away. I turned to her, afraid to ask, "What was that about?"

"We ran into each other outside my bedroom this morning. He wanted to train, but I told him I wanted to eat and change first. I told him I would meet him when I was done, but I guess he couldn't wait."

"Why didn't you tell me?"

She puts her fork down beside her plate, "I just did."

"I mean before he came over?"

She lets out a sigh, "I was going to tell you when we got back to the room. When I was done having breakfast."

I close my eyes for a moment to clear my head. When I open them and look back at her I realize the weight that was on my chest is now gone. "I'm sorry. It's just that he makes me uneasy. He brings out a side of me I'm not too fond of."

"I know the feeling."

She leans over and gives me a kiss, stands and takes me by the hand. "Come on."

"Where are we going?" I ask as I stand and start to follow her.

She looks back at me with a devilish look in her eyes, "My room."

"Say less." I smile, and grab her by the hips and push us faster.

"Well, that didn't take much."

I smile. "Should it have?"

She laughs. "No."

"Then be happy I follow instructions."

She looks back at me seductively. "Oh, I am."

"Woman, you'll be the death of me."

"In a good way, I hope."

I smile devilishly at her. "Very much so."

"I doubt anyone's ever complained about dying from pleasure."

"Pleasure, you say."

She shines her pearly whites at me. "Yes."

"There's nothing I want more than you, and if I die then, at least I'll die a happy man."

She smiles at me and then starts laughing. "Logan."

We laugh together as we make our way to her room. On the way I can't help but feel like we are being watched. I turn to look behind us more than a handful of times until we finally make it to the door, and she grabs me by the collar of my shirt and pulls me in for a kiss. She opens the door behind her back, and we practically fall through it laughing.

* * *

Julian

Seeing them together makes me sick to my stomach, but this is what I wanted isn't it?

I can't help but watch them as they walk down the hall together, holding hands, and laughing. It makes my stomach do somersaults. When they get to her door, he turns around to look in my direction once more, and I move behind the wall closest to me.

When I peer back around it, I see her grab him by the shirt and pull him in for a kiss, and I hear a low growl escape between my teeth.

As hard as I try, I can't help feeling angry. Her lips on his, his hands on her. That was supposed to be me. But you messed that up, remember?

I hoped I could bridge the gap, could fix this, fix us but the more time that passes the more I'm beginning to realize that may not be possible.

This is my new reality.

My new world.

Amberly and Logan.

I find myself wishing more than ever that I could take back the last few days.

Chapter 27

Amberly

I walked outside the cave entrance to look for Julian so we could start our training session, and I couldn't be happier. Things with Logan are better than I ever thought they could be. I never knew I could be this happy. I was so unsure about giving this a try, but I am happy I did.

"Better late than never I suppose."

I turn around to see Julian leaning against a tree, and if it's possible he looks smug.

"Sorry, I told you I wanted to change."

"Yeah, because that's what you were doing?"

I can feel the blood rushing to my cheeks, "What are you talking about?"

"Never mind." He stands up straight and starts walking in my direction. He stops in front of me and looks down, "Let's just train." He says the words almost in a snarl.

He brushes my shoulder with his on his way past, and a surge of hot energy radiates from where our shoulders touched, and then it spreads through my whole arm. I really hate that feeling, and I hate that he can still give it to me after everything.

I follow him deeper into the woods until he stops.

"So, we are going to work on your shifting today."

I tried to hide my excitement at his words, but I couldn't be more ready for this. It didn't go over so well last time, but now I'm ready. I know what to expect, I know the amount of intensity from the pain coming, so I can handle it this time.

"Take a seat on the ground."

Without looking in his direction, I do as he says.

"Now close your eyes."

I do.

"Listen to my voice, and I want you to focus just like Aaron taught you."

I take in a slow deep breath and let it out the same way. I do it a few times, letting everything else leave my mind.

Vladimir.

Logan.

Julian.

Gone.

"See your body, every muscle, see it stretching, changing." He starts to circle me just like my father did, "See your hands start to change, shift. See your nails growing long as they form into claws, and then your hands change to paws. See them completely formed as they find their place on the cold dirt floor. See yourself look to the sky as if you might howl. As you do, your back arches, feel every bone, every muscle inside your body start to shift."

My muscles start to ache, start to burn, and I fight back the urge to cry out. I can feel the change, right there at the tips of my fingers. Yet, nothing. I keep trying repeatedly. I see it clear as day in my mind. My hands are no longer hands but paws. I see me running through the woods on all fours with the cool air kissing dirt under me, and the cold wind hitting me like daggers. I can feel my fur slowly emerging from every piece of my soft skin until it engulfs my entire body. Knowing it's the only thing keeping me warm as it protects me against the harshness of the night air.

And still. Nothing.

I open my eyes and stand up fast. Anger and frustration radiating off me.

Out of the corner of my eye I can see Julian looking at me, but he's smart enough to know to keep his distance. I pace back and forth wondering if I should just give up, and move on for the day before I get too annoyed to want to do any more training.

"Close your eyes." He whispers.

I glare at him.

Unfazed he repeats, "Close your eyes."

"Julian, I don't..."

He cuts me off and more sternly says, "Close your eyes."

I let out a long-annoyed sigh and do as he says.

"Count back from ten. Slowly."

I do as he says.

"Clear your mind."

I go through the same steps again.

"Imagine every cell in your body turning warm. Feel that warmth moving towards the surface of every inch of your skin. Feel it begging to come out."

I can feel it.

"Now release it."

I feel the heat like fire in my veins working its way to the surface, I feel the ache in my muscles turning into a weight I've never felt before. I can feel my body starting to move closer to the earth's floor against my will.

The pain surrounds me, and I can't help but release a whimper in pain.

I hear Julian start to walk closer to me.

I open my eyes and he sucks in a breath as he stops dead in his tracks. "Your eyes."

I don't have time to think about what he's talking about. I look down at my arm and see my bone snap back and I bite down on my lip to keep from screaming out.

"I know it hurts. Try to slow your breathing. Breathe in and out as slowly as you can. Feel the change, embrace it."

I know he's only trying to help, and more than that, I know he's done this a million times himself so he knows what he's talking about, but no matter how hard I try to focus on him and his words I just can't.

This time when I look down at my hand, I can feel something itchy making its way to the surface of my skin. Moments later, I see fur start to take over the top of my hands, and at the same moment, my nails start to form into claws.

If the pain wasn't so intense, I would be smiling right now. I'm doing it, I'm shifting. Without warning my back arches out and my spine feels like it's being snapped in half, and this time I can't help it. I look to the sky and open my mouth as I let out a pain-wrenching scream.

* * *

Julian

Her scream fills the air around us. I can feel the intensity of it in the vibration it is giving off, and it takes everything in me not to run to her. I stand in place and wait, knowing she would kill me if I did anything else. It is hard to sit here and do nothing. Amberly has never been one to show pain, so when she does, I know it's bad. I try to remember what it was like for me the first few times I shifted, but that was so long ago that I cannot recall how painful it really was.

I look on in wonder as her skin starts to disappear as her fur coat emerges. I find myself watching her in awe. Her body finishes taking on its new form as her wolf form sits still against the earth floor. I watch her keeping my distance, remembering that the first few shifts can leave you disoriented.

She's about four feet in height and at least five feet in length. One of the biggest I've seen in the females in our pack. Her fur coat is a bright silvery white with light brown markings on her paws, unlike anyone else's in the pack.

As I take a step forward, she starts to stand slowly. She turns in my direction and snarls. I raise my hands to show I'm not a threat. I look her in the eyes to see they are the color of a burning sun. Without another thought, I look to the ground.

Her snarl disappears as she moves closer. Starting to feel uneasy, but I don't move as she approaches me. Before I have a chance to react her muzzle brushes my cheek. As fast as it was there it is gone again and when I look up, she's nowhere in sight.

* * *

Amberly

Somewhere between my scream, and Julian yelling my name, I completed the shift. I couldn't tell you when because the next thing I remember is this moment, now, me running through the forest on all fours. I look down at what used to be my hands to see they are now a light shade of brown and white. I look forward and see the forest laid out in front of me and if a wolf could smile, I would be right now.

This feeling is like nothing I have ever had before, and if someone asked me to describe it for them all I would be able to come up with would be one word...

Freedom.

It's so freeing to be out here. Being able to run without a care in the world. It feels like nothing can touch you. And I don't want it to end. At this moment, I find myself not wanting to go back.

Everything feels right, it all fits. I feel at complete peace like this is always what I was meant for. The forest has always called to me like a mother calling her child home. It always felt like my home and now it is.

Suddenly, I become very aware of the chilly dirt as it finds its place between my paws, but I don't stop running. I peer up at the moon still high in the sky and I find myself wondering if everyone else is awake yet. I know I should get back and continue my training, but I want to enjoy this moment. It is something I've thought about for a long time, and now that I'm here, now that I did it, I don't want to change back. All I want to do is keep running and never look back.

Chapter 28

Julian

I look at Aaron, almost unable to keep my pride inside. "She did it."

He looks at me surprised. "What?"

"Amberly, shifted."

He stands up with a smile on his face and Johnathan, Aayda and Serenity all look at each other and smile. If I didn't know better, I would say they were all communicating with each other like we do as a pack.

Aaron's words draw me back to him. "When did this happen?"

"About five minutes ago. And Aaron. She's a natural."

I can see the pride in his eyes and my smile only grows.

"I knew she could do it. She just needed the right push." He says as he looks over at me.

My smile fades as I ask, "What do you mean?"

"She needed someone she felt a real connection with to push her. I knew you would be the right person for the job."

"I think you're thinking of someone else. She hates me now, remember. She can't even stand to be in the same room as me."

He smiles. "Exactly."

"What?"

His smile grows, and with it so does my temper.

"It means if she didn't still care, then what happened wouldn't still be affecting her, meaning she wouldn't care to be around you."

"So, you're saying what?"

He shakes his head from side to side in disbelief. "Meaning my daughter still cares for you, even though she doesn't want to admit it to herself."

"Well, it's one thing to care, and it's another to want to be around the person or with them for that matter."

He places a hand on my shoulder, "Trust me she does. She just needs some space and some time to move past it. And she needs to know she can trust you,and rely on you again." He removes his hand and flashes me a know-it-all smile, "Which is why I wanted her first time shifting to be with you. It's a good bonding experience."

I can hear the surprise in my voice. "You did it on purpose."

"Well, I had to do something. Leaving you two to figure it out for yourselves was getting us nowhere. Wouldn't you agree?"

I don't know whether I'm more annoyed or thankful. "You know she's gonna be pissed, right?"

He flashes me a devilish grin. "Who says she ever has to know?"

"Aaron, it's Amberly. I think she will figure it out."

He looks back at the table where the others are sitting. "I don't think so because I have my cover right here."

I look around him and back at the table. When I look back at him, he's smiling, and I can't help but do the same. He turns back to the table, where he got up from with the others, and retakes his seat before turning to look in my direction. "Now go back out there and wait for her. Trust me you will be glad you did."

* * *

Julian

Heading outside as Aaron suggested I find my mind in a whirlwind of thoughts and emotions. It is nice to know without a doubt that Aaron approves of me being with his daughter, even after what I've done. But it doesn't matter because as much as we both try, she isn't ready. I know he thinks by pushing us together it will change things, but after last night, I don't see that happening. She's with Logan, and more than that she seems happy and I don't want to take that away from her. As much as my heart aches for her I can't come between her and something that makes her smile. Maybe if Aaron knew the truth, he would stop pushing us so hard. If I'm being honest, being around her and not being able to touch her hurts too much, and more than that, last night is stuck in my mind. Knowing she was with Logan makes it hard for me to look at her. I know it's my fault, but it hurts just the same. However, I can't tell Aaron.

My thoughts end when I find a nice boulder to sit on. I look to the night sky wondering what time it is now. Somewhere during our training everyone in the cave woke up so it was nearing morning. I look to the sky again and see the light blue creeping across the horizon. I hear branches and dry leaves in the distance, and I see Amberly running up the path with excitement written all over her face. I can't help but smile at her as she looks to her feet as she slows to a walk.

For what seems to be the first time, she realizes I'm here and she looks at me and her smile widens, she picks up her pace once more until she reaches my side. Without a word, she throws her hands up and around my neck pulling me close.

Without any hesitation my arms go around her like they have so many times before.

She whispers in my ear, "I did it. I actually did it."

We stand there in an embrace for what feels like forever, but in the same instance, as fast as her arms were there they are just as quickly gone. As she pulls away from me slowly our cheeks touch. She keeps her hands on my shoulders as we look each other in the eyes. Without thinking I start to lean in towards her and when our lips are just about to touch, she pulls back and drops her hands to her side and smiles at me.

"We should head back."

I rub the back of my head before answering back, "Yea, I guess we should."

She smiles at me one more time and then starts to walk back in the direction of the cave. For a moment I found myself lost in her presence. Not thinking about what I'd done, that we weren't together, or her and Logan. Seeing only her and me and our lips. This is going to be a lot harder than I originally thought.

I sigh in frustration as I take my first step towards home.

* * *

Logan

It's been a few hours since Amberly went to meet with Julian to try to learn how to shift. I would hate to say that I'm feeling a little jealous, but I am. I will never be able to share that part with her or know what it feels like, not like I always have, and I think that's the hardest thing to admit to myself.

I walk into the kitchen just in time to see Amberly about to pick out a seat for herself. She looks up in my direction and a smile washes over her face, and I can't help but smile back. I start to walk over to her, but I guess I'm moving too slow because she starts to run towards me, and I can see the excitement in her eyes as she approaches.

She places her hands in mine while saying, "I did it."

I smile at her, not too sure what to say. I can see her smile starting to fade so I grab her by the hand and start to walk back over to the table I saw her eyeing up moments ago.

"What was it like?"

I can see the hesitation in her eyes, or maybe it's something else. "Well. It was rough, I'm not gonna lie, but once I finally changed it was amazing. There's nothing like it in the world."

Just what I was afraid of. Something I can never experience with her so something I can't really talk with her about and act like I understand what she's going through or experiencing.

"I'm sorry it was so rough."

"It was worth it. Being able to run like that and feel the breeze in your hair, or should I say fur." She laughs.

"Yeah."

I can see the disappointment in her eyes. "You OK?"

"Yeah, I'm fine. Just a little tired. I'm sorry."

She places her hand on my lap. "I totally understand. Why don't you go get some rest?"

"It's a little early."

She laughs. "Precisely, it's not even eight yet, more than half the pack is still asleep so if you're tired you should rest, while you can."

I look at her in surprise. "What's that mean?"

She flashes me a devilish smile. "Well between our late-night activities and training for the big fight coming, I think you could use it."

I look at her as my smile reaches my eyes. "And what about you?"

"Oh, I've got more than enough energy for the both of us." She says as she practically bounces up and down in her seat and I can't suppress my laugh.

"Don't laugh at me." She says playfully as she comes to a stop.

"Hey I'm allowed."

Her grin turns to one of pure enjoyment. "Just because you're my man doesn't mean you can make fun of me now. You're not Troy."

"Thank God for that."

We look at each other and laugh.

She forces the last bit of food in her mouth and as she's still chewing, she grabs me by the hands, stands up and takes me with her.

"Where are we going?"

"You said you were tired."

I hold back my smile. "Amberly, I don't think you coming with me is such a good idea."

She stops walking and looks back at me. "Why not?"

I rub at the hair on the back of my head nervously. "I don't think I'll want to sleep if you're there."

She smiles when she realizes what I'm saying. She moves over next to me and stands up on her tippy toes and kisses me. "Then maybe we won't sleep."

"You're killing me, you know that?" I say with a smile.

"All in the right ways, I'm sure."

"You know my weakness and that's not fair."

She grabs me by the hand and pulls me along after her. "I didn't know I would be considered a weakness."

I sigh. "You know what I mean."

She looks back at me with a smile that reaches her eyes. "I know. I promise just a little make out session and then I'll put you right to sleep."

"Amberly." I say as she pulls me along.

Man, this girl will be the death of me but at least I'm going to die happy. She knows all the right things to say and I couldn't be happier in this place with her and I find myself hoping it never ends. Because now that I know what it's like to be with her, I don't think I could ever be without her.

Chapter 29

Amberly

I've spent the past week training with literally everyone in the cave. Every day someone different in the pack would take time to spar with me, and then later in the day I would train with my mom or dad, and at the end of the day, it would be with one of my closest friends or Johnathan. And let me tell you no one pulled any punches, that's for sure. My bruises have bruises, and I don't think I've ever been this tired.

But I can feel how much stronger I am because of it. I've also mastered a lot of powers that I didn't even know about. I've perfected my levitation, telekinesis, mind reading, dream walking, astral projection, even my new powers like invisibility, and this shield protection thing I have going for me. I've even perfected my wolf abilities. However, I still can't control my premonitions, but they are far and in between anyway.

"Amberly?"

I turn around to see Serenity standing behind me.

"Hi."

"Do you mind if I sit with you?"

Surprised, I answered, "No, please." I gesture to the seat next to me.

"Thank you."

We sit in silence for a few moments before she finally looks at me and says, "I don't know what Johnathan has or hasn't shared with you yet, but I wanted to let you know that you aren't just a descendant of the originals. You are also a direct descendant of Johnathan, Aadya and me."

She can see the surprise on my face, and if not, she can definitely hear it in my voice when I ask, "How is that possible? None of you have any children."

"That is correct but because we are all a direct descendant of the original you have our power too."

"But wouldn't that mean I have all of the seven's powers?"

She shakes her head, "No, not really. See the three of us are the only ones of the last group of seven that were a direct descendant of the originals."

The wheels start turning in my head and I can't help myself from blurting out, "Wait, does that mean I can control the elements like Aadya can?"

She nods her head in agreement.

"Well, I need to get on that. I need to train, that could really come in handy."

I stand up and she gently grabs my wrist, "Please sit with me a few more minutes. I can understand your eagerness to train and learn more, but there is something I must share with you first." I sit down slowly as she continues, "It's not only her and Johnathan's powers you share, but mine as well."

"Oh, yeah I forgot I'm sorry. You're the healer, right?"

"Yes. But with this power comes a lot of understanding and," she pauses for a moment, "limitations."

"Limitations?"

"Yes. And I would like to talk to you more about them, and the power, so you can fully understand how it works before you go and try to use it on your own."

I can feel my necklace fall out of my shirt and before I can place it back Serenity grabs it lightly. "This can't be…"

I look at her confused. "What."

"This was made by the originals. They foresaw the hardship that was to come, with Vladimir and the other battles ahead and so they made this."

I catch myself looking down at it like a long-lost friend. I wear it every day so most days I forget it's even there.

She continues, "This is a very strong pendant."

"My mom just gave it to me and told me never to take it off. She said it would protect me."

She nods her head, "That and so much more."

"Like?"

"This amulet was made for more than just the protection of the wearer but first I want to explain something. Yes, it does protect whoever owns it but that doesn't mean you can't get hurt or even die."

I think back to the night I was attacked by the wolf and almost mauled to death and I suppress a shudder. I look at her and all I can manage is a nod to let her know I understand what she's telling me.

She continues. "It can sense when you're in danger, it will change different colors depending on how much of a threat and by how close the threat is. It also enhances your powers and can sometimes make you use the right one at the right moment. Meaning it will bring out the power that is best suited to protect you or cause the most damage."

I nod my head in agreement, once again while I recall the encounter with the wolf and how I started running faster than I ever had before and then the energy blast that came after.

Before I can stop myself, I ask her, "But it takes all of your energy after. How is that supposed to be a help?"

"The more you connect with it and use it the more it will do the opposite."

I don't let her finish before I interrupt again, "Meaning?"

She smiles, "Meaning at the time I'm assuming it was helping you, you didn't really know about its power, so you weren't connected which is why when it came to your assistance it took all your power to help you, in I'm guessing one attack."

I nod my head.

She looks down at my pendant again and continues, "But now that you know more about it and you can accept its help, it will do the opposite. Instead of only helping with one attack it will help you through the whole fight. And instead of it taking all your energy it will only make you feel more awake and alive and ready for the battle you're in."

"Well, this thing definitely did more than my mom and I thought."

Now it is her turn to nod her head.

I look at her questionably, "But how is this meant to help me defeat Vladimir or even the other seven when the time comes?"

"The pendant is so much more than what we've been told. Once you connect with it, its powers become almost unlimited. Just take the time and practice with it, use it and learn how to really connect and then you will see how it can help keep you safe. You'll then understand how with its help, and your careful planning of each attack that everyone will find it much harder to defeat you in a battle."

I touch the object around my neck once more and a sudden calm washes over me for the first time since my dream. I might be able to do this.

I can sense Serenity looking at me so I look back at her and smile, "Can you teach me?"

"Yes, along with many other things. But first I want to talk to you about your other powers and then we can talk about the training that's to come."

I nod letting her know to continue.

"As you know I'm the healer, and Aadya is the natural. I want to tell you what that means and what powers you will have because of it. But I also

233

want to stress your limits and the repercussions of using curtain powers."

"Limits?"

She almost looks sad, "Yes."

And just like that, I don't feel as sure.

"Our powers are truly amazing but like everything, power comes with a price, as I'm sure your mother has taught you."

I only nod, seems to be my only reply lately.

"Well with my power comes the biggest price."

"Amberly." Logan's voice seems so far away but when I turn, he's standing right next to me with Angela, Tory and Amara.

"Hey, guys."

Amara continued, "We've been looking for you everywhere."

"Really?" I say with a little sass in my voice and realize maybe I'm not totally over what happened yet. I smile at her to let her know I didn't mean it.

Angela steps forward, "We wanted to see if you wanted to head out and do some training."

I almost jump up but look back at Serenity who has stayed quiet, I feel like she doesn't do well with crowds. I turn back to my friends. "I would love to but I'm a little busy right now."

Troy's sarcasm cuts through everyone, "What are you too scared to come train?"

"Troy shut up."

"What? We haven't seen much of you since the party gone wrong, which makes me wonder if you're getting scared."

"Me scared?" I let out a laugh, trying not to let the fear show through, I hate admitting when Troy is right.

"You know it would be ok if you were, I'm pretty sure we all are."

Logan steps closer and places a hand on my shoulder, "Take your time, finish up and come meet us outside."

I look up at him, "Sounds like a plan."

Before I can say anything else, he leans down and kisses me and when he stands back up everyone is looking at us in surprise. My eyes come to rest on Angela and there in the background across the room I see Julian, and I can see his sadness from here. He turns away and continues back down the hall. I turn my attention back to my friends in front of me and realize for the first time since Logan and I started dating that no one else really knew. We were never together in front of them. Always training with different people at different times.

I turn my attention back to my friends. "I'll see you guys in a bit."

They make their way to the exit and I see Julian emerge from the hall he goes down and heads outside with them. I return my attention to Serenity, "I'm sorry about that."

"No, it's good to have that many friends and for them to care enough to train, and to train with you at that. You're going to need that and them when the time comes."

"I was really hoping to keep them out of it."

I can hear the surprise in her voice, "You know that's not possible."

I look back at the exit and let out a sigh, "Yes, unfortunately."

"They are stronger than I think you're giving them credit for. With them all being part of the seven I wouldn't expect them to go down so easily."

"They all are part of the seven?"

She looks at me surprised again, "Yes. Couldn't you sense that? You should be able to sense who else is in the seven. The only thing that's hard is to tell which are good and which aren't."

"No, I couldn't. But it's not like I ever tried to. But then again not like I knew that was something I could do."

"Just something else I can teach you." She smiles at me. "So, where were we? Oh, yes, my powers. So, let's start at the beginning. First, you should know you get your power of premonitions from me."

I know the surprise is all over my face because she pauses and releases a small giggle, "Well, where did you think they came from? Every power you have, or anyone in your village, they all originate from someone in our seven, you're one of the only ones who has ever been connected to more than one."

"I mean I figured they all came from the original witch."

She shifts herself in her seat to get a more comfortable position and I see something like pain on her face at the motion. "Yes, for most that is correct. There are few in your village who would be connected to me or any of the other seven. Your mother and your friends might be the only others."

"My friends?"

She reaches up to tuck a piece of her straight gray laced auburn hair behind her ear, "Yes, other than them being part of the seven a few of them are connected to more than just the person their village is connected to."

I find myself wondering which ones, but I know we have more important things to talk about right now. "So other than the premonitions."

"Well, I also have a shielding power, the one that Johnathan taught you, that comes from me."

"Well, that's a handy one to have."

She nods, "Yes, it can definitely come in handy, and the more you use it the stronger it will become, just like the rest. Once you've mastered it, you can shield others around you as well."

It's my turn to fidget in my seat a bit.

"But that's a talk for another day. The main thing I want to talk to you about is your healing power."

"I have that one too?"

She lets out a small laugh at my reaction, "Yes, you have every power that we have."

"I think I'm starting to like my odds," I say sarcastically.

"Well let's not get ahead of ourselves. Remember I told you with powers come the limitations as well."

More than interested I ask, "And what are ours?"

"The first thing you need to know is you can heal anyone, even yourself, of anything as long as it's not life-threatening."

"I've always been curious; does that mean anything from a cold or sickness to a cut or bruise?"

"Anything." She nods her head in agreement.

"Wow, that's pretty awesome." I pause and look at her once more, "But the way you said it." I stop.

She almost looks sad when she continues, "Like I was saying, we have our limits."

Almost afraid to ask, I say, "Which are?"

"For starters, you can only bring the same person back from the dead so many times before they can't be brought back again."

"How many times?"

"Seven."

I look to the ground. "Well, that's appropriate."

Serenity laughs, "I guess you could say that."

I look back up at her, "what else?"

She looks sad again, "If someone has a life-threatening wound you can heal them, however."

I know I'm not going to like what comes next.

"When you heal them, you take on that wound yourself. You will heal, at first, you'll heal so fast you won't even notice the wound transferred to you. But after some time, you will start to heal slower and slower until."

She pauses and I'm afraid to ask but I do anyway, "Until?"

She lifts her shirt slowly to show the skin of her abdomen, it's torn to shreds and I suppress a gasp. "Oh my God what happened?"

"The limitations." She returns her shirt to the place it was only moments before but not without wincing.

"We need to get you help," I say as I start to stand but her hand gently finds my wrist and leads me back to my seat.

"Part of these limitations is whatever you heal, and take from someone, and transfer to yourself, your body has to heal for you. No one can do it but you."

Understanding is clear on my face I'm sure when I say, "Meaning no one can help?"

"Correct. All they can do is bandage it up and maybe give me something for the pain but that's it."

I look back to where Johnathan and Aadya are sitting, "Do they know?"

"No."

I turned back to her. "Do they know about the limitations?"

Again, she gives me a one-word answer, "No."

I can feel the anger rising in me, why wouldn't she tell them?

Almost as if she heard my thoughts she says, "They don't need to know."

"How can you say that?"

I can see the sadness forming in her eyes, "Because there's nothing they can do to stop it, like I told you, and I don't want them blaming themselves."

"You healed one of them, didn't you?"

She nods her head.

"Who? And if you knew what would happen. why?"

"It doesn't matter who, and I thought of all people you would understand the why. Tell me, if it was someone you loved, one of your friends, one of your parents, wouldn't you do the same thing?"

Well, she's got me there.

"I just wanted you to understand this power before you start to use it, and with the battle ahead, I know you will."

"How long?"

She looks confused, "How long what?"

"How long do you have, and how long were you able to heal before this started getting this bad?"

"My body isn't healing anymore. so it's only a matter of time. I'm hoping to help in the fight and take some down with me before I go."

I feel the anger surface again, and I have to push it back down. After all, how could I be mad at someone so strong and caring? She knew what would happen and she healed them anyway, and even now she's thinking of them as she prepares for the fight.

"As for how long, I was healing before this started. I healed a lot of people over the years. What you need to pay attention to is once you can start to feel them forming on yourself. That's when it's time to slow down, or to stop altogether, because once you start taking on the wounds yourself it only gets worse from there. I don't know how fast it would happen for you, but for me it was fast."

I'm sure the sadness is clear in my voice when I say, "Thank you for telling me."

"No need. I knew when I saw you, you had the same powers and so I knew I had to get you alone, and tell you before you learned about the power another way."

"Do you need anything? I mean, before I head out to start training, is there anything I can get you?"

She smiles. "No, but thank you."

"I wish there was more I could do."

"You remind me a lot of myself at your age."

I flash her a big smile before I say, "I'll take that as a big compliment because you are one of the most unselfish people I've ever met. And it takes a lot of courage to do what you did."

She looks over to the table where Johnathan is sitting with Aayda. "Courage has nothing to do with it. When you love someone, you would do anything you could to protect them." She looks back at me, "They are my family and without them I wouldn't have a place left in this world, so I'm honored to be the person to make sure they continue on living in this world together."

I turn to glance over at them. They look so happy. He has his arm draped around the lower part of her back as she slightly leans into him. They are smiling and laughing, almost like they don't have a care in the world and that a huge battle isn't right around the corner. I find myself envying them and wishing I was a bigger person.

"You should go meet your friends; your training is very important."

I turn around to face her once more and find her smiling at me. I get up slowly as I smile back at her. "You sure there's nothing I can get for you before I go?"

"No. Thank you."

"Please, let me know if you change your mind, and take it easy while you can." I turn to walk away but pause, "Thank you for the talk and for letting me know the truth about my powers, I'm sure it wasn't easy to talk about."

She nods. "We will talk more and find time to train you on your amulet and a few other things. For now, go teach your friends a thing or two." She winks at me.

I turn around and I'm about to walk away when her words stop me.

"Amberly. Please, remember what we talked about here today. Carry it with you OK?"

"I will, I promise."

Chapter 30

Logan

I hear Amberly approaching behind me and I get distracted as Troy throws a right punch and it connects with my face. My hand extends up to cradle my chin as I glare at him.

"Sorry, maybe you should pay more attention." He grins.

"Oh, don't worry I'll get you back."

I see his mouth gaping open as I turn my back on him with a smile spread wide across my face. The one thing about Troy is he can be a handful and overstep a lot of the time, but he knows how in a second I could take him to the ground if I ever needed to. I leave him stewing as I approach Amberly.

"Hey, what were you talking about with Serenity?"

"Right to the point, aren't you?" The curve of her mouth turns up into a smile.

I shrug. "Well, I figured we should get the small talk out of the way first. Plus, I'm interested to know because I've never seen her take part in a conversation since she arrived here."

"Yes, she is very quiet."

She seems like someone far away. "Amberly?"

She looks at me and I see a fake smile take its place on her face, "Sorry. She was telling me more about her power, or maybe I should say my power."

Intrigued, I push further. "Which one?"

"Apparently, I can heal people like she can, among other things. She told me I'm a descendant of her line as well as the others."

"What does that mean?"

She knots her hands up in the hem of her shirt as she kicks around the dry dirt at our feet. "It means again I'm something different, stronger than everyone else. It means more powers I need to learn how to use and control before they consume me."

I place my hands on her shoulders and wait until her hazel eyes come to meet mine. "And you will. You're the strongest person I know and with all of us on your side," I pause to look around at all of our friends, minus Julian, I smile, "there's nothing you can't overcome."

Her smile returns as she looks at me with love in her eyes. "I know, but she also told me the limitations of some of my powers. I mean I know that is normal, but hers seem so..."

She looks off into the distance and I can see her getting lost in her thoughts. "So, what?"

"So final." She whispers.

"What do you mean?"

She looks over at me. "She's dying, because of her power she is dying. She healed too many people and now she is taking on the repercussions of it."

Surprise takes over. "She's dying?"

She nods. "I would like to train now. I don't want to think about it anymore, OK?."

I can only nod at her as she walks over to where Angela and Amara are sparring. The more she seems to learn about herself, I see her lose a part of who she's always been. More than that. With each new power, I find myself growing more nervous for her. I know she's strong, but no one has ever had these powers before. How can she possibly be strong enough to handle them without it killing her?

I look over to see her kick out her right leg in Angela's direction, but she moves in time as Amberly does a 360 spin and sweeps her leg under Amara and she falls to the dirt floor.

* * *

Amberly

Training.

Round kick.

Punch.

Dodge.

Stay focused.

Don't think, just act.

I'm finding it hard to evict my conversation with Serenity from my mind. She's dying and there's nothing we can do to stop it. Someone so kind is going to be leaving this world and all because she cared a little too much. How is that fair? How does someone like Vladimir get to continue living when someone like Serenity doesn't?

"Ouch!"

Ripped from my enraged thoughts I look down to see Angela cradling her right arm. I try to remember what just happened, but my mind is blank. I reach out my hand to her. "I'm sorry. I...what happened."

She looks up at me, her face is a mask of concern, as she places her uninjured hand in mine. "You don't remember?"

I look at her sheepishly.

"Where did you go just then? I could see something dark in your eyes."

Embarrassed, I say, "I was thinking about something."

"Talk to me. Maybe it will help to get it off your mind."

I shake my head sadly, "A conversation isn't going to make me feel any better. It's not going to change things."

She looks at me with sadness in her eyes and I can see hesitation in them. "Is it about Julian?"

I look at her in surprise, "What? No!"

She throws her last hand up. "I was only asking."

I rub my eyes feverishly. "I'm sorry. I'm not in the right mind space right now."

She places her hand back at her side while her other is wrapped in front of her chest till. "I can see that, so please let me help."

Knowing no matter what she says it's not going to change anything I sigh. "It's Serenity. She's dying."

"What!" Angela's eyes went wide as she looked back at the cave behind us. "Do the others know?"

I shake my head. "No, and she doesn't want them to. There is nothing they can do. It's because of her power. Like everyone tells us, powers come with a cost and well this one is hers. She healed too many people and now she's paying the price." I feel the daggers poking the back of my eyes and I look away from Angela, "I was thinking how someone as sweet and kind as Serenity is going to die while Vladimir gets to live," I look back at her with my eyes stinging, "and I got lost in it. My anger started to overpower me, and my body was acting out without me knowing." I look down at her arm as my vision starts to blur and I know the tears are right around the corner.

"I'm sorry I didn't mean to hurt you."

She flashes me a reassuring smile. "I'll heal in a few minutes, it doesn't matter. But Amberly I've never seen you like this. Why is this bothering you so much? I mean yes death is never a happy thing and we don't want to see anyone go but."

"I barely know her. I know."

I see something like shame in her eyes. "I didn't mean to suggest that it doesn't matter or that you shouldn't feel something."

I force a smile. "I know you didn't."

"I wish there was something I could do. Something more."

For the first time, I think back to the first time I met Angela. It feels so long ago, and I remember the story about how my father found her and brought her to live with him, just like Julian and now Amara. All at the hands of Vladimir. So many families are torn apart, separated and lost.

"It's just another reminder to me about how unfair life can be and how we really have no control over anything. You can be the strongest one in the room and still lose the fight."

She places her free hand on my wrist gently. "If you're thinking you're going to lose again to Vladimir."

I brush her thoughts off. "No. It's more than that. I have the same power as Serenity, as all of them really. There's no one else like me and I can feel it." I break off looking in the direction of the boys, not wanting to admit what I'm about to. "I can feel my powers getting stronger and I feel myself getting weaker."

Angela's eyes widened. "Amberly, no. You're stronger than you think. You're just tired, as you should be. You've been training nonstop for weeks now. Your body needs a break, that's all you're feeling."

I look at Logan and then to Julian sitting on the sidelines watching Logan and Troy sparing. "I don't know. I hope you're right." I turn my attention back to her. "But what if you're not?"

Chapter 31

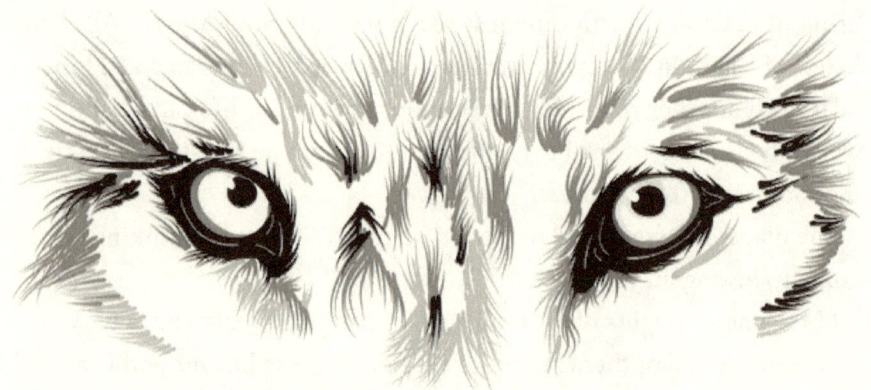

Amberly

The training was brutal. Just when I thought I had enough bruises covering my body, I added more. Talking with Angela did make me feel a little better about all the chaos in my mind. However, I'm still worried about my powers taking over. That's why I keep pushing myself, trying to get stronger, trying to keep up with the powers growing inside of me. Since my birthday I've felt it, the power, strength, multiplying everyday inside of me. I don't want what happened to others before me to be my fate. I want to be stronger than what's growing inside of me. That's why I never stop training and pushing myself. It's not only to prepare myself for the fights ahead but to grow my strength, so my powers never overcome me like they have so many others of my kind in the past.

With these powers, I can do so much good. I could change things for everyone in the forest. I'm not only meant to lead over my village but I'm also the next leader of this pack. I still have no idea how I'm going to pull off running two villages at once, but I figure we can cross that bridge when it comes around. After all, I have a few things that I need to deal with first. So, I know now is not the time to let up, it's not time to rest, not yet.

Well, maybe just a little.

Returning to my room for some serious R and R might be the smartest move. Like Angela said, I'm tired and can't put everything into my training, and getting stronger, if I'm not at my top form. Time is running short but it's better to be smart and take the time I need to get back to the top of my game before trouble comes knocking at our door. Which will be any day now.

I can sense Vladimir's men and I know they are closing in and faster than we all thought. I just pray we are ready to fight them when the time comes. The thought of losing anyone is hard to stomach but one thing I do know for sure is in war there are always casualties. But this time, I pray that we can change that outcome, that I can change my vision.

Tonight was brutal, from the talk with Serenity to the training with everyone. But the worst part would have to be Julian. Seeing him is hard to deal with, but seeing him and knowing he's in pain because of me and I'm happy, well it's hard. I know I shouldn't care, not after what he did, but I can't help it. I'm always going to care for him and seeing him hurting is harder on me than I thought it would be. I distanced myself from Logan because I didn't want him to feel like I was flaunting my relationship in his face. I also didn't want to see the hurt in his eyes. I've witnessed the last few days whenever he saw us together.

I make it to my room and once my bed comes into view, I'm more tired than I realized. I can feel every muscle in my body screaming to lie down and relax. I make it to the edge of my bed, and I fall into it without thinking.

Knock. Knock.

Ugh. "Come in."

I hear whoever is opening the door slowly, but I don't move.

"Someone's tired."

I smile when I hear his voice.

With my face in the covers, I reply, "I'm dead."

Logan laughs as he walks over to the bed. "Maybe I should let you get some rest?"

"Don't you dare."

I can feel him sit down next to me and with my hand, I feel around until I find his. I turn my face to the side so he can hear me. "Come lay with me."

Without a moment's hesitation he gets in the bed and lays behind me. In seconds, every inch of him is touching me and his arm is wrapped around my body and I couldn't feel more at peace.

"I'm glad you came."

He whispers into my ear, "Always."

* * *

Amberly

I feel my body being sucked into the dark and I already know where I am. I'm back in the enemy's camp. Once my eyes adjust, I look around until I see them. They are about twenty feet from where I stand. They are out of earshot, so I close my eyes and focus on my wolf hearing. Take in a deep breath, exhale, and open my eyes.

Mumbles.

Whispers.

And then.

"We will be there in the morning so make sure everyone is ready," Aidan says.

"Yes, sir."

Tomorrow? But they were still weeks away when I last dreamwalked. How could they have come so far so fast? They should still be a few days out. The other man walks away and heads into the camp. Aidan starts to walk in my direction, and I move back slowly.

"I know you're there; I can sense you."

Surprised, I think maybe he's talking to someone else, so I don't move.

"Amberly."

Not possible.

"Come out, come out wherever you are."

I stay silent.

"Doesn't matter, we will be seeing each other soon enough."

I can feel all the hairs on my arms starting to stand straight up. Tomorrow.

"One way or the other we will be seeing each other. Whether it's now or tomorrow doesn't make a difference to me. Just know you can't escape the inevitable. We are coming for you."

I want to say something, anything. I want answers, but I don't want to risk him knowing where I am, as he is so powerful. For all I know even in this dream state, he could take over my mind, my last encounter makes me almost sure that's possible, and I can't take that chance. Since the last time he threatened me, I have trained hard with Johnathan and the others to keep people out. However, I'm not ready to test my mind out.

"It's time for you to join us, to return to where you were always meant to be."

His words ring through my ears.

What is he talking about?

"Curious yet?"

Still, I stay silent. But that doesn't stop him.

"You were never meant to grow up with your mom. You were meant to be here, with me, with us. But the stupidity of people cost us that."

I remember Onyx and Lurch and my body involuntarily starts to shake.

"They weren't meant to kill you. They were meant to simply get information

and to make your mother vulnerable."

Vulnerable. That's why they killed the guards and my grandparents.

"They made her vulnerable for sure but when they went back to collect, a few short months later, they forgot one particularly important thing. You."

I can feel myself starting to hyperventilate. All I want to do is wake up.

"So now it's time to collect. One way or the other you will be leaving with me tomorrow and no one can stop that."

I close my eyes trying to get myself to wake up, but I'm stuck.

"You'll wake up soon but not before I'm done. All I want to do is talk."

My ass.

"I know you've felt like something's been missing all these years and what if I could tell you I know what that something is."

I try to shut him out but it's hard. It's like he's reading my mind.

"What if I tell you I've felt the same way all these years?"

"Amberly."

I hear Logan calling my name, but he sounds so far away.

Aidan starts to look around as he smiles. "I guess we will finish this conversation tomorrow."

I feel the magnetic force that's been holding me in place snap back as it releases its grip on me. I take in a deep breath as I feel my body growing lighter and the world around me starts to fade.

* * *

Amberly

My body throws itself forward as my mind is thrown back inside. Logan is sitting next to me with a look of concern on his face. Without thinking I throw my arms around him and pull him close.

250

"Hey. What's wrong? Sorry, I had to wake you, it looked like you were having a pretty bad dream."

I whisper. "It was more than that."

Slowly he pulls back just far enough to look at me. "What do you mean?"

It's time to tell him. "I've been having these dreams. Kind of like I'm dreamwalking, I guess. I've been seeing Aidan."

I can feel his body stiffen next to me.

"He's closer than we thought."

He takes in a slow deep breath. "How close?"

For the first time, I look him right in the eyes. "He will be here tomorrow."

He jumps up from the bed and he's out the door before I can say another word and for the first time, I feel unsure, I feel unready and unprepared.

Chapter 32

Amberly

I lift my hand hesitantly and it hovers just over my parent's door. I'm not sure where Logan ran off to, but I know he went to fill someone in, the question is who. I knock, no answer.

"Amberly?" I hear Angela's voice behind me.

I turn around and force a smile on my face. "Hey."

"Hey, yourself. You alright?"

I laugh. "Aren't you getting tired of asking me that?" She looks at me concerned and my smile disappears. "Sorry."

"Don't apologize. But something is wrong I can tell."

"I had another episode."

Realization is clear on her face. "Dream walk or premonition?"

"I'm pretty sure it was a dream walk."

She nods. "What happened?"

"I...I saw Aidan. He's closer than we thought."

I can see the panic in the features of her face. "How close?"

"He will be here in the morning."

Angela has never been on to show signs of fear or panic, but I can see it clearly now in her features. But fear and uncertainty are only the start of my feelings. Confusion is at the top of that list. I think about what Aidan said to me while I was under and I wonder if I should say anything about it.

"Amberly?"

I look at her stunned. "I'm sorry."

"Tell me."

I look down at my hands. "It's just something Aidan said on the walk."

"What?"

I look up to see her face is unchanged. "He said something about how I was never meant to be here. I was meant to be there. Almost like he was telling me that Lurch and Onyx weren't meant to kill me all those years ago but instead they were meant to take me back. Back to Vladimir."

She turns her back to me as her face goes to work. She's thinking, thinking hard. "That doesn't make any sense though."

"But doesn't it?"

She faces me once more, her face a mask of uncertainty and longing to understand. "How so?"

"Think about it. What has everyone been telling us about the seven and how there are two groups born at the same time."

She nods her head. "Seven good and seven evil."

"Yes. So, what if Vladimir was trying to tip the scales?"

Her eyes go wide. "By taking you!"

I nod.

"Oh my god you're right. If he knew you would be one of the strongest of the next generation and somehow knew you would be on the side of good," She stares at me intently, "he would know if he took you for himself that you would surely tip the scales in his favor."

"Yes. However, something doesn't quite add up to me still."

Her eyebrows meet in the middle as her face becomes a mask of confusion.

"If he doesn't want me dead, why would he want to take me now? What would be the point? I'm all grown up now."

She looks at me sadly. "I don't think it matters. With someone as strong as Aidan on his side maybe he thinks he can still get into your mind. Still take you over and make you fight on his side."

"Well, that's a scary thought. I know this guy is strong. I've sensed it." I looked at her fiercely, "I don't know if I could fight him off."

"You can. Have faith in yourself. You're stronger than you know."

I place my hand gently on hers. "I need you to do me a favor. Make me a promise."

"Anything."

"If the time ever comes. If he is about to win. I need you to kill me."

Shock spreads through her facial features as she takes a step back. "Amberly, you can't ask me to do that."

I keep her in place and squeeze her hands lightly. "Please, if he takes over my mind you know no one will stand a chance. Everyone here will die and every village that is still left in the forest will be destroyed if they don't follow Vladimir's ways. We can't let that happen."

She looks at me sadly and I can see the moisture forming at the surface of her eyes, "Do you understand what you're asking of me?"

I nod.

She sighs. "I can't make you any promises that I'll be able to go through with it, but I promise if there comes a time where I think we can't save you, that we can not undo what's been done, and you are lost to us. I promise to try to do what you asked."

I smile at her weakly. "Thank you."

She looks away as I see a tear make its way down her cheek. "Don't thank me." She starts to walk away as her hand slips from mine. "Maybe we should go fill everyone else in. It's time to prepare for war."

Chapter 33

Amberly

After filling my parents and everyone else in on the dreams and letting them know we have until tomorrow to prepare, I decide to go off on my own for a little bit. I walk into the forest and look up at the moon as I take in a deep breath of the cool night air.

Tomorrow.

Tomorrow, everything comes to a head. All the training, and preparing. I hope it was enough.

"What are you doing out here all alone?"

I turn around to see Angela and I flash her a smile. We haven't had a moment alone together since before she threw me the party, well other than our training sessions but they don't count to me.

"I needed some fresh air."

She walks up next to me as we both look up at the moon. "I know that feeling all too well."

"I never got the chance to thank you for the party."

I can see her grin out of the corner of my eye. "No need. I was more than happy to do it."

"It meant more to me than you know."

"Good. I was a little worried because everyone kept telling me how much you hated your birthday, and you don't like to celebrate it, but I felt this was a birthday that couldn't be passed over. For many reasons."

I close my eyes. "I agree."

We stand in silence looking at the sky for a long time. I never feel more at peace than when I'm out here in the forest and ever since I shifted it seems to mean more.

I look over at Angela afraid to ask but knowing I need to hear the answer from someone other than myself. "Be honest. Do you think I'm ready?"

The smile leaves her face. "There's no real way to know. I don't know how strong they are, I only know how strong we are."

I look back to the forest. "I hope we all trained hard enough to walk away from this."

I can see in her eyes she's thinking about our earlier conversation when she replies, "As do I." She reaches over and takes my hand in hers. "You want to go for a run?" She smiles at me, "heard you can do that now."

I smile back. "I would love that. I think that's just what I need."

I head into the forest, but her hand stops me.

"Can we talk for a minute first?"

Unsure I answer, "Sure."

"I know it might not be my place, but I wanted you to have all the facts before things with you and Logan get too serious, and there's no going back."

I think that ship has already sailed.

"All the facts?"

I've never really seen Angela sad, other than my very first day here when we were talking about her village and all the loss she had to go through.

"Julian. He came to me."

"About?"

"You."

I wish he would stop talking to everyone about me other than me. "What about me?"

"Julian and I grew up together, there's nothing I don't know about him, nothing that I haven't felt before. Like you with Logan, that's me with Julian."

My eyes open wide. "Oh, you love him?"

She looks both surprised and horrified by my statement as she starts to laugh. "Yes. But not in the way you're thinking."

"I'm sorry I'm a little confused then. What are you trying to tell me?"

"What I'm trying to say is I've watched him grow up, I've seen him be angry for most of his life and I've seen him with women."

I find myself turning away from her without thinking about it. I didn't realize I still cared this much. I knew I still felt things for him but things with Logan and I have been going so well that I thought it had lessened my feelings for Julian.

"He never cared enough for any of them. Not until he met you."

"No offense Angela but what is the point of this conversation?"

"What I'm trying to say is with you, things were different. He became someone else. The best version of himself came out."

Trying to hide my annoyance, I say, "OK."

She says her next words fast, "He loves you."

I close my eyes before saying, "You don't hurt someone you love. Not like that. Not on purpose."

"He did it because he thought it was the only way to save you more pain later on."

"I know. He told me all about it. Told me about how we couldn't be together and the rules of the pack and how he thought that kissing Amara was the only way I would walk away from him."

In a whisper, she says, "I know, he told me that he told you."

"Then why are we having this conversation?"

She shifts her feet in the dirt below before continuing. "The point is I know you still love him."

I look to the cave entrance to make sure no one else is coming outside. "So, what if I do? It doesn't matter he made the choices he made and by doing so he made the decision for us both. I'm with Logan now and I'm happy."

"He did what he did for you. And if you think it didn't hurt him just as much as it hurt you, trust me you're wrong."

I can feel the anger boiling inside my stomach. "For me? You don't hurt someone as a favor."

"You weren't brought up with the pack, so you don't understand how it works. He was doing what needed to be done."

"Are you seriously justifying what he did to me?"

She shakes her head from side to side slowly. "No, that's not what I'm trying to do. I'm trying to get you to understand before it's too late."

"Understand what?"

She lets out a long sigh. "Other than me and Aaron, Julian has never put anyone else above himself. He always took what he wanted and did not care about the consequences of his actions."

"OK?"

She closes her eyes. "Until you." She smiles lightly at me, "He cares about you more than you know."

My heart skips a beat and in the same moment I release a long breath. "What do you want me to do with this information?"

"I want you to remember how you felt about him only a few weeks ago. Remember how he made you feel. And I want you to ask yourself who you want to be with."

I close my eyes and let out another long sigh. "Angela, the decision has been made, I'm with Logan now. He's my best friend. He's always been there for me and he's someone I can always count on."

"I understand. And I know you've known him your whole life and you've known Julian only a few short months. But in those short months, I saw you come to feel for him the way you do for Logan. Don't you think that means something? That it happened so fast for the two of you for a reason?"

I don't want to think about Julian anymore, it hurts too much. I look up at her before I say. "It did happen too fast, he felt it just as I did. I'm not saying what we felt for each other wasn't real, but maybe because of that it wasn't meant to last either."

I've never seen Angela look so defeated. "That's where you're wrong."

I try to search for something to say, anything, to make her feel better. I don't want her carrying around my choice like it's her fault I didn't choose to be with Julian. That's no one's fault but his. But I can't seem to find the words.

She flashes me a genuine smile. "Let's go for that run."

She takes off into the woods and I try to smile as I run behind her and for the first time, I find myself asking a question I never thought would cross my mind again.

Did I make the right choice?

* * *

Amberly

The change came on faster this time and was a lot less painful. I look down at my tan-covered paws and I feel my muzzle pull back into a smile. Being in the forest has always made me feel at peace but being out here like this, it's something else. I feel like I've finally come home and found the most important part of myself. Throwing one paw in front of the other, running deeper and faster into the dark brisk forest I throw my muzzle into the breeze and release a freeing howl into the night air all around me.

There's nothing like it.

I forgot Angela was here with me, I turned my head to look in her direction to see her beautiful light gray coat moving in the wind. For a moment I wonder how fast we could be running, or how long we've been running for that matter.

Only a couple of minutes.

I glance over at it and then it dawns on me. I forgot we can read each other's minds in this form.

Don't worry, it took me some time to get the hang of things too. You'll catch on in no time.

I sigh, so anytime any of us is in wolf form we can all hear each other's thoughts?

Not entirely. You must focus on the person whose mind you want to communicate with. I'm glad it works that way. I mean could you imagine running with the whole pack and having to listen to everyone's thoughts at the same time? You would never be able to tell them apart.

I nod my muzzle in agreement.

Angela?

Yea.

About earlier.

I can hear her chest rumble next to me and I realize she's laughing. Which conversation are we talking about?

All of them, I guess.

She looks to the moon and then back down to her paws. I'm sorry if I overstepped with Julian. I just want you both to be happy and I think you're lying to yourself if you think you can walk away from him. Having the feelings you have for him, it's not something you can close off at will.

I know. It's going to take some time.

They might never go away completely Amberly. I need you to think about what you're doing to yourself as well as Julian and Logan. It's not only going to hurt you in the end.

I know.

She looks forward once more. I'm sorry. I did it again.

No, it's fine. You're right. It's just not an easy decision to make in general let alone right now.

I know it's the furthest thing from your mind.

I nod my muzzle again. I don't even know if I'm going to make it through the next week so right now the most important thing is to focus on that.

I agree.

I glance in her direction. But I did mean what I said earlier.

I know you did, and I promised if the time came, I would do my best to do what you asked.

That's all I can ask.

We become silent then, concentrating on running, listening to the noises in the night, and our paws each time they land on the dirt floor. This is just what I needed. Not ready to go back to reality just yet but I know it's time. I turn to look at Angela and I can see in her eyes she knows what I'm saying without a word. We both look to the moon and howl to our heart's content.

Chapter 34

Amara

Over the last week I've felt myself getting stronger, becoming the old me again. All my bruises have healed, and I feel like I'm ready for battle. Which I guess is a good thing since it's only a matter of hours now before I need to be ready . I never would have thought this is where I would have ended up but I'm happy I did. I've never met a pack more connected than this one and I know if anyone had the chance of fighting off Vladimir it would be them.

Other than training this last week I've come to know everyone a little better. Logan is one of the nicest men I think I've ever met and I'm happy Amberly has someone like him in her corner. But then there's Troy. Weird, yet sweet and very funny. I never saw him being someone I would find myself attracted to because let's face it he's not really my type. I don't tend to go for blondes but there is something more about him. Something deep down inside that I can tell he doesn't let many other people see.

"Hey there."

I turn around to see him walking up in my direction. Speak of the devil.

"Hey, Troy."

"You seemed lost in thought, hope I'm not bothering you?"

I smile at him. "Never. I love your company."

Really, Amara? Way to stay aloof. I mean you've already locked lips with one man here that was connected to Amberly don't push your luck. As I'm mentally beating myself up for my careless words, I can see something like excitement on Troy's face and I wonder if it's because of what I said. No, it can't be.

"I enjoy your company too." He says with a smile that reaches his eyes.

Surprised I say. "You do?"

He shrugs, "Sure what's not to enjoy? You're beautiful, smart from what I can see, you're funny and you can definitely kick some ass." He chuckles.

Could he really be interested in me too? No, Amara, get your head out of the clouds, there is a fight coming to stop daydreaming about things that aren't important. "So, I take it those are things you like in a friend?" I laugh as I turn to start walking down the hall.

He follows slowly behind me and says at a whisper. "Not really. I can be friends with almost anyone as long as they are a decent person." He reaches my side and looks down at me unsure. "Those are things I look for in a woman." I looked up at him, surprised and unsure if I heard him correctly. He looks forward again as his smile grows. "Those are the characteristics that attract me to a woman."

Baffled, I choke on my next words. Unable to form them, unable to think. I face forward once more, putting one foot in front of the other. I hear Troy laugh as he reaches for my hand. I look down at them now interlocked and I can feel the blood rushing to my cheeks.

"I hope this is OK?"

I look forward again and manage a nod. I hear a chuckle erupt from his chest before he says. "Good."

Should this be OK? What would Amberly think? I shake my head lightly trying not to draw Troy's attention. I free my mind of all thoughts related to him. I need to get my head in the game. I need to prepare myself for battle. However, my body doesn't agree as I feel my hand squeeze Troy's lightly and his smile grows wider as he squeezes mine back.

* * *

Amberly

Running with Angela was amazing. Just when I thought it couldn't get any better. Running with someone from the pack somehow makes you feel more around you. Like the earth beneath your feet. It's like you're more attached to the world when you're together. And then the telepathy thing doesn't hurt either.

Until this moment I never really thought about why we can't communicate in our human bodies like we can in our wolf forms. I mean Julian and I can, and I start to wonder why it's different for us.

"Hey, Angela."

She turns to me with a smile on her face. "Yeah."

"I was thinking about something."

"What is it?"

I stop and she mimics me. "Why can't we communicate in this state?"

"You mean telepathically?"

I smile. "Yeah."

Her smile widens. "I'm not sure. It's always been like that."

"But me and Julian can communicate when we are humans."

There's no surprise on her face which surprises me. "I know."

"You do?"

She turns away from me. "He tells me everything."

"But what does that mean?"

She looks back at me and the sadness is clear on her face. "I don't think you really want to have this conversation?"

I take an involuntary step back. "Why wouldn't I? I asked the question."

She lets out a sigh. "Because it has something to do with the two of you. And I know you really don't want to talk about that subject again."

I look at my feet before answering. "Well, I want to know."

She pauses for a good moment before she gives me an answer. "Aaron and I think it's because you're foreordained."

"I think Julian mentioned something like that. What does that mean?"

Her smile returns. "It means that you two are destined to be together. That's why Aaron stepped aside."

I start walking again unsure what to say next. I know one of his powers was to read minds, but I shouldn't have been able to hear his back. At least now I have an answer to at least one thing in my life.

She continues, "Amberly."

"Yeah."

"Talk to me, please. I'm here and I want to help you. There isn't much I can do for everything else going on in your life. I can't protect you from the things coming, but this, this I can be there for."

I turn to smile at her. "Thank you, Angela, that means a lot." I stop and really look at her for the first time, "I just don't know what to say. I don't know what I'm thinking let alone what I'm feeling."

"I'm sure it can be very confusing. I can only imagine what you're going through."

I start walking again. "But this foreordained stuff. Does that mean I have no say in who I choose to be with?"

I can see the wheels turning in her head. "Not necessarily. All it means is in our world you are meant for each other so if you want to be together you can and there's nothing the pack or Aaron can do to stop it. It's in our laws."

"So, what would happen if I chose Logan and didn't want to ever be with Julian again?"

Angela looks at her feet as we walk. "Honestly, other than Julian staying miserable I don't know. Maybe nothing."

"He's miserable?"

She turns her attention back to me. "Sorry, I didn't mean to say that."

"Is he?"

"Yes." She looks away from me before she continues, "I've never seen something affect him like this. He's always been so reserved, strong, and angry. He's never really been hurt. He would never let himself get close enough to anyone because it wasn't something he wanted to feel. He doesn't like being vulnerable."

"Yeah I noticed that much about him." I look over at her as we continue walking, "I did notice he seemed more closed off and sad the last few weeks and I had a feeling it was because of me but I didn't want to let myself care." I pause and look in front of me again, "But I can't help it. I don't like seeing him hurt and it sucks knowing there's nothing I can do to help him because I would be lying if I said I didn't want to."

Chapter 35

Amberly

Angela and I talked for a long time. It was nice to be able to talk to someone around my age who was a girl. I never really had a girlfriend growing up, it was always me and the guys, so this is something new to me. It's something I didn't even realize I needed until now. Having someone understand you is a big part of being able to talk to them and no one can understand a woman more than another woman, so it was nice to be able to talk to her about all the things that have been on my mind. Even though I could tell she was a little biased it was nice, and I can't say I blame her. I know if it was Logan or Troy who was hurting and in this kind of situation, I would do what I could to see them happy again.

I make it back to my room and once again drop into my bed and don't move. As I can feel myself drifting off as I think about my conversation with Angela some more. As sleep starts to overpower me, one thought continues to occupy my mind and the harder I try to fight it the more it enslaves my mind. One person, one thought, as I drift off into sleep.

Julian.

* * *

Amberly

I know I've fallen asleep from the darkness around me but also because of how heavy my body feels once again. Every time I find myself in this place, I feel like I'm being weighed down by cement. However, this feels like a vision more than a dream walk. I'm starting to be able to notice the difference between the two, which can make going through the motions much easier.

"Hey, beautiful."

I hear Logan's voice and I turn to look in every direction until my eyes locate him. His shoulder-length raven hair is slicked back out of his face and his emerald eyes shine as they catch the light rays. His navy blue beater shows off all the definition of his muscles and I find myself forgetting to breathe as my mouth starts to salivate. When he reaches my side a smile automatically spreads across my face, but he keeps walking until he passes me. I turn around to see where he's going and there standing only five feet away from me is Angela.

Did he just call her beautiful?

Too stunned to move I watch as he walks up to her and takes her in his arms and the next thing I know they are kissing.

Kissing!

What the hell is going on?

Without thinking I run over to them to demand answers and then I trip and go flying, right through them, and end up on the ground. I turn around and look up at them but only to get a different view of them making out.

This can't be happening, not again. What is wrong with me? I look away as I can feel the tears starting to stream down my face.

"This is how it's meant to be."

I turn around to see Johnathan standing next to me.

I get up fast and look at him. "You can see me?"

He nods his head.

"What did you mean when you said this is how it's meant to be?"

He looks sad. "This was something I didn't want to tell you before because I knew you weren't ready. But remember the conversations we've had with you and how we told you that those born with the mark are strongest when they pair up with who they are meant to be with?"

Hesitantly I answer, "Yes."

"You aren't meant to be with Logan," he nods his head in Logan and Angela's direction, "She is."

I look over at them as sadness fills my heart. Logan is something I've wanted for longer than I can remember and since we've had each other things felt right, felt safe. And now I have to give that up. I have to give him up. How is that fair? I look back at them for a moment as they rest their foreheads together and smile. I can see they are happy and that's all I want for my friends, isn't it?

My voice comes out shaky and at a whisper, almost as if it's a secret. "I know Logan, he won't let go so easily. He won't just fall into Angela."

"Yes, he will."

I stare at him with pain-filled eyes. "What makes you think so?"

"Because it's how it works."

"If that's so then why didn't he feel pulled to her when they first met?"

He looks at me with sorrow-filled eyes. "Because you were still there, front and center. *You were all he could see because you wanted him as much as he wanted you. Once you remove yourself from him-* "

"*You mean once I break his heart?*"

He nods sadly before continuing, "*Yes. Once you do that his eyes and heart will no longer be clouded with you. They will feel the pull towards each other fast and strong. They may even come to question how, but it will be so.*"

"*Why? I don't understand. Why can't we have a say in who we choose?*"

He glances over at Logan and Angela, "*In a way you do. Your souls are already locked together. You're each other's perfect match in every way. So, one way or another you will find the person you are meant to be with. It will be thrown in your face until you accept it.*"

"*If that's so then how come the rest of the seven never paired up?*"

He rests his eyes on me once more, "*Because they turned away from their feelings and because of that they became weak. I know you love him, and you always will but the love you feel isn't for your soul mate. You need to stop standing in his way and yours. You need to release you both.*"

"*I.*"

I don't know what to say. I love Logan, but Johnathan is right, I never felt for him what I feel for Julian. "*If I remove myself, will Logan and Angela find their way to each other?*"

"*Yes. The pull will take them fast because they've already been around each other for so long. It won't take much time for them to let each other in.*"

I look away from him as tears sting the back of my eyes. "*Fine. I'll do it.*"

"*And one last thing. You know who you're meant to be with, and I think it's time you stop fighting it.*"

I look over at him as he starts to fade away. I turn my attention back to my friends as they too start to do the same.

* * *

Amberly

I can't remember the last time waking up was so hard. Everything in me was fighting it, not wanting to return to this reality knowing what I had to do. The next conversation is going to be one of the hardest I've ever had in my life and I don't even know where to start. Should I tell him the truth? He will think I'm crazy and he will fight my decision. But I've never lied to him either. But I need him to be as safe as possible and this is the only way to make sure he will be. Like Johnathan said we are at our strongest when we are paired together with the partner we were born to be with. Even if that person isn't me. I'm happy it's Angela. I love her like a sister and if I can't be with Logan, I couldn't have chosen someone better than her.

But I won't lie, this still hurts like hell. How am I supposed to give up on us when it feels so right? When we are both happy and whole. How are either of us supposed to just walk away from that? I know it's what we have to do, not because we don't love each other and not because we aren't good together but because we are better off without each other. For us to be the strongest we can be and have a better chance at a longer and happier life, like Johnathan and Aayda, I need to do this.

I close my door behind me and rest my head against it as I close my eyes. I can feel the tears already starting to form behind them and I know I need to do this and soon or I won't be able to make myself.

How much heartache can one person take before their heart stops?

I never thought much about whether I believed someone could die of a broken heart but now, standing here, feeling my heart breaking again, I believe it to be true. For the first time, I wonder how much more mine can take.

"There you are."

Logan rounds the corner and smiles at me and I try my hardest to smile back but to no success.

"What's wrong?"

He reaches my side and places his hands on my elbows pulling me in close.

"We need to talk."

"Ok."

I move away from him slowly and turn back around to my bedroom door. Not once looking back at him.

"Amberly?"

"Once we are inside. I don't want someone to overhear our conversation."

Without another word we walk into my room and I still can't face him.

"Amberly, what's going on?"

I don't answer.

I don't turn around.

I can hear him walking across the room until he reaches my side and places his hands on my shoulders. He slowly turns me around to face him, but I continue to look at the ground as the tears start to fill my eyes. Without a word or a second thought, I throw my arms around him and pull him close. I put my head on his chest and I could hear his heartbeat. The thought of losing this and possibly losing our friendship is killing me.

"Amberly talk to me please."

"I." I barely get the word out and even as I do it's muffled from my face being buried in his chest. He moves me away from him slowly and lifts my face to look at him and I'm sure he sees the tears that are forming there.

"What is it?"

I do the only thing I can. I say the words fast knowing it's the only way I'm going to get them out. "We…we need to break up."

Well, that could have come out better.

He looks shocked. No, it's more than that and more than hurt. "No, we don't."

"Logan, we have to."

I pull away from him and face the bed.

"Why are you doing this? We've been great. I don't understand. Did I do something?"

All I can do is shake my head from side to side, hoping that that is enough to let him know he didn't do anything.

"Then tell me why."

I can't say it. He will think I'm crazy or worse he will fight me on this decision.

"Is it because of Julian?"

His name makes my heart skip a beat.

If I say it's because of him he won't fight me as much, but I will also lose Logan for good and I don't know what to do.

"Just tell me the truth. I promise I'll understand."

I turn around to look at him for the first time. Trying to keep the tears in my eyes. "You're always so understanding, and I love you for that."

He takes in a slow long breath preparing himself.

"You know I love you both."

"I know."

"But."

The next words get stuck in my throat.

"It's ok, just say it."

The hurt is radiating off him and it is killing me knowing that I'm about to cause him even more pain. I'm doing the same thing to him that Julian did to me, minus the make-out session. I never really let myself understand his reason for doing what he did, but now, I understand it completely, and I know the pain he felt. .

I look up at Logan knowing what I have to say, but fighting myself every step of the way. How can I hurt my best friend? I know he needs to hear it, but I also know, there is no going back. I hope he can forgive me in time and after all the hurt we can find our way back to each other and what we once were.

"I do love you, Logan. More than you will ever know. But." I pause again and close my eyes because looking at him hurts too much, "but I love Julian more. I can't let him go. I'm not ready."

"I understand."

I look at him with tear-filled eyes and as one makes its way down my cheek she lifts his hand and rubs it away. He smiles at me sadly before he takes my hand in his and brings it to his lips and places a soft kiss on the bottom of my palm.

He lowers my hand to my side and heads for my bedroom door. He opens it slowly, looks over his shoulder at me, and whispers, "I love you. I always will. Don't ever forget that and no matter what I'm always here for you." His eyes find mine for a moment as he says in a much lower voice, "Always."

Chapter 36

Amberly

The room feels empty, dark and lonely now that Logan isn't here. Even so, I can still feel his pain like it's my own and knowing I'm the cause is killing me. There's nothing I wouldn't do for him but knowing that this was something I had to do to protect him and to better his chances at a long life and future, it was still the hardest thing I've ever had to do.

I return to my place on my bed and wrap my arms around my knees. Trying to hold myself together and I'm barely succeeding.

*** *** ***

Angela

"Hey, Logan was just coming to get you and Amberly."

He turns to look in my direction and I can tell something isn't right.

"What's wrong?"

He looks away from me and chokes on the following words, "Amberly and I just broke up."

I pull him in close for a hug. "I'm so sorry."

I remember mine and Amberly's earlier conversation and I mentally kick myself. I never meant for anyone to get hurt and I never once thought about Logan and how he would feel if she ended it. Suddenly I'm angry with myself. I put Julian in front of everyone else. I knew Amberly still loved him, but I knew she loved Logan too and by medalling I hurt them both.

"What happened?"

He pulls away and turns his back to me as he answers me with one word. "Julian."

I look at my feet and let out a sigh. "I'm sorry Logan."

"It's not your fault."

If only he knew.

"You know she loves you right?"

"I know but sadly that's not enough."

I look at the cave exit. "Hey, want to go for a walk? We can talk, or we can just walk in silence. Whatever you need."

He looks down at me and for the first time, he smiles. "I'd like that."

We make our way out of the cave and as I walk behind him, I can see the pain in every movement he makes. It's in his stance, his muscles, the lines of his face. The pain is on every inch of him and I feel my heart breaking.

* * *

Logan

I never thought it could be so easy to talk to someone other than Troy and Amberly. I mean talking with Troy wasn't always easy but after some time it became like second nature and then there was Amberly. I've always been more comfortable around her than anyone else. But Angela, I've only known her a few short weeks. So, this feeling is foreign to me.

"How are you feeling about tomorrow?"

Her question pulls me from my thoughts. "Tomorrow?"

She looks scared when she answers, "The fight. Do you think we are ready?"

I look away from her and further into the deep dark forest. "It doesn't matter if we are or not, we have to be. We don't have a choice."

"I know life has been crazy lately, but I want you to know I wouldn't trade having met you, Troy and Amberly for anything. If tomorrow is… war, we need to face it, I am thankful for knowing you all and I would do it all over again."

Surprised by her words, I ask. "Why? You barely know me. I understand Amberly, she's part of your pack and you've known her longer."

She looks almost embarrassed when she answers. "I've watched you, Logan. You're one of the nicest men I've ever met. You're kind, sweet, funny, and you'll do anything for your friends. It's been an honor to get to know you."

I flash her a smile. "I would have to say the same."

I take notice of the blood rushing to her cheeks and I can't help but find it cute. "Thank you."

"You've been such a good friend to Amberly. I wanted to thank you for that. For being there for her. She's never really had another girl around to talk to, so I'm sure that helps. I know it helps me sometimes to have Troy. I mean it's Troy." I laugh. "But having another guy around to talk about things is nice. So, thank you for being there for her."

I can see the surprise on her face. "You don't need to thank me. I'm happy to have her in my life. She is an amazing person. You all are. I can see why you've all been so close for so long."

I choose my next words very carefully. "Angela, I need you to do me a favor."

I can see the uneasiness starting to take place in her expression. "What is it?"

"I need you to be there for Amberly now, more than ever." I pause but only long enough to close my eyes and take in a breath. "I need you to be what I was for her." I open my eyes and look down at her. "I need you to be her best friend." I look over at the cave entrance and feel a tug at my heart. "I can't be that for her, not anymore. At least not for a while."

Next thing I know her hand is in mine. I look down at our hands and I know this is just a comforting gesture, but I find myself feeling something more. Something I've never noticed around her before. Something that shouldn't be possible given the limited time we've come to know one another. But she feels like Amberly made me feel. She makes me feel safe, makes me feel like I'm home. And suddenly I feel angry with myself. Amberly and I just broke up. I shouldn't be looking at anyone else this way, let alone Angela. I don't want to hurt her, and I know right now I'm in no place to have anything serious with anyone. I need to find a way to bury myself in something to keep my mind from Amberly and to take the time to heal. I've never really been one of those guys to throw myself into another relationship right after, just so I can feel something. I don't want to be that guy, because in the end, the other person is always the only one who is left feeling like you were when you entered into the relationship. They end up being nothing more than the rebound.

I look down at Angela once more. I want more than that.

Chapter 37

Amberly

Needing to get out of my room, I decide to go for a walk, one last walk before all hell breaks loose tomorrow. Before I know it somehow, I find myself outside. I've been walking for a while now but I'm not too sure how I got here.

I look around the forest to see how empty and dark it is. I hear nothing, everything is sleeping. My eyes continue to wander around the forest and then they come into view.

Angela and Logan.

At first, I wonder what they are doing out here this late and by themselves and then I feel a little spark of jealousy at the sight of them together. I mean we just ended things. And then I see it, their hands, interlocked together.

We just broke up.

I want to scream but then I remember I did this, and I remember why. It needed to be done. But I just thought it would take a little longer than an hour for them to end up here, in this place, together.

I feel my heart starting to ache as I look at them and realize it's only a matter of time before this is my reality. I turn away and head back inside, not ready to live in that moment. Suddenly I find myself thinking about the one thing I'm not ready to deal with. The one person who I have tried so hard not to think about for the last few weeks. Then I whisper one word, one word that makes my heart skip a beat, one word that makes my world both rise and crumble. "Julian."

* * *

Julian

I can't get the thought of tomorrow out of my mind. I can feel how nervous and worried everyone is and it's only making me more nervous than I already am. I don't care about myself, I just worry about failing and something happening to Amberly, or someone else in my pack. I have this pit in my stomach that's telling me something is going to go wrong tomorrow.

I never let myself get close enough to anyone, romantically. Never let anyone in, other than Angela and Aaron. I always kept everyone at a distance and only worried about myself. It was always easier that way. Number one rule: worry about yourself.

I never wanted to feel the hurt that came along with caring for someone. Once you let someone in you worry about them, you care for them and their feelings, their wants and needs. I never wanted to be burdened with that. But somehow, she got through all the walls I put up. She did it without me even noticing and without her even trying.

She stole my heart from day one.

She stole it before she even knew me.

She had it and she has it still.

There's nothing in this world I want more than to see Amberly happy, and lately, that's what she's been. Happy. So, I need to find a way to let her go, to let her be happy and I need to find a way to be happy without her.

I can't help but feel angry. From the moment I felt the pull that led me to her, I always thought we were meant for something more. Something different than where we are now. After I kissed her, I never wanted to stop. In her arms and by her side was the only place I wanted to be. So how did we end up here? How did it all turn out so wrong?

If my feelings for her were wrong, then I don't want to be right. What we had, what I still feel, it's real and no one can tell me differently. It's something I've never felt before, it can't be normal and because of that I know we are meant to be something more. I know in my heart we are meant to be together.

No.

Stop it.

Enough is enough.

I close my eyes and let out a sigh. I can hear the pain in it. I can feel the pain in every muscle. It's killing me, not being near her, it is killing me. I feel drained, I feel weaker than I ever have in my life and I know without a doubt it's because I'm without her.

I meant what I said, I want her to be happy. But at the same time, I know with every cell in my body that she isn't meant to be with Logan. She's meant to be with me. So, the only thing I can do is give it time. Let her do

whatever makes her happy. The only thing left for me to do is one thing.
Wait.

Chapter 38

Amberly

The only thing I want tonight is to be left alone, meditate and ready myself for tomorrow. But first things first, sustenance. I head to the kitchen for dinner, knowing it's the perfect time because everyone else would have eaten by now.

I enter the dining room and see Angela is about to sit down and I really don't feel up to dealing with anyone right now, especially her. I try to sneak back out, but she sees me at the last second and flags me down.

"Amberly."

I know it's too late to walk away without her thinking something of it, so I turn back to the dining area.

"Hey."

"I've been looking everywhere for you."

Sure, you have. "Well, here I am."

Her smile fades. "I heard about you and Logan. I'm so sorry."

"Hey, it is what it is right."

I can see the confusion in her eyes. "What's that supposed to mean?"

I shake my head. "Nothing. Sorry. So, what's up?"

"I just wanted to make sure you were OK."

I force a smile. "I'm fine."

"I know you well enough to know that's not true. You love him."

I look away. "Yeah, well turns out love isn't enough."

"Or maybe you just love someone else more."

I turn back to look at her.

"Logan told me."

"Of course, he did."

She sits down. "I'm sorry. I know that it wasn't an easy decision and so does he."

"Relationships aren't always forever, tomorrow's never promised."

She pats the seat next to her as she tries to hide whatever she's thinking about the words that keep coming out of my mouth. I hesitate but sit down next to her.

"Amberly."

"Yeah."

She pauses. Thinking about the right words, I guess. "Why did you break it off? I mean why now? Is it because of tomorrow?"

I know I can't tell her the real reason. I can't mess with what's supposed to happen in the future. So instead, I say, "Partially, I guess."

"Maybe you should sleep on it. I don't think you're thinking rationally, and I don't blame you. Tomorrow isn't something small to deal with."

"I don't want to sleep on it. It needed to be done. So better to do it now."

"Is there anything I can do?"

I think for a moment, but I know what to say. "Yes."

For the first time, I see excitement in her. "Anything. What do you need?"

"I need you to look after Logan for me."

I see confusion all over her face. "What do you mean?"

"Tomorrow during the fight take care of him, please. I won't be able to watch out for him."

"You got it."

"And one more thing," I pause trying to think of the best way to word what I'm trying to say, "I also need you to be there for him. Be what I was. His friend, his shoulder. I can't be that anymore. At least not for a while."

She pauses and gives a little nod, "Are you sure this is what you want to do?"

"No. But it's what needs to be done."

"I'll do my best."

I look at the exit and whisper. "Thank you."

"You know it's kind of funny."

I look at her surprised. "What?"

"You two."

"What about us?"

"You're more alike than I thought, and I think more than you both realize."

Confusion is all over my face I'm sure. "What are you talking about?"

"What you just asked me to do for you. He asked me the very same thing. And you both worded it the same way too."

I try to hide my surprise. "He asked you to look after me?"

She nods her head. "And to be your friend. Until you two find your way back to each other of course."

I smile. It's nice to know even though I hurt him he still cares enough to make sure I'm ok. It's going to be hard without him around for a while, but I need to let him be and do what's best for him. He needs this.

I look over at Angela.

He needs her.

And I can't let myself get in the way of that.

* * *

Julian

I see Logan out of the corner of my eye, but I turn the other way.

"Hey, mate."

Ugh.

I stop.

He walks up behind me and I turn around to face him. "Yes?"

"Well, you win."

Confused, I ask. "What are you talking about?"

"Amberly."

I rub at my eyes feverishly. "What about her?"

"We're done. She broke it off. She wants you. So, you won."

My heart stops and in that moment time freezes. His words take a second to really register in my mind.

They broke up.

He turns away and starts to walk away from me, but I run to get in front of him. "Wait."

"Why? Shouldn't you be running off to find her and rejoice, and throw it in my face that I was never the one she wanted?"

"I wouldn't do that. I'm sorry I really am. I know she loves you. You have to know she does."

The sadness is radiating off him, and it reminds me of the pain I've been living with myself up until a moment ago, and I can't help but feel for him.

"Yes, I know she loves me but it's not enough." He pauses to look at me for the first time. "I love her like she loves you, and I love her too much to stand in the way of her being happy. Even if that means she's with you."

"Listen no matter what she chooses, I would like us to be ok with one another."

He gives me a look of annoyance. "I don't know if that's something I can do."

"Can you at least try, for her?"

He looks past me. "For her."

Before I have the chance to say anything else, he's gone.

Chapter 39

Amberly

As I round the last corner to my room there he is. This is starting to become a regular occurrence. I watch him pace back and forth as he talks to himself. As I continue to watch him, I suppress a laugh. I would be lying if I said I was ready to deal with whatever the next step is in my love life. Right now, the most important thing is tomorrow, we need to prepare. Julian and I can wait. Plus, I need time to deal with everything that just happened with Logan. I don't want to be the girl who goes from one man to the other. And more than that I don't want to throw it in Logan's face if he sees us around the cave together.

Not this soon.

I walk up ready to tell him we can talk tomorrow after we don't die but as I open my mouth the words don't come out as he locks eyes with me. I haven't seen him look like this, happy, hopeful in weeks. What's changed?

He looks up at me. "Hey."

"Hey, yourself."

"I was hoping to talk to you if you were up for it."

I play dumb as I cross my arms over my chest. "Why wouldn't I be up for it?"

"Come on, don't do that."

"Do what?"

"Act closed off, and like I don't know you well enough to look at you, and know somethings going on."

I lower my arms. "You knew me Julian, but I've changed a lot these last few weeks."

"I know."

"How could you?"

He looks at me sheepishly. "I watched you. I was always there, even when you didn't see me."

"Way to sound like a crazy stalker."

He laughs. "No, I just want to make sure you're safe. And."

"And what?"

He looks at me with sad loving eyes and my heart skips a beat. "And I can't stay away from you." He looks down at his hands. "It's hard to explain, but I feel less heavy when I'm near you."

"What does that mean?"

"You calm me Amberly."

Trying to stay strong I say. "Well, I'm sorry I can't be that for you, not anymore."

"I know it's going to take time for you to trust me again and I'm willing to wait and work on it if you can give us that."

"I don't know, Julian."

I can still see the hope in his eyes as he whispers. "I do."

In the next moment, his lips are on mine and his hands are hard on my back pulling me in closer and closer until every inch of our bodies are touching. And I just melt into the kiss, into his lips, into him.

* * *

Julian

Never letting our lips part I place my hand on her doorknob, turn and push the door open, holding onto her tightly with my free hand. We almost fall through the door as we giggle under each other's lips and the vibration sends chills down my face into my neck. I slowly trail my hands down her back, past her butt to her thighs and grip them up and lift her to my waist. Her legs wrap around my torso in earnest as I slowly make our way over to the bed. I guide our bodies gently down to the cotton-covered platform. I gently place myself on top of her until every piece of exposed skin is touching and it sends a flaming inferno through my skin and into every nerve. I moan in pleasure against her lips and she returns one of her own.

It is not enough.

I want, no I need more.

Without hesitation, I sit up straight, slide my shirt over my head, and discard it to the floor below. I look down to see her auburn hair, a knotted mess and her cheeks flushed, and I've never found her to be more beautiful than in this moment. I glance at her shirt buttons, and place my hands at the top one and start to work on undoing them as I kiss her neck feverishly.

I need more of her, need our skin connected. I undo all the buttons and slide her shirt off to expose a lavender-laced bra and a light growl escapes from between my lips.

I trail kisses come her lips to her cheek, down her neck to her chest and I feel her body arch upward begging for more as she moans again. I trail my hands down every piece of exposed skin, leaving fire in its wake. Not wanting to stop, not knowing if I could, I took a fistful of her hair and gently pulled her head to the side, exposing more of her bare skin. I smile as I trail feverish kisses along her jawline and neck. I'm so lost in this moment, touching her, the heat, that I don't hear her say my name. Not until the third time. I pull away and look down to see the sadness in her eyes. I pull back further.

"Did I hurt you?"

She whispers "No."

I sit back away from her; it takes everything in me to do so. "What's wrong?"

"I."

I lightly place my hand on her cheek trying to comfort her. "Please tell me."

"I want to slow down."

I would be lying if I said I wasn't surprised, but I smile at her as I reply, "OK."

Her voice sounds husky as she says, "I'm sorry."

"Hey, don't apologize. I understand."

She places her hand on me hesitantly. "I don't want to jump into this again. I just ended things with Logan. I don't want to be that girl."

"Is that all it is?"

She looks away from me. "That and, I just need time. I need my head in the game for what's coming, I can't be lost in this. In us. I need to focus."

"I understand."

Chapter 40

Julian

Amberly and I stayed up for hours talking. We talked about our past, our future, and how we got so off track from each other. She told me she wanted to take things slower this time around and not rush into anything. She said she needed to focus on the battles ahead and not worry about where we stood, and I agreed.

Remembering last night, each kiss, each touch, every word, I look down at her as she sleeps soundlessly. I wonder if she's even asleep as I remember how loud she snores, and I can't help but smile.

I know I should wake her because the sun is now high in the sky, but I can't help but want to sit and watch her sleep a little longer.

"Will you stop staring at me?" She says in a low whisper as a smile spreads across her face.

"I knew you weren't still sleeping."

She moves the hand from in front of her face and looks up at me. "Liar."

"No really. I was just thinking about how you weren't snoring."

She slaps me playfully. "You were not?"

"Sorry to say I was."

She sits up resting on her elbow to face me. "Do I really snore?"

"When you're deep in sleep, yes."

"Oh, man." She falls back to her pillow embarrassed, hiding her face behind her hands.

"Don't be embarrassed, it's kind of cute."

"See you said kind of."

I laugh at her as I answer. "Anything you do is cute to me so what does it matter? I wouldn't change a thing."

She peers at me from behind her hands. "Really?"

I smile. "Really."

"How is it that you always know the right thing to say?"

I look at her sadly as I say, "Not always."

She removes her hands from her face and places it on mine. "Julian, let it go. I'm trying to."

"I know. I just hate myself for being so dumb."

She smiles at me. "You weren't dumb you knew me well enough to know I wouldn't just walk away."

"But I should have just talked to you about it, we are adults after all."

I smile at her devilishly.

"Define adults." She laughs.

"Well, we are both eighteen so I would say we are in adult territory."

"At least our age is."

I pull her hand to my lips and press a light kiss on her warm skin. "I've missed this."

"Me too."

I look up at her. "Don't just say that."

She looks at me sadly. "I'm not. Yes, you hurt me, but I always thought about you."

"Even when you were with him?"

The words come out before I can stop them, and she looks away.

"I had to give Logan and me a chance."

"Why?"

She looks up at me with serious eyes. "I had to know for sure."

"Know what?"

"That it couldn't work with us. I had to know I gave it a shot before I could ever think of going back into this with you."

Confused, I ask. "So, what changed?"

"Huh."

"Why did you break up with him?"

She looks away and her face becomes a mask of secrets. "It's a long story."

"I'm all ears."

"For a few reasons."

I lean down on the bed to be closer to her. "Which are?"

She sighs. "Well, the most important thing would be that even when I was with him, even though I loved him, I couldn't get you out of my head and that wasn't fair to him."

"And the other?"

She closes her eyes. "Isn't that answer enough for now."

"For now," I say as I kiss her forehead lightly.

We sit there in silence for a while until she breaks the silence and pulls me back to reality.

"How is it possible that so much has changed in a few short weeks?"

"Change is good."

She looks at the ceiling. "Yes, it can be, but I mean just a few months ago I was fatherless and didn't know anything about myself. I was in love with one guy, the same guy, my whole life." She pauses to turn back in my direction, "Then I met you and everything changed. I have a father. A crazy man is hunting me and wants me dead for all I know. But more than that." She pauses as she closes her eyes. "I went from loving my best friend to falling in love with someone I barely knew. I fell and fell hard. Then I learned the friend I loved all my life loved me back and I was stuck in this loop. I went from him to you, back to him, and now back to you. All in a matter of weeks." She looks back at me, and I can see something in her eyes that I've never seen before. "It's just a lot."

"I know."

"Do you?"

I sigh, "Yes. That's why I said I understand you want to take things slowly. Like you said, a lot has changed in your life, in a short time, and I appreciate the need to sort everything out and to make sure the next move you make is one you feel right about."

She looks to the ceiling again, "It's more than that."

I wait for her to continue but when she doesn't, I ask. "Like what?"

She looks at me sadly. "I need to know I can trust you this time."

Her words hit me harder than I thought they would. I know what I did, and I know she didn't forget about it, but after last night part of me did. It felt like we picked right back up where we left off. Like nothing had even happened. So, her words took me by surprise.

I look at her and give her a reassuring smile. "I know words are just words and that actions can be different than what someone says they plan to do. But I promise you, I will never be the cause of your hurt. I will never hurt you again. I can't."

"You say that, but you never know."

I take her hand in mine. "I promise you I do. I did what I did because I didn't see a future where we could be together and instead of you fighting to find a way and drag out our hurt, I thought what I was doing would save us more hurt. I never thought Aaron would say we could be together. But now that we can there is no reason for me to ever hurt you again. No reason for me to walk away."

"But what if in a year you meet someone else or your feelings for me change?"

"I promise you my feelings for you will change." I can see the fear in her eyes, so I keep talking. "Since the day I met you every day my feelings for you have only grown. There has never been anyone else for me. Only you and there never will be anyone else. You're it for me. I've been with girls," I can see in her eyes she doesn't want to hear this part, so I make it fast, "I've had girls love me and I mistreated them, tossed them to the side, or did just enough to keep them where I wanted them without really ever feeling a thing for them, and never wanting what they wanted. I tried to never get close but also to fill the void that I felt. The void that you were meant to fill and have. I don't want anyone else. You have changed my world, Amberly. In ways that I could never really get you to understand and I didn't really see it for myself for a long time. I didn't want to see it. I wanted to keep you at arm's length just like I had everyone else over the years. But something about you wouldn't let that happen."

"What makes me so different?"

"Honestly, I don't know."

She closes her eyes. "Are you happy?"

"Very."

She looks at me and smiles.

I ask. "Are you?"

She nods.

"You sure?"

She laughs. "Yes."

"Good."

"Oh really?"

I look at her seriously. "Yes. Because I don't intend on letting you go, not this time."

She rolls to her side. "Good."

I mimic her earlier response. "Really."

She laughs. "Yes."

We look at each other, each waiting for the other to fill the silence. She starts to open her mouth but gets interrupted by a knock at the door.

She looks at me apologetically. "Come in."

"Amberly I," Amara pauses in the doorway, "Sorry didn't know you had company I can come back."

She smiles at Amara. "No, you're fine. What's up?"

"Troy and I wanted to see if you wanted to join us for breakfast. We all need as much energy as possible today."

"You're right. Sure. When were you thinking?"

"We were going to head there in about an hour to fuel up."

"Sounds good."

Amara looks at me for the first time. "I guess we will see you there then." I nod.

"Ok, I'll let Troy know," Amara says as she heads out the door again.

I turn back to look at Amberly. She smiles and says, "I feel like I haven't seen Troy in forever. I was beginning to wonder where he had been hiding."

"I guess with the new girl." I laugh.

"Doesn't surprise me."

"Why is that?"

She looks at me as the smile grows on her face. "Troy and she are a lot alike. I guess it was only a matter of time before they hung out."

I look back at the door. "Really." I turned back to her. " I don't see it."

She laughs. "You just don't like Troy."

"And?"

She smiles. "You never even gave the guy a chance."

"Do I have to?" I ask in a playful voice.

"It would be nice."

I pick up her hand and place a light kiss on it. "Well for you then I will."

"Smart man."

I laugh. "Is it really that easy to make you happy?"

She nods.

"Well, then I'm at your service." I look at her hungrily, "Whatever my lady may need."

"Oh really?"

I let a low growl escape my chest as I crawl over to her on the bed.

She giggles and I can't hold in my laugh anymore. We sat there laughing and lying with each other. These are the moments I fight for.

"Amberly."

"Yeah."

"I love you. I had to say that at least once before everything changed."

She leans over and looks down at me as I continue to lay on the bed.

"I love you too."

She leans down and our lips touch for a moment before she pulls back and smiles down at me.

"We should get ready."

I smile not wanting this moment to end but knowing she's right. "Yeah we should."

Chapter 41

Amberly

Julian and I head to the kitchen to meet Troy and Amara but when we walk through the door, I see it's not just them sitting at the table but now Logan and Angela have joined the group. I pause but Julian continues walking until he realizes I'm not behind him. He turns around to look at me.

"What's wrong?"

I look from the table to him and shake my head free of the cobwebs. "Nothing."

I take him by the hand once more and walk over to the table with him.

Angela sees us first and smiles. "Hey, there you guys are, we were just about to send out a search party."

Julian laughs. "Well wouldn't have taken them very long to find us now would it?"

"I guess not." She laughs back at him.

Julian turns to me and puts his hand out gesturing for me to sit. Once I do, he sits next to me.

"So, what did we miss?" He says to no one in particular.

Troy speaks for the first time. "Nothing much we were just talking about what we think might be best to eat considering today's later events."

Julian answers back, "Well we want something very filling but something that won't slow us down."

Angela speaks up. "That's what we were getting to."

I look around the table at everyone. They are all getting along. I was always worried about how the people from my two worlds would work together, but it seems I worried for nothing. Even Troy and Logan are being nice to Julian which is definitely a surprise.

"Amberly?" Amara pulls me from my thoughts.

"Sorry. What did you say?"

She smiles at me. "Was wondering if you wanted to come with me to get everyone something to drink?"

"Sure."

We get up and head to the drinks station.

"How are you doing?"

I turn to her and smile. "I'm fine, how about you?"

"I'm good."

I look back at the table and see Troy looking over at us. "Seems you and Troy are getting pretty close."

"Oh, man don't tell me he's an ex or something."

I laugh at her. "No. Just a friend. More like a brother."

She lets out what feels like a gust of air in relief and I must stop myself from laughing harder. "Oh, thank God, I was thinking I overstepped again."

"No, you're all good, I promise."

I see her relax. "Good. Because I think I really could like him."

"Good I'm glad. He's a little rough around the edges," I laugh, "but he's a really good guy."

"Yeah, he is, and he's pretty funny too."

"I guess."

She looks at me surprised. "What, you don't think he is?"

I laugh. "Maybe I'm just used to it."

She smiles. "Well, he makes me laugh."

"Good. That's always a good thing to have in a man."

"It sure is."

I look at her with concern, "So how are you doing?"

She looks confused. "What do you mean?"

"With Vladimir coming."

I can see the hair on her arms stand up. "I'm fine."

"It would be understandable if you weren't."

She smiles and sticks out her chin. "I know but I'm good."

"So, you're ready for a fight?"

She shines me her pearly whites. "Born ready."

I laugh. "Good."

I grab all the water and tea I can carry and start to head back to the table, but she stops me.

"So how are things with Julian?"

It takes me a second to register her question. "They are good."

"Good I'm glad. I felt horrible after everything."

"I know."

She looks at me sadly. "I really didn't-"

I cut her off. "I know."

"I would never have-"

"I promise we are good."

She smiles at me shyly. "Good. Because I've come to think of you as a friend."

"As you should."

"And I wanted to thank you."

"Thank me?" I ask confused.

"Yes."

"What for?"

She laughs. "For everything. For finding me, feeding me, and giving me a home again."

"You don't need to thank me."

She stops walking. "Yes, I do. You've done more for me, a stranger, than most friends I grew up with."

"Well, I would do it all again."

She smiles and starts walking to the tables again. "I just wanted to let you know I'll never forget it, and it meant more to me than you know."

Speechless I continue walking until she breaks the silence once again.

"So, you and Julian, me and Troy, and Angela and Logan. Who would have ever thought that's how it would pan out?"

I try to hide the little bit of sadness that creeps up at the sound of Angela and Logan together.

"Yea who would have thought."

Chapter 42

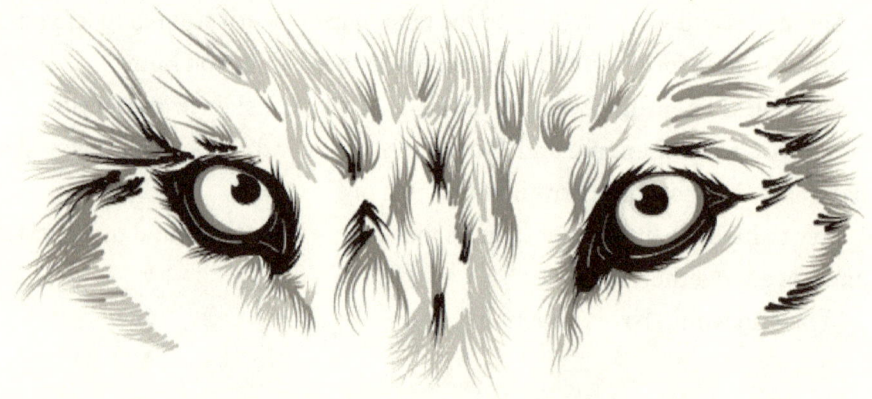

Amberly

We ate as much as we could and then headed outside to find the rest of the pack and my mother and her guards. When we arrived, everyone was already outside and on alert. I look over at my parents and then turn to Julian.

"I'll be right back."

He nods his head and I walk away.

"Hey mom," I look over to my dad who is wearing an expression I rarely see on him and I can tell he's worried. "Dad."

They look at me and smile. My mom answers, "Hey, honey, where have you been hiding out?"

"We were in the dining hall. Getting fueled up."

Her smile widens. "Smart but you know that's not what I meant."

"I was dealing with some life stuff."

She nods in understanding. My father steps forward and lays a hand on her shoulder as he looks at me and asks. "Are you ready?"

I know he's talking about the coming battle and all I can manage is a nod.

"I want you and all your friends to stay behind me and the rest of the pack. Hopefully, it won't last long enough for them to reach any of you."

"Dad."

He cuts me off before I can say anything else. "No. I don't want any of you to have to fight unless you must, I'm going to try to prevent that at all costs."

"You might not have a choice."

He walks to my side slowly and puts his hands on my shoulders. "I may not but I plan on doing everything I can to keep you out of harm's way. You're too young to have to worry about such things."

"Age doesn't matter. The point is none of us should be dealing with these things. We should be able to just live together and be happy now that we are finally together, sadly that isn't a reality, but hopefully, once this is behind us it will be."

"Sometimes you still surprise me. You act well beyond your years." He paused to look back at my mother. "You will make a great leader one day."

He looks back at me as my mother does the same and they both share the same proud look. I smile and then look away to my friends. "I guess it's time to join the troops."

"Just be sure to stay behind us."

I nod at him and walk over to where my friends are standing. Angela is the one to notice me first. "Take it you heard?"

"Yeah."

She smiles. "I can see you're not too happy about it."

"That obvious huh?"

"Well, I know I'm not too happy about being kept on the sidelines so I can only guess how you're feeling."

I look behind her to see everyone else in a separate conversation. "This fight has come to our doorstep because of me. It's not right that I can't take part in it." I look back at her, "but as for the rest of you. I'm glad my father made that call. I don't like the thought of any of you being put in harm's way."

I can see the sadness starting to cloud her face. "If you're in danger, we're all in danger."

I smile at her. "Thank you but it's not that simple."

"It is. You are a part of our pack, and more than that and more than being the next pack leader, you are our friend and there's nothing we wouldn't do for you."

"But dying. That's not something I'm OK with."

"Who said anything about dying?" She flashes me a reassuring smile.

"Angela, I'm being serious."

Her smile disappears. "I know you are but so am I. We are stronger together. I know what's coming is big, and they are stronger than anything we've ever fought before, but I know together there's nothing we can't walk away from."

I look around at everyone and whisper. "I hope you're right."

* * *

Julian

I look over at Amberly and ask, "Are you ready for this?"

She lets out a sigh. "As ready as I can be." ·

I look down at her hand and take it in mine. "I know what you're going to say but I can't help but say it. Your father is right in putting you on the sidelines and I hope you won't have to fight. I want you to stay in the back with Logan, Troy and Amara."

She squeezes my hand lightly. "I can't do that."

I can hear the pleading in my voice. "Please. I can't fight to my full ability if I'm worrying about you. The rest of you aren't like us."

I can see a flare of anger boiling inside her. "What's that supposed to mean?"

I smile at her as I rub her hand. "I only mean we were trained to fight our whole lives; we always anticipated a fight because of how we came to be a part of this pack. We knew long before anyone in your tribe about what was taking place in these woods, and because of it we trained all these years. You haven't and I'm glad that wasn't your life. But I can't go into this fight knowing these things, and knowing you're right there in the middle of it. I won't be able to watch my own back because I'll be too busy keeping an eye on you. Can you try to understand where I'm coming from?"

The understanding becomes clear in her eyes but all she does is nod. I pull her into my chest and hold her there as I whisper just loud enough for her to hear me. "Thank you."

I know it's hard for her to sit on the sidelines, but I'm happy she agreed because I meant it when I said it would be hard for me to focus if I knew she was right in the middle of it all. The thought of her being hurt, taken, or killed weighs me down more than I admit. It's something I haven't been able to stop thinking about for a while now.

I feel her hand touch my shoulder. "Hey, what's going on in your head?"

I smile down at her. "I'm simply happy you agreed to go to the back with them. I've been worrying about this day for a while and I was worried you wouldn't agree to it." I can see she's about to rebut me in some way, so I quickly add, "The thought of something happening to you has been something I can't seem to control in my mind." I look at her sadly before I continue. "If anything were to happen to you it would kill me, Amberly. I don't know what my life is without you in it."

She places her hand on my cheek. "I know the feeling."

"You've been a big part of my life for longer than I can remember. When I first saw you in these woods something shifted in me and the need to see you more and more only grew." I pause and close my eyes. "And the thought of not seeing you anymore has been something I've been wrestling with since I first learned you were Aaron's daughter."

I open my eyes to see the sadness that hides in hers. "You're not going to lose me."

"I almost did. Twice."

She smiles at me for the first time. "Well yea you were cutting it close with that wolf but hey I couldn't leave you here to fight in a battle I've been begging to be in." Her smile lessens as she says, "And as for the other thing. Even then you never lost me."

I look at her and I know she wants to take things slow but considering we both might not walk away from this I can't help but lean down and kiss her. I throw my arms around the lower half of her back and pull her in close. Kissing her sends warm shocks through my whole body. It's something I've never felt with anyone else before. She makes me feel more alive than ever before and I feel this power growing inside me. I know I have something worth fighting for and I intend to do just that.

Chapter 43

Amberly

The pain is overwhelming. I pull my hand away from my side and see it's covered in blood. I look around at my surroundings trying to make sense of everything. It all happened so fast.

Julian and I were holding each other and then the next thing I knew we were surrounded, and the pack went flying in every direction. Most of them were knocked out on impact but those that could get up were killed in seconds by the group who had invaded our home. Through all the chaos I lost track of my parents. As my eyes were searching for them Angela and Julian moved ahead of me and joined the fight.

I focused on them long enough to see Julian look back at Logan and with one look it was like Logan knew what he was asking for. Next thing I knew Logan was grabbing me by the arm and pulling me backwards. I screamed at him to let me go but he didn't stop. We reached the spot where Troy and Amara were and then we all started fleeing, with much fighting on my behalf.

We reach behind the cave, but Logan doesn't stop pulling me, not until he's ripped from my side and thrown twenty feet away. I turned around to see where the attack came from and that's when something hit me, and I went flying through the air landing not far from where Logan's limp body now lays.

Holding my side, I look around at my friends lying all over the ground. I don't know how Amara and Troy went down but they are also unconscious not too far away from where I now sit on the ground. I try to stand but I fall to my knees. I look over and try to crawl to where Logan's body is lying. I need to know he's OK.

I don't make it five feet before someone I don't recognize reaches me and grabs a fistful of my hair and punches me in the face. I fall back to the cold dirt floor once more.

"Sage, take it easy. You know what Aidan said."

The girl who hit me turns around to look at the men approaching us but then her gaze comes to rest on the one who addressed her recent actions.

"One punch isn't going to kill her."

The man reaches our side. "Well let's hope that wound doesn't either."

Sage scoffs. "What would it matter? If you ask me, she's better off dead."

"Don't ask me, that's a question for Aidan. But our directions were clear. Amberly was not to be hurt."

The redness of her hair almost matches the color of her cheeks and I find myself wondering if it is from the cool air or is she really mad about her orders?

"Grab the girl and let's go." The tall man says as he starts to walk away from us.

Sage looks down at me with a smile as she grabs me by the hair once more. "Get to your feet."

I grab at her hand trying to free my hair from her grasp. When that doesn't work, I focus. It only takes me a few seconds before I send her flying. She passes the man and lands on the ground in front of him as he laughs. The other men stare at me in awe as the head one turns around to look at me. "Well, I guess you're going to put up a fight after all."

"Bet your ass I am."

I stand up as his feet leave the ground. He looks down and then back at me and smiles. "Well, I guess your powers weren't over-exaggerated after all."

"Wanna see more?" I say with a smile.

"Give it your best shot."

I can feel the anger taking over and I have to push it back down deep. I don't want to lose myself in this fight. Once I feel the calm wash over me, I open my eyes and smile at the unknown man who still sits in the air above me. His arms crossed over his chest like he had no worry.

I reach out with my mind. Trying to control him. I remember my mother telling me the stronger the mind is the more of a fight it will put up against my powers and some people I won't be able to control no matter how hard I try. I can feel the push coming from his mind, but I keep trying until there's a snap and I grab my head in pain and he falls back to the earth with a huge grin on his face.

"Is that the best you got?"

"I'm just getting started." I smile.

He lifts his hand and gestures for me to move forward. I focus all my energy to my hands and lift them in his direction as hot blasts of energy leave them and hit him square in the chest and he flies through the air and hits the rock wall of the cave and then crumbles to the ground, lifeless. The rest of their group takes off running to the other side of the cave. Once they are out of view, I reach out sensing if he's alive and he is, and I feel relief wash over me.

I walk over to Logan to see he's still unconscious but he's fine and so are Troy and Amara. With my mind I lift them all and move them to the far end of the forest and cover them with branches and leaves so that no one can find them. Hoping this will keep them safe until this fight ends. I turn away and run to where I can still hear the fight going on. I round the corner and find Julian in a fight with two men and my mother and father right next to him also in a fight of their own. I look around real fast and I see Angela is doing the same. I let out a long breath I didn't realize till now that I was holding. Just relieved they are all safe.

I take a step forward and two men stand in my path. It takes my mind a moment to catch up and once it does, I realize I recognize these men.

"Hello, pretty." Lurch's voice hits me hard in the face.

I turn to see Onyx smiling triumphantly at me like he knows something I don't. His raven hair is longer than the last time we met. Now shoulder length, and he is skinnier too, almost like he hasn't been eating. I look back at Lurch and notice that once shoulder-length chocolate brown hair is almost a buzz cut but I can still make out the grease in it. His scar stands out more than ever as he looks almost sickly and I find myself curiously wondering what became of them after that night that they failed. From the looks of it, Vladimir wasn't at all happy with their failure.

Lurch smiles, defining his scar that much more, as he takes a step towards me. I smile back and reach out with my mind calling on the earth for strength. Moments later Lurch is on the ground wiggling around frantically as Onyx looks on at him in horror. Lurch looks down at his legs to see the roots of the nearby tree wrapped around his ankles and moving up the length of his body in a quick motion. He looks back at me frantically trying to remove the tree roots from his body, but to no avail. He glances at his partner as he says in panic. "Stop her."

Onyx moves towards me, "You."

I close my eyes, focusing, making myself feel lighter and lighter. I release a breath as I open my eyes and look at Onyx with a smile and wink. He looks at me stunned as I vanish before his eyes. He looks around him frantically.

"Where did she go!"

Lurch wiggled around on the ground still ripping at the roots that are now around his torso. "I don't know, I'm a little busy."

He looks down at his friend and takes a step towards him. He reaches out to aid him as I throw a punch in his direction, not seeing it coming it collides with his face and his body jolts backward.

Cradling his now bloody mouth he looks around him frantically. "What!!!"

I punch him once more before sending him flying into the nearest tree. I release a breath as I let my invisibility cloak vanish from around my body, taking with it a good amount of my energy.

I reach Lurch and kneel down beside him. "Where's Aidan?"

Frantically he answers. "On the battlefield."

"Where? Point him out."

He looks down at his ensnared arms pleading with me. I smile down at him as I stand up straight. "Never mind. I'll find him, you stay right there."

I turn away from him as I search the area hoping I will be able to tell which one is Aidan when my eyes come to rest on him. I pass over Julian to see he's not faring well in a standoff with two men. I reach out with my mind once more to one of the men who's fighting with him, but nothing happens. Almost like the man sensed my attack coming he looks over at me and smiles. Why aren't my powers working? Julian sees the man smiling and follows his gaze in my direction and I can see concern written all over his face as the man leaves him and starts towards me. Julian tries to go after him but the other man he was fighting steps in his way and punches him square in the jaw.

Julian looks back up at me and I can see the fear in his eyes as he yells. "Amberly, behind you."

I see the man who left Julian's side, his smile disappearing as something like anger takes hold of his features. Before I get the chance to turn around, to see what they could be looking at, a searing pain shoots through my abdomen. I look down at my stomach and see a sharp object poking out of it. A moment later a crippling pain shoots through my whole body as the object disappears. I look at Julian as he screams my name and I fall to my knees.

Sage comes around to stand in front of me. She looks down at me with a smile on her face and a long crimson-covered knife in her hand. I glance down at my stomach as blood pours out between my fingers and then I realize the blood on her knife is mine. She lifts the knife high ready to drive it home. I hear Julian yell my name once more as he tries to run past his foe and gets a punch to the gut.

Sage is about to drive the knife down when I put my arm in the air just above my head. The knife comes down but stops in midair, only inches from where my arm hovers. Sage looks down at me as anger takes over her expression. Confused, she pulls the knife back and tries again. But the same thing happens.

I smile, thankful for all my recent training because without it I never would have known about my shielding power, let alone how to use it. I look at Sage and reach out with my mind with every bit of energy I have left. I call on my amulet to give me more strength. In seconds I feel energy wash over my body, and I smile up at her.

Her walls come crumbling down.

I smile.

"Do as I say."

She looks at me awaiting her orders.

"Lower your knife."

She does as I say.

"See that man coming our way?"

She turns to look at him and nods.

"Disable him."

"As you wish."

I fight to keep my eyes open as I say. "And when you're done move on to the man fighting Julian and then the men fighting my parents."

"As you wish."

She runs forward at full speed, goes to her knees, and slides along the ground as she lifts her arm and the knife as she passes by the man. Pain is clear on his face as he looks down and blood covers his abdomen, he drops to his knees. She doesn't stop as his body drops to the ground. She makes her way to the man who has Julian in a chokehold. She steps behind him and pulls his head back and runs the blade along his neck. The man releases Julian as he grabs at his wound. Julian falls to the ground gasping for air. Sage continues over to the men fighting my parents. But Julian takes my attention as he looks across the battlefield at me and smiles as he stands and starts to run in my direction.

He gets sloppy.

He only sees me.

He doesn't see the man about to be in his way. A man who looks familiar. The man looks back at me and smiles.

Aidan.

"Julian, look out."

Aidan turns his attention back to Julian as I yell out his name again, but Julian doesn't hear me. He's too focused on reaching my side. I try to reach out with my mind, but nothing happens, he's too strong for me to control. I try to send him flying but nothing works, somehow, he's deflecting all my attacks. I try to get to my feet, to make my way to Julian but my legs aren't working, and pain is all I feel.

Aidan is fast and my eyes and all my focus is on him. Everything happens too fast. I'm watching Aidan as he continues to walk in my direction, he reaches Julian and in a moment Julian's smile is gone and it's replaced with pain. But it wasn't Aidan who inflicted the pain on Julian as he still continues to walk in my direction. I look past him at Julian as I see blood starting to stain the front of his shirt. It takes a lot of focus for me to see her. Standing there, behind him.

Sage.

"Julian!" I scream his name. An ear-shattering scream.

Sage removes the knife from Julian's back, and he crumbles to the ground.

I try to get up again, but my feet buckle under me. Before I realize it, Aidan is on top of me.

"Hello, sister."

I look up at him in confusion.

Sister?

Julian...

And then the darkness engulfs me.

Chapter 44

Logan

My head feels like someone took a bat to it as I slowly open my eyes.

It's dark.

That's not possible.

I put my hands above me and feel something rough. I push at it and the light seeps through. It's so bright I have to close my eyes. Once they adjust, I look around and see I'm outside and I'm lying on the dirt-covered ground. What I pushed off me were branches that fell from the trees above me. I look around and see Amara and Troy on the ground next to me. I can sense they are only knocked out and I let out a sigh of relief.

I look around trying to find Amberly but she's nowhere in sight. I jump up and start to walk slowly in the direction of the fight. I round the corner and there she is lying on the floor unconscious. I see blood all over her shirt and my heart sinks.

I run over to her side, unaware of the man standing above her as he speaks. "And who do we have here?"

I quickly stand putting myself between her and the unknown man.

"I'm guessing you must be Logan."

I look at him confused.

"I'm Aidan."

Uneasiness washes over me.

"So where have you been hiding?"

I don't answer.

"It doesn't matter. You're of no concern to me."

He starts to move towards us, and I take a fighting stance.

He laughs. "You're no match for me. If you know what's best for you, you will keep moving."

"In your dreams." I turn to look at Amberly. "You're not touching her."

"You think I wish to hurt her?"

I know confusion is plain on my face when I ask. "Don't you?"

He laughs out. "No."

"Then why are you here?"

He looks past me to Amberly, still lying on the floor.

"I've come to take her home."

My body stiffens. "You're not taking her anywhere."

He turns his attention back to me. "She doesn't belong here."

"Well, she sure as hell doesn't belong with you."

He smiles. "She belongs with me more than she does you trust me."

I hear Amberly moan behind me and I turn around to see she's waking up and the next thing I know I'm being thrown across the field as I hear Aidan say. "You're in my way."

* * *

Amberly

The pain is crippling. I feel almost lifeless as I feel the blood continuing to leave my body. I reach out with my mind to my amulet asking for help, for power, for strength to heal myself. I know if I don't stop the bleeding soon, I'm not going to make it. I feel the amulet warm against my exposed chest and I feel the blood flow starting to slow. I open my eyes slowly. Unsure of how much time has passed or if what I recall even happened. I look to the battlefield and see Julian face down.

"Julian!" I scream.

"Don't worry about him. You have enough to worry about."

I look up at Aidan and say between my teeth. "Get away from me."

"Oh, but you didn't ask nicely." He smiles down at me.

I try to stand but with no success.

Aidan looks at me for what feels like the first time as anger takes over his expression. He leans down and removes my hand from my stomach as I wince.

"Who did this to you?"

I pull my hand out of his. "One of your lovely assassins." I laugh.

He looks me in the eyes. "Who?"

I look at the crowd and when I locate her, I reach back out with my mind, using what I know is the last of my energy. I order her in my mind to kill

Aidan. I look up at him and smile.

"She did."

He turns around to look at Sage just as she's about to apply a deadly blow. He smiles as her blow stops short and her hand freezes in dead air. She blinds a few times and returns her hand to her side as she looks around.

"What happened?"

Aidan turns back to me and smiles. "She got in your head."

If looks could kill Sage would have struck me dead. "You."

She steps forward and Aidan gives her one look and she freezes. He stands to face her. "You did this?" He says to Sage as he looks down at me.

She doesn't answer.

"Answer me." He almost screams.

She looks to the ground in shame. "Yes."

"Were my orders not clear enough for you?"

She looks back at him. "No. They were."

"Then why did you not listen? Did I not say no harm was to come to her?"

"You did."

He stands there waiting for her to explain. But she remains quiet.

"Then please tell me why she is bleeding."

She closes her eyes like she's waiting for a blow. "I feel like your judgment is clouded when it comes to her...Sir."

"That's not for you to say now is it?"

I can see something that looks like hurt forming in her eyes. "No."

He turns his attention to me as he applies pressure to my wound, and I cry out again.

Sage pulls me back from the darkness that is starting to take hold. "I just thought because we..."

Aidan cuts her off. "We are nothing. Don't take a few nights together and make it into something it's not. You were there to warm my bed and give me pleasure, nothing more."

The hurt is now clear on her face as she looks away.

"You know what the price is for disobeying a direct order."

Fear takes over the hurt on her face. "I was only..."

322

"It doesn't matter what your intentions were. You will be dealt with when we return home. But you better hope she survives because if she doesn't your fate will be worse than death, I can promise you that."

Confusion is plain on her face. "I don't understand. Why does she matter so much to you? She's better off dead. She's the only one who can take down Vladimir." He doesn't answer as she looks from him to me and back again before she says. "She's making you weak."

He turns on her with a look of anger. "Don't ever accuse me of being weak."

"I only meant I've never seen you like this."

"I don't know what you mean."

She looks down at his hand on my stomach. "You're applying pressure to her wound like you care."

I can feel the darkness taking hold of me again. I know I'm about to lose consciousness. I look at Julian still on the ground. I reach out trying to find his heartbeat and I sense nothing.

He's dead.

I feel the tears rolling down my face as I start to sob uncontrollably, and my body begins to shake from the blood loss and my sobs.

Aidan looks down at me and holds me in his arms as I start to fade. And finally, he says, "You'll be good as new when you wake up. Close your eyes."

Sage speaks again and I can hear what I think is annoyance in her voice. "Why did we come here for her? Really."

He turns to look at her. "Because she's my sister and we've come to bring her home."

I hear Sage's voice in the darkness. "Sister?"

He looks down at me and I look at him in confusion. So, what I heard earlier wasn't a dream. But what he's saying isn't possible. My mother and father never had any other children. Just as I'm about to fill him in on how crazy he sounds the darkness engulfs me and I've never been more afraid in my life. Fear of the unknown. Fear of never waking up. Of being lost. But most of all the fear that this wasn't all a horrible dream and that I've truly lost Julian.

About the Author

Laura Lukasavage started writing shortly after her mother's passing when she was only fourteen years old. She remembered how her mom would write 192 About the Author poems and letters to her stepdad and as a way to feel close to her mother she took up writing. She started with poems in eighth grade and short stories in high school. Once she started college in 2009 at Neumann University in Aston, PA her interest only grew. By the time she would transfer from Neumann to Rowan University in Glassboro, NJ in 2011, after her father's passing, is when she knew what her passions truly were. She majored in Radio, TV and Film productions with a minor in creative writing. She found her love of film and writing meshed together and this is where she felt at peace. Laura writes as a way to escape from reality but to also deal with life as a whole. She writes hoping that one day her books will be an escape for someone needing them just like the books she read in high school to escape the recent loss of her mother.

You can connect with me on:

 https://publishingdreams20.wixsite.com/my-site

 http://www.insmtagram.com/lauralukasavageauthor

Also by Laura Lukasavage

Moonlight Secrets (Book 1)

Amberly's world is forever changed when she discovers she has the power to communicate with wolves telepathically. To learn how a witch can have this power Amberly embarks on a journey of self-discovery, world-altering love, and the truth about who she is and what she is meant to do. Every answer leads to another question that takes her closer to the truth behind her past and what darkness now awaits the future for her and everyone she loves.

Excited to have answers she has searched for her whole life; she soon questions if her life and everyone in it would have been safer if she had stayed home learning how to control her powers as her mother taught her all she would need to know to take over as the leader of the witches one day.

From discovering the truth about who her father is, finding love where she least expected it, and learning she is the key to giving the supernatural world the unity it needs, there is no shortage to the twists and turns.

Moonlight Legacy (Book 3)

Serenity: It's all happening as I've seen in my dreams. Amberly learned who she was. Was united with those she should have known her entire life. Met her true mate. And then was torn from us all. But hope still springs, because in being lost, Amberly will find answers and learn the true strength of her heart. The last battle might have been lost, but the war has only just begun. And Amberly's choices from here on will send out ripples that will shape the future of our world. But can an eighteen-year-old choose the right path when darkness and grief obscures every way forward?

See You On The Other Side

Blissfully happy, newlyweds Sam and Jane are looking forward to years of building their life together. But the reality they thought would be theirs is shattered by tragedy when Jane dies. Now both Sam and Jane are lost in the darkness alone. Unable to see any way forward. Only by finding her way to peace can Jane help pull Sam out of the depths of his grief. But can he be saved when the love of his life has been ripped away from him, taking the future they planned together with her?

Enough Is Enough

My name is Elena and I have put a plan in motion to escape my abuser and recurring nightmare. However, there is that old saying about the best-laid plans going awry... Escaping your abuser only to have new obstacles laid out in front of you. Now not only does my body need to heal but my mind as well. Beaten, torn down, and broken. I'm no longer the woman I once was and to find her again will be no easy task. Anxiety takes over my mind and body whenever any man gets too close. Even if it was someone I knew would never hurt me. Can I overcome this fear? Can I get close to a man again and live out the rest of my life in peace, or am I destined to be alone and afraid for the rest of my days? A story of a broken woman fighting to stabilize her life after ending her abuse. Can she silence the fears in her mind and allow herself a happy ending with her lifelong friend Jason, or will the anxiety and fear her husband beat into her win out? Jim has become Elena's living nightmare but today everything changes. Elena has put her plan in motion. A plan to take back both her life and happiness.

Will's Awakening (Book 1)

Will Walker's life is about to change forever as destiny finds us all one way or another. His life shattered to pieces the day his older brother West was murdered, and their father disappeared from his life overnight. His mother is the only person left in his life until his childhood best friends, Thea and Trey, fight to make amends. Will is facing demons of his own that he fears he can't outrun and that may keep him from the normal life that he craves so badly. He's being hunted in his dreams by the Company and their leader Morpheus and soon realizes that there was more to his brother's death than anyone knew, but Will holds a more profound secret. Will soon discover he may be the only hope the world has against Morpheus. Will he be the world's savior or their doom?